IGOR ZAVILINSKY

A DREAM
OF ANNAPURNA

A DREAM OF ANNAPURNA

by Igor Zavilinsky

Translated from the Russian by Michael and Jonathan Pursglove

First published in Russian as
Не смей сдыхать, пока не исполнил мечту in 2019

Proofreading by Richard Coombes

Russian text © Igor Zavilinsky 2019

English translation © Michael and Jonathan Pursglove 2024

The translators acknowledge with gratitude the help given them
by Ksenia Papazova of Glagoslav Publications
and Dmytro Drozdovskyi of *Vsesvit Journal*, Kyiv.

Book cover and interior book design by Max Mendor

© Glagoslav Publications 2024

www.glagoslav.com

ISBN: 978-1-80484-164-8
ISBN: 978-1-80484-165-5

First published in English by Glagoslav Publications in November 2024

A catalogue record for this book is available from the British Library.

IGOR ZAVILINSKY

A DREAM
OF ANNAPURNA

TRANSLATED FROM THE RUSSIAN
BY MICHAEL AND JONATHAN PURSGLOVE

GLAGOSLAV PUBLICATIONS

CONTENTS

Dedicated to my sons and their dreams

With gratitude to two charming old Italian gentlemen whom we met in November 2015 on the trek to Annapurna base camp.

Separate thanks to the owners of Agriturismo Sanguineto, where we spent a splendid four days by the walls of Montepulciano in the summer of 2016, and where I, without their asking, "located" the heroes of this story.

To Igor Tunik: thank you, friend, for your support and faith in me!

To Igor Chaplinsky: thank you for the inspiration from our friendship and travels.

With love to Tuscany. Missing Nepal.

I

1955. MONTEPULCIANO, ITALY

Don't dare die till you've lived your dream

"Angelo!"

It seemed to Angelo that he had not yet managed to shut his eyes. To be more accurate it didn't "seem"; he was absolutcly certain that it was all a horrible mistake and they were summoning someone else, or a completely different Angelo, of whom there were more than a few in these parts. It couldn't refer to him personally because... well, it just couldn't and that was that. The boy turned over irritably onto his other side and lay still, in expectation of a miracle: they wouldn't summon him any more, they'd lay off him, or the whole thing was a dream. The feeling of pent-up expectation began to subside and blissful sleep to return joyously. His legs relaxed from their tense, curled-up position, and his body began to adopt its usual pose, stretched diagonally across the bed. And at that moment, like a death sentence, louder than before, and divided into syllables, no doubt in the hope of greater understanding, the word rang out: "An-ge-lo."

Angelo woke up. At least the bit connected to reality did. There was no doubt it was definitely him that was being summoned; he fully understood that his friend Vito was downstairs; furthermore, Angelo had guessed how cross his frozen friend was and was full of sympathy for him. But the commands went no lower than Angelo's head; all the signals and impulses being actively sent out by his brain to his body, fizzled out at the very place where his neck disappeared beneath the warm woollen blanket, and he remained motionless. Angelo knew very well that he would get up but was absolutely certain that five minutes from now it would be significantly easier to do so. It was a very happy idea – not to refuse to do his duty by a friend, but simply to postpone its implementation.

"Angelo, you idle bastard. I'm cold!"

Vito, for it was he, was standing beneath his friend's window. Vito hated the cold, even in a Maytime manifestation such as this. The boy was ready to endure hunger, weariness from long hours of walking, and even toothache, but cold he could not bear. Cold paralysed his body and his thoughts, forcing him to think only of one thing – warmth. What was most hurtful was that inability to endure cold was universally treated as a sign of being spoiled or excessively soft. For a lad who had grown up surrounded by four women this was always very painful. Furthermore, from early childhood he had also been teased for his always impeccably ironed clothes, which in these parts were regarded as foppish, for the satisfying lunches in his school satchel, and for the tight schedule by which he lived, which left him no room for manoeuvre. Then there was the cursed, almost total, intolerance of cold. All attempts to conceal this failing, so injurious to the reputation of a sixteen-year-old adolescent, were futile. In this village, in response to an inopportune nocturnal bark, everyone called on the dog by name to desist.

"Angelo! Come on!"

Vito's voice had gone beyond the angry stage and was becoming more and more plaintive. The last "come on" simply beseeched Angelo to have pity and, if not to emerge at once, at least to give grounds for hope that his friend's pleading had been heard. Younger than Vito by a couple of years, Angelo naturally knew of the complicated relationship between Vito and the cold, but always kept quiet about it, not so much from fear of receiving a poke in the eye as from tact, possibly innate, or instilled in him by his grandfather. Even at such a young age, the boy wisely considered that everyone was entitled to their own peculiarities. In the final analysis, his own fear of heights was not a sign of cowardice as a whole, but merely a specific attitude to a very specific situation which, like Vito's love of warmth, in no way depended on him himself. It came from God, as they say.

"Stop yelling! You'll wake everyone up! I'm coming," Angelo at last replied, his intonation suggesting that he wasn't averse to getting up and his friend was making all this racket for nothing and was threatening the implementation of all their plans for the night.

Having convinced himself that Angelo had woken up, Vito fell silent. Hearing the floor creaking, which confirmed the imminent appearance of his friend, he tried to distract his attention from the cold, and contemplated the unusually starry sky. There was much to contemplate; after two weeks of non-stop rain, this was perhaps the first clear night. The stars, like children who had spent a fortnight in stuffy houses, playing and replaying games both possible and impossible and driving their parents mad, had broken free and were scattered about the sky in a multitude of combinations.

Unlike city children, for whom a starry sky, polluted by the light of the megapolis, can, in moments of rural revelation, claim the status of a "wonder", Vito did not perceive the night sky as something distant and boundless. On the contrary, he thought of it as the wholly real and tangible roof of his small world: the cosmos covered their village like a large cup, with stars painted on the bottom of it. It was beautiful and even enchanting on such nights, but in the mind of a country boy it evoked wholly earthly thoughts about the next day's weather, and did not take him off into the cosmos.

"Well, have they arrived?" Vito asked in the direction of the staircase, which was creaking beneath Angelo's feet.

"Yes, late in the evening. What time is it now?"

"Half past one," Vito's voice rang out as he tried to conceal a shiver. "What are they doing?"

"Nothing in particular for now," Angelo replied hesitantly. His information about the goings-on in the bar were two hours old, the two hours during which he had managed to sleep. "They're getting washed. Genarro is cooking something for them."

Angelo never called Genarro grandfather. Come to that, he, in his sixty plus years, did not particularly resemble a grandfather; he was a strong, stocky man, whose age had only managed to claim for itself the grey hairs on his head and in his short stubble-cum-beard. Genarro always lived by his own rules, refusing to acknowledge authorities or the opinions of others; in his time, this had enabled him to avoid Mussolini's populism. However, living in an Alpine village in the north-west of Italy, at the intersection of three countries, Genarro had not given the Duce the slightest chance of winning over his heart with his dazzling speeches. Nationalism was alien to Genarro, as was monogamy. The colourful nature of his ancestry was like the variegated nature of his personal life. This was not a matter of frivolity or licentiousness but simply that Genarro saw his life as being like a hotel in an alpine resort: there was room for everybody there, everybody was warm and comfortable, but, once the holiday was over, the "residents" came together – some till the following year, some for good. His life ran very smoothly and successfully. Over time he acquired some small five-room apartments which, together with the services of a mountain guide, allowed him to have a wholly respectable lifestyle even when Europe fell into the grip of war. On the whole all the years of his life were reasonably stable and, in a way, even monotonous; only one year, 1943, broke the mould and seem to come from someone else's life. That year two remarkable transformative events befell Genarro, two startling leaps: he became a hero of the anti-fascist resistance without once picking up a rifle, and he became a grandfather without being a father.

Well, everything in its own good time. Being indifferent to the Italian fascists, and even more so to the German Nazis, in the torrid 1940s Genarro took a contemplative position, judging people with reference merely to himself and not to their political affiliation or convictions. Over the course of many years in the mountains, among his few friends and large number of residents, there were all sorts of people – from the children of Jewish industrialists from Genoa to officers of the Bundeswehr who came to sharpen their alpine skills.

But one day in March, French partisans arrived and he didn't even think of refusing them. Anyone who knocked on his door was his guest and could count on his help, both in his home and in his mountains. Thus, what was subsequently treated as heroism was simply a matter of principle. Of course, if partisans had been found in his house, no one would have found his actions exquisite and the result would have been dire. Genarro understood this very well, but stubbornly continued doing things his own way even if this posed a risk to his own quiet life.

In time, his little hotel became a safe refuge for members of the anti-fascist Francs-Tireurs et Partisans,[1] with whom Genarro sympathised and whom he helped, not so much because of their convictions but because of their youth. After the war the grateful communists who had formed the core of these bands made much of Genarro's modest contribution to the defeat of fascism and even managed, without his permission, to make him a member of the French communist party.

Truth to tell, by this time Genarro had no time for glory – after all, a grandson had "landed" on him. To be more precise, in that year of 1943 a hitherto unknown daughter had "landed" on him. An eighteen-year-old girl, already with a round little belly, stood in the doorway of his hotel and looked at Genarro with the eyes of his late mother. The resemblance was so obvious that the newly-minted father assumed his new obligations without misgivings or delays. The poor man was so carried away by his new duties that it was two days before the question was asked about the mother of his daughter. It wasn't that he didn't hazard a guess as to who this might be but, let's put it this way, there were two or three possibilities. As for the future of the child-to-be, Genarro didn't even enquire. A couple of months later this whole newly-minted family had to flee: the partisans warned him that information about his friendship with them had somehow reached the authorities. This was advance notice, and had Genarro been on his own he would certainly have ignored the warning. However, his mobility and, to a certain extent his audacity, had sharply decreased with the appearance of his pregnant daughter and the father-cum-grandfather, always quick to make decisions, left the hotel to a young neighbour who had been helping him for several years, and went south.

....

[1]   An armed resistance group formed by the French Communist Party during World War Two.

They had brief stints in several towns, but circumstances, in the shape of Sofia's swelling belly, forced Genarro to settle somewhere. "Somewhere" turned out to be a little village in the middle of Tuscany, just south of Siena. Some savings and a small income which he continued to receive from his Alpine hotel, together with low wartime property prices, allowed them to buy a two-storey house, with the prospect of opening some sort of drinking establishment on the first floor.

Whether the information about danger had been erroneous or whether Genarro's simple manoeuvre had thrown his pursuers off the scent, nothing more disturbed the peace of the newly-minted father. Plans to return north, if they had existed in Genarro's head at first, fairly quickly evaporated amidst the worries about Angelo, who had just made his appearance in the world, and about his new business. Although at the time it was difficult to call it a business, it simply managed not to make excessive calls on their existing resources. The restaurant was worth its keep later, after the war, when Genarro managed to sell the Alpine hotel at a profit to an American.

"How many are they?" asked Vito in tremulous voice, not so much for information but in order to distract himself from the cold.

"I saw two."

"F-French people?"

"Yes, but one was speaking Italian."

"Are they here for long?"

"Don't know."

"Is that their Peugeot over there?"

"Uh-huh."

The boys went up to the first floor. The interior window of Angelo's room gave a superb view of the whole bar room and bar. The window itself was in the corner and remained unlit. Maybe at first Angelo felt the superiority of his room's layout. Up until now he had never seen at such close range the drawbacks of the restaurant's layout: without leaving his kitchen, Genarro could summon him on account of a plate which, in the old man's opinion, had been badly washed up, and there was nowhere for the boy to hide.

The boys moved up to the window and began to watch what was going on inside the restaurant. At a table in the centre two men were sitting – Genarro in his chef's apron, and one of the Frenchmen, dressed military fashion, although not in a military uniform. There was no sign of the second guest; he'd evidently already gone to bed. The Frenchman was noticeably younger than Genarro; he was scarcely pushing forty. From the window all one could see was his brightly lit face, a determined face with a square chin, a pencil moustache above his upper lip and an ironic look. Vito looked reproachfully at Angelo, who had slept through the first part of the conversation and, trying not to make a noise, sat down on a stool by the window. Angelo, fearing lest he was again smothered by sleep, remained standing behind his friend. The adults' conversation was in full swing.

"… I tell you, Maurice, never in my life have I seen such a crooked mug as on that Pierre. And you know I've seen everything," Genarro was saying, choking with laughter.

"Then I asked him: 'What the hell are you doing in the mountains, soldier. There's enough work in the town," replied Maurice in a strong accent. "But do you know what his answer was?"

"Go on."

"The air is cleaner in the mountains!"

Both speakers began to guffaw. Maurice put his hand on Genarro's shoulder, and with the other, beat time to the laughter on the table. Vito and Angelo were dumbstruck; by the light of the lamp they saw that the Frenchman had no fingers at all on either hand. The boys exchanged glances as if checking whether they had seen one and the same thing. Genarro, continuing to laugh and, afraid lest he wake up the sleeping boy he thought of as his grandson, tried to catch hold of the hand the Frenchman was banging on the table; having caught it, he hesitated somewhat – instead of fingers he was holding in his hand only a wrist which resembled a small pancake. The old friends calmed down, sobbing from time to time and evidently recalling the face of the wretched Pierre. Genarro, as if by way of apology, nodded towards the Frenchman's hand.

"A mere trifle, my friend. Payment for the last expedition to Annapurna," replied the guest, calmly and without regret.

"Wasn't that too high a price?" From beneath a scrap of cloth thrown over a basket Genarro took out a large chunk of cheese and began to slice it up deftly on a board. Maurice watched the rapid movements of his friend's strong hands spellbound and said nothing until preparations were complete for a simple hors d'oeuvre to go with a second bottle of wine.

"Well, no one warned about the cost," said the Frenchman, coming back to reality and switching his attention to the cutlery. "However, I got off lightly. Well, it's not for me to tell you…"

"I understand."

"Good Lord, Genarro, why do you have cutlery like this in this hole?" said Maurice, unexpectedly changing the topic of conversation and trying to turn over a knife which was lying on the table. On the first floor Vito coughed and, frightened by the noise he'd made, jumped up and retreated quietly into the depths of the room.

"Do you like it?" asked Genarro proudly, taking the knife, wiping it on the towel at his shoulder and laying it on the Frenchman's palm. "Stainless steel."

"So it doesn't rust?"

"That's what they promise…" said the old man guardedly.

"Who do? The Americans?" Maurice persisted.

"No, these are ours. Italian," Genarro countered uncertainly, fully aware what his friend was driving at.

"Well that clinches it," said Maurice with a laugh. "But look, there's already a mark."

"Where?" asked Genarro with a frightened twitch.

At this Vito, who had returned to the window, gave a start, having banged his head painfully on the window frame.

"No, I think it's the remains of ketchup," the Frenchman continued mockingly, but he took pity on the sincerity of his friend's feelings and added in business-like fashion, "but the cutlery is really good. After the war I managed to do a bit of trading in kitchen ware."

Genarro raised his eyebrows interrogatively.

"I'm no expert, but I do know something about it," the guest continued, maintaining his business-like tone. "Don't be offended if I say I didn't expect to see such knives and forks."

"Yes, there's a whole story behind those knives. I'll tell you another time." Genarro wanted to get back to the topic of Annapurna. "How's your partner?"

"Louis? Well, he also caught it. Although he had more luck. He only got it in the legs," said Maurice almost casually.

"You got it in the legs too?" Genarro couldn't help casting a glance at his friend's stylish shoes.

"Uh-huh," the Frenchman continued in the same calm fashion, as if the subject was not his body but the imperfections of a suit he'd bought. "So I've got enhanced streamlining."

Maurice looked up at Genarro as if testing the quality of his joke. But the old man sat silently, not knowing how to react to the Frenchman's rather cruel jokes at his own expense.

"Maybe I can do some swimming?" Maurice made another attempt to prod his friend into action.

"Yes, or some politicking!" Genarro finally came to life. "To my shame I found out too late. Information takes its time getting here. I dare say you were already at home."

"Probably." Maurice examined his hands as if hoping to see some improvement there. "Those bloody mittens!"

"What's wrong with them?"

"Everything was all right with them – things were bad without them."

Maurice hid his hands in his pockets, as if the flood of recollections had made him freeze up. "Like a fool, I lost them."

"How so?"

"When we got to the top, we were elated." The Frenchman's eyes flashed, as if he were again standing on a summit at eight thousand metres. "Only where did we get the strength from to be elated?"

Maurice picked up his glass in both hands and took a large gulp of wine. He took his time with the story, trying to prolong his recollections and not switch to a less pleasant part of the narrative. But then, with a sigh, he continued. His speech was somewhat ragged – he was clearly embarrassed by his carelessness, faced with such an experienced companion.

"I tried to take a couple of pictures with my camera. But it was completely frozen up and I couldn't feel the buttons through my mittens. In a moment of euphoria I took off my gloves and clicked away to right and left. Then it was Louis' turn. We were like children. We realised we had to get away quickly. The window was closing. And you couldn't really call it a window. The weather was lousy. I looked all round me – the mittens were gone. Already covered with snow, you see. I searched but it was no good and there was no more time. I had to go without them," the Frenchman said, emphasising every word, like a schoolboy reporting to his father on the low marks he's received.

"I can imagine."

"How sorry I was that you weren't beside me then, my friend. With your daft habit of carrying spare pairs of mittens and socks." The tipsy Frenchman laid his damaged hand on Genarro's shoulder.

"Two pairs, my boy. Always two pairs."

"Well, to cut a long story short," Maurice said with a start, reverting to his usual ironic tone, "Jacques had to give me a manicure at base camp. He couldn't do anything else."

With a sad smile the Frenchman blew on his imaginary fingers, like a woman drying varnish on her nails.

There was a pregnant pause. Both speakers had their own thoughts.

"Good Lord. You did that. Eight thousand metres." Genarro poured the wine, trying to imagine himself at that height.

"Eight thousand and ninety-one metres, Genarro."

"I always knew you were the best. I've told you that before."

"You alone were better, Genarro. However, not the best, in any case," said the Frenchman with a laugh. "There was that New Zealander climbed Everest two years ago."

"Yes, I know. All the same, you were the first at eight thousand metres."

"Well, yes. Now I can do nothing for the rest of my life but tell that story."

"Yes, it's just about you!" laughed the Italian. "Or else I don't know you! By the way, what's that lorry?"

Maurice nodded, making it clear that he would answer as soon as he'd eaten his hunk of cheese.

"I'm carrying tyre samples!"

"What?"

"I'm a partner in a company now and am in sales."

"Is that so?"

"A potential client, a big one, has appeared in Rome, so I decided to call in on you at the same time." Maurice continued eating his cheese and gesticulating in delight. When he'd finished the last piece, the Frenchman adjusted his chair, as if he wanted to move on to a more important part of their conversation.

"In fact I found out where you lived last year, but I didn't want to simply write. I'd wait until I was in your part of the world."

"How did you find me, you vagabond?"

"Well, if it hadn't been for your glorious communist past, it would have been more complicated."

"A communist! Yes, I'm still one of those!" The friends burst out laughing again. "Except I yield to you in ideological fervour."

"You're a rubbish communist – forgive me! But you're still on their books, so your comrades-in-arms quickly gave me all your details."

"There you go. Someone still remembers the old man." Genarro stood up and went behind the bar in search of a new bottle. "I'm grateful to them for that. To tell the truth, I didn't think we'd meet again."

"I never doubted it." As he got more tipsy, Maurice's Italian got worse and became mixed up with French words. "I needed you."

"And why do you, the conqueror of Annapurna, a chevalier of the Order of the Cross, need me?"

"You know why!"

"I'm sure that thirty or so years from now will just be the beginning of a catalogue of your achievements, my dear fellow!"

"Thank you, my friend."

"So what do you need esteemed Monsieur Old Man Genarro for? Well, apart from getting drunk for free in his bar?" asked the Italian, indicating with a gesture that he should pour drinks from the new bottle.

"I should have told you…" Maurice collected himself and took a big swig of wine. "There's one small fact you don't know. Nor does anyone else."

"You're gay, Maurice?" yelled Genarro, already rather drunk, in mock horror. "You'd have been better to give me the news by letter!"

Vito and Angelo burst out laughing in surprise and almost gave away their presence.

"No, Genarro, I definitely wouldn't have come to see you with such news! There's something else." There seemed to be a catch in Maurice's voice.

Realising that it was a matter of some importance, Genarro instantly grew serious.

"You saved my life, old man."

"Somehow, Maurice, I don't remember that. If the communists told you that, don't believe it. It's not the first time they've told fibs about me..."

"We'd got stranded on a slope," the French man continued, ignoring his friend's joke and recoiling. "Night had fallen."

"What height were you at?"

"Difficult to say, but we weren't that far from the summit. We were simply being blown off the mountain, literally blown off. Do you understand? Annapurna was avenging herself on us for losing her virginity. There was nothing for it but to spend the night in a crevasse. We had one sleeping bag between four people."

The smile on the Frenchman's face expressed simultaneous hatred and delight at these memories.

"For four people?"

"Yes, there was Gaston and Lionel too. They were behind us. We turned them round. They wouldn't have made it anyway. It was suicide. However, at that moment I was sure I was saving their lives. Or increasing very slightly their chances of survival." Maurice paused for a second, then added: "You know, sometimes I think I tried to increase my own chances by picking up two soldiers."

"Don't argue. You saved them. You all got down, didn't you?"

"Yes, yes. They're all alive," continued Maurice thoughtfully. "But that night... Honestly, Genarro, by morning I'd given up. You know that's not like me, but I'd reconciled myself to death. And I simply decided to go to sleep. No, that's rubbish... I didn't decide anything, I simply let go of everything. I didn't feel any pain, and at some point I wasn't even cold. I was simply drifting off. Everything was somehow peaceful and calm. The thought of death didn't frighten me. Not at all. You know, I understood there that death is not frightening in itself. People are afraid of pain, not death. There was no pain. Nor cold. After hours of torment, the absence of pain and cold was almost happiness."

"Maurice…"

"Listen. They say that normal people at such moments remember their family, wives, girlfriends," Maurice resumed his habitual ironic tone, "but not your humble servant."

With a nod the Frenchman indicated his empty glass to Genarro and said nothing while the latter filled it again.

"What were you imagining, you French debauchee?" the barman impatiently urged his friend. "Not Laurent again?"

"Good Lord! You still haven't forgotten!?"

"You don't forget things like that, my friend!" laughed Genarro. "You must agree, Laurent was pretty rough-looking."

"No, brother! You won't believe it, but before my eyes rose your snout, not, forgive my saying so, the most beautiful I've ever seen in my life!"

"Well, yes. Where's this leading?"

"Do you remember, one day during the war we were sitting in the cellar at your place and discussing important things?"

"You know you talked of nothing else the whole time, so I don't remember."

"I too hadn't remembered until I started dying. Then it came to me so clearly. In that cellar we ardent brats discussed death. We all argued about what was easier: to get a bullet in the chest or be blown up by a mine. There, lying in the crevasse on Annapurna, I remembered our stupid argument. I thought too that the variant that had befallen me was not bad – was much better than what had befallen many of the lads who had argued in your little Alpine house." Maurice raised his glass, indicating that he was drinking to the comrades who had died in the war. Then he went on:

"Then you used to listen to us without butting in. You kept grinning into your moustache – you didn't yet have a beard – and it was only when you were closing the cellar trapdoor for the night that for some reason you turned to me specifically and came out with: 'Maurice! Don't dare die till you've lived your dream!' and left."

"Maurice, I don't remember that."

"Why did you address it to me specifically, old boy?"

"If I really did say that, it's probably because, Maurice, I knew about your dream. And for me your death, even the most heroic of deaths, would have been a betrayal. A betrayal of your dream and of those talents which the Lord had endowed you with."

Maurice fell silent, as if he were again reliving those minutes. Then, after a swig of wine, he went on:

"I think at that moment I was already asleep. Then I saw your face, just like in the cellar; you were looking at me from above, through a half-closed opening. The light was pouring through it, dazzling our eyes, which had become accustomed to the darkness. You were saying: 'Don't dare die till you've lived your dream!' Genarro, it was like an electric shock. Annapurna wasn't my dream! We hadn't set out to climb it."

"Meaning?"

"That's a separate story. We had planned to climb Dhaulagiri, but when we got there, we realised that wasn't possible, and went to Annapurna."

"I didn't know."

"Well, you understand how it is: journalists need lovely stories about how dreams are fulfilled. Two Frenchmen, one a hero of the Resistance, went and opted for his second choice," laughed Maurice. "All in all, I got really angry. What the hell am I doing here, I thought? I tell you, my dream of you came just in time. My colleagues were already asleep. How I bashed them, Genarro, how I bashed them. It's lucky I couldn't feel my hands by that time. Just imagine, I'd split Gaston's eyebrow."

"I suppose he doesn't hold it against you."

"He'd have tried. That lucky blighter's split eyebrow was his only injury from the climb. The rest of us had something cut off and that son of a bitch got a bloodied brow. If I'd known, I'd at least have broken his nose. That's the story, old boy." Maurice put both his crippled hands on Genarro's. "Thank God, you haven't figured in my dreams either before or since."

The friends burst out laughing, their foreheads pressed together, their hands clasped. Vito and Angelo, shocked by the story, sat in silence.

Genarro clapped the Frenchman on the shoulder, and poured the remains of the bottle into his glass. Holding the bottle between his two palms, Maurice proposed a toast;

"Don't die till you've lived your dream!"

"Don't even think of it!"

Somewhat embarrassed by the pathos of the moment, Maurice hastened to continue:

"I've got a present for you."

"You should have started with that, you greedy frog!"

"It's a great shame that not a single photo from the summit came out. I'm not very good at it and don't know why that happened, but in the event all the film came out black. So there's only one left from that film. I left it in camp before the climb."

Maurice dived into his travel bag, which had been dumped under the table and, not without some difficulty, fished out a photo.

"That's her?" asked Genarro.

"That's her. That's us at base camp with Louis looking at the summit. Here's our tent. You know, I look at that photograph and try to remember what I was thinking about at that moment. And I can't."

"It doesn't matter what you were thinking about 'before'. What matters is that you're able to do it 'after'. Thanks. If you don't mind, I'll hang it in the most prominent place in the bar."

"Of course, my friend. A second one just like it hangs in my study."

"Then sign this one."

"It's already got a signature: 'Annapurna. 1950'."

"I want something from you." Genarro put a pencil into the Frenchman's hand.

"Will that do you," the Frenchman asked and, with surprising dexterity, holding the pencil between his hands, drew some letters in the corner of the photograph. The two friends laughed and embraced.

The children waited for another fifteen minutes or so until the comrades-in-arms went to their rooms, and after this went downstairs and eagerly began to examine the photograph. Angelo was somewhat disappointed with the external appearance of Annapurna: his childish fantasy and innate fear of heights had, as the Frenchman's story progressed, created a picture of sheer cliffs and a pointed peak at the summit. Undoubtedly the photograph showed huge mountain, which was nevertheless a long way from what the boy had imagined. Vito looked at the two mountaineer figures in sweaters who had crawled out of the tent and were gazing at the snow-covered peak as if pondering whether it was worth continuing. From the sharp ridge leading to the summit the wind was dislodging huge snow prominences, the sight of which made Vito cower. As Maurice had said, in the bottom corner of the picture was printed ANNAPURNA 1950 and a little higher, in block capitals, an uneven inscription had been added: "DON'T DARE DIE TILL YOU'VE LIVED YOUR DREAM! MAURICE HERZOG, 1955."[2]

....

[2]   Maurice Herzog (15.01.1919–13.12.2012). French mountaineer and politician. After completing his studies, he fought with French partisans in the Alps. Although himself unsympathetic to left-wing ideas, he served with the Francs-Tireurs et Partisans communist brigade. After the war he was awarded the Croix de Guerre. In 1945 he began working for Kléber-Colombes, a tyre-manufacturing company and took up rock-climbing. He later became co-owner of the firm and headed it until 1958.

On June 3 1950 Herzog, together with Louis Lachenal became the first men in history to conquer an eight-thousand-metre peak when they climbed Annapurna 1 in the Himalayas, the tenth highest mountain in the world.

The return from the summit turned out to be a severe ordeal. Light boots and Herzog's loss of his mittens at the summit, and a night spent in a glacial crevasse on the descent, with one sleeping bag between four (Louis Lachenal, Gaston Rébuffat, Lionel Terray and Maurice Herzog) led to severe frostbite. The two who had reached the summit (Lachenal and Herzog) lost all their toes; in addition, Herzog lost all his fingers. The quick spread of gangrene forced the expedition's doctor Jacques Oudot to do urgent amputations in field conditions and without anaesthetics.

From 1958 to 1966 Herzog was French Minister for Youth and

Sport and from 1968 to 1977 Mayor of Chamonix. From 1970 onwards he was a member of the International Olympic Committee, and from 1995 an honorary member of that committee. He was a Grand Officier de la Légion d'Honneur (2008).

On December 30 2011 he became a Chevalier de la Grande-Croix de la Légion d'Honneur.

2

FEBRUARY 2015. NEW YORK, USA

"Angelo!"

"Mr De Rossi!!!"

"What's the matter?"

"Phone for an ambulance!"

"Doctor!"

"Mr De Rossi!"

A moment before, Angelo had been pacing the length of a large conference table, loudly proving his case, with true Italian gesticulations. In his imagination it ought to have looked like the roar of a leader who is ready to scatter a council of directors gathered for a meeting and has, for some unknown reason, failed to do so. In reality everything was quite wrong. As the temperature of his speech rose, Angelo's pacing became more rapid, which produced the opposite of the desired effect, and he more and more came to resemble an old and nervous animal driven into a corner. Angelo was not roaring, but merely snapping. For the first time in thirty years, he was talking about what must not be done, without a word about the direction which should be taken. At first Angelo was defensive. This appeared so pitiful that to lose the thread half-way through a word just before it became totally comical was not the worst outcome.

At first it seemed that Angelo had dried up as he pondered the next word: he leant one hand on the table and clutched his temple with the other, as if that was precisely where the decisive argument had lodged and he was trying to seize it with the tips of his fingers. But then all the functions of his organism cut out, as happens in the cinema when the all-powerful cyborg's feed button is switched off. Angelo went floppy and slid smoothly, and even, one might say, gracefully, under the table.

No one said anything for several seconds. There was no surprise on their faces, mostly because the majority of the conference attendees had not been listening very carefully to their chief and were preoccupied with their own thoughts. This was not the result of disrespect but merely of weariness with an old argument which had been going on in the company for the last six months. Everyone already knew the arguments on both sides and did not expect anything new. What had started as a highly professional argument from one of the top Manhattan investment analysts had turned into a banal slanging match and a recruitment drive for supporters. When it became clear that neither side had the upper hand, the majority of members fell into apathy, relying on the fact that the opinion formers would either agree or devour one another and a decision would appear of its own accord.

It was for precisely this reason that at first only the senior vice-president noticed Angelo's fall. Being the leader of the young opposition, Steve had just been readying himself to enter the already traditional fray, which was more and more like the mating call of birds in the spring, and was merely waiting for a pause in Angelo's emotional speech. When such a pause unexpectedly arose, Steve was about to open his mouth, but the start of his speech was interrupted by his boss's fall. In the heat of the war of words Steve even managed to get angry, as if saying. "All right, Angelo! You might at least hear me out before hitting the deck!" A second later, humane instincts prevailed over predatory ones and Steve jumped up from his place in genuine horror and was the first to yell: "Angelo!"

Angelo was lying on the floor in a beautiful pose – full length, with his arms flung out. If it had been a scene from a film, the critics would have pulled it to bits – everything was painfully staged; arranging the film's hero like that would have taken an hour's work on the part of wardrobe assistants, laying out fold by fold the jacket and trousers of an expensive suit, and on the part of make-up artists working on the face of an adult actor in order to preserve the balance between the natural traces of ageing and noble beauty, with overtones of the best golf course tan, and beauticians would have spent a considerable amount of time in achieving such an effective spread of long grey hair. The spot from which Steve was looking at his chief when he leapt to his aid was ideal for taking a photo: the back wall of the room against which Angelo had been moving was fully glazed and now, when Mr De Rossi, the managing director of the DRI group, which incorporated his first two initials in its name, lay full-length, the illusion was created that he was lying right on top of Central Park, occupying a good third of its southern sector.

By their passive behaviour, the conference attendees merely added to the cinematic nature of the scene; they all froze as if expecting the director to call "cut!" afraid of spoiling by word or gesture the Master's great idea. But then, as if an invisible director really had given the command, they all broke out yelling:

"Mr De Rossi!"

"Angelo!"

"What's the matter?"

"Phone for an ambulance!"

"Doctor!"

"Mr De Rossi!"

It seemed that the fall of the eternal and evergreen De Rossi could not be imagined, either figuratively or actually. Despite the fact that Angelo had recently celebrated his 70th birthday, the age of the famous New York financier existed, as it were, separately from De Rossi himself. However, it couldn't be said that he looked like a forty-year-old, but when he got to sixty, Angelo had stopped ageing, having become the happy possessor of that noble old age about which many dream, but very few achieve. Of course, besides the high quality of his heredity, the chief himself deserved the credit for this; he had not indulged himself either in sport or in food and, it must be admitted, had made regular visits to an elite spa, where, once a week, either Thai or Filipino girls cooed over his expensive personage. However, there were two sins which even his will power could not overcome. Firstly, Angelo could not relax; even arranging a normal day off was an insoluble problem for him. This was not so much the needs of productivity as habit – from childhood Angelo had had no school holidays, spending all his spare time earning pin money in his grandfather's Tuscan bar. Many people, especially Angelo's wives and girl-friends, had at various times, but inevitably with negative results, done battle with this phenomenon; they all came independently to the same conclusion that, to all appearances, Angelo simply lacked the "relaxation" option. Angelo himself felt no ill effects from this; he thought that all he needed to restore his strength were several hours of sleep at night and a daily game of tennis. Yes, there was golf as well, of which he was not over fond because of its static nature but which he was compelled to play, regarding it exclusively as an instrument of business communication.

His second sin was exclusively Italian – his native Tuscan cuisine. He was willing, if not to sell his soul, then to exchange a controlling share in his company for the smoked Finnochiona sausage which the Salumeria[3] restaurant on Upper West Side regularly delivered to him. However, as a true financier, Angelo did the opposite and expressed his love for the place by opening his own restaurant and calling it by his own name. Angelo's GP and friend from his school days, Aaron Gudhartz once said:

"You know, for some of my patients who are suffering from dementia, I order a medallion with their home address engraved on it. But when the time comes, I won't do this for you because I know where to find you: Salumeria – that'll be the last thing that fades from your memory!"

"Can you hear me, Angelo?!"

In the now empty conference room a paramedic was bending over Angelo.

"Who are you?" was the rather brusque response from Angelo, who had come round.

"Your fairy godmother! Don't you recognise me?" The dark-skinned medic answered the brusqueness with mockery.

"Yes, go to..." said Angelo faintly, trying to work out where he was lying.

....

[3]   Salumeria Rosi: one of the most popular Italian restaurants in New York and recipient of numerous culinary awards.

"Curse away – that's good," the medic went on cheerfully as he got his dropper ready.

"But if I bang your eyes – would that be still better?"

"It's all the same. It'd be something else to show that you haven't had a stroke."

"I haven't had a stroke."

"And you hid under the table from angry shareholders?"

"I didn't…" Angelo gradually began to recall the chain of events which preceded his fall. "Hell, it would have been tiresome to die like that."

"Same." The medic was looking at Angelo, testing the symmetry of his face and it wasn't clear whether what he said related to this process or to discussions about causes of death. "Death is a nuisance in principle, but that said, not a single corpse of all the ones I've seen complained about the way it had become one. So the most natural and positive factor now is that you're still alive."

"Where's Steve?" said Angelo with some agitation.

"Who's that?"

"Call Steve!"

"I can't for now. I'm dealing with you," said the medic, deftly finishing with the dropper.

"Stern!" yelled Angelo angrily after reading the medic's name on his uniform. "Call Steve! It's urgent!"

"Your sight's all right – that's good too. You get a prize for that. Call Steve!" he shouted towards reception.

"Stern…" Angelo called out faintly.

"Yes, sir."

"Are you German?"

"On my father's side," replied the medic with a broad smile; his face had no shade of pale in it.

"My eyes have gone dark somehow. Maybe it really was a stroke."

"I'd have been worried if you'd said you'd come out in spots. As it is – it's fine. My father was adopted by a family from Hanover," the medic explained with a laugh.

"What good luck…"

"I agree, sir."

"Angelo, you were calling me?" Steve had run in.

"I want no one at this level."

"You mean this level?"

Angelo wearily ignored Steve's question.

"I want no one to see me!"

"I understand, boss."

Steve hurried to carry out his instructions, but when he'd got as far as the door, Angelo stopped him.

"Steve!"

"Yes, Angelo," said Steve from the doorway.

"I've snapped ligaments in my leg," said Angelo, trying to catch his breath. "Tennis…"

"Understood, boss!"

Angelo had already been placed on a stretcher, and Stern was about to have him carried from the room.

"Wait! Everybody leave!"

"And are you going to kill everyone who was at the conference?" the medic grumbled, somewhat irritably, aware of the importance of every second.

"I'll think about it… Meanwhile, let's leave through the garage."

Stern, realising the futility of arguing with the patient, picked up his radio.

"Ron! We'll leave through the garage! You're already there? How did you know? Got it."

Stern rolled the trolley into the corridor and hurried towards the lifts.

"Not bad, Steve…" murmured Angelo, wearily closing his eyes.

3

FEBRUARY 2015. MONTEPULCIANO, ITALY

"Can you hear me? Massimo! I've told you more than once. This won't be a spa resort! This is a vill-age!" Vito felt round his chair with his hand, looking for the bottle of wine he'd started. "This is a farm. Always was and always will be. I won't let a third of the land (its best third!) to be used for a foundation pit."

The old man was sitting in his traditional place – inside an old gazebo which gave an excellent view of the fortress wall of Montepulciano. In view of the seriousness of the conversation, his sons weren't allowed in, and resembled schoolboys being ticked off by the headmaster for being late, there in the doorway. In addition, the eldest, – Alessandro – was gazing demonstratively into the distance, while the younger – Massimo – was constantly on the move, clearly feeling the awkwardness of the conversation.

"For a swimming pool." Thirty-year-old Massimo punctiliously corrected his father.

"What?"

"For a swimming pool, Dad. Not a pit."

"You're still putting a jacuzzi under the olive trees!" Vito continued to address Massimo, completely ignoring the presence of his other son. Massimo thus understood that he had not lost hope of coming to an agreement with his father.

Mention of the jacuzzi rooted Massimo to the spot, and he cast a horrified glance at Alessandro. The latter did not turn his head towards his brother, but merely nodded, giving him to understand that this was a very bad moment to discuss his father's surmise, which was very close to the truth.

"Father," Alessandro cut in, despite being ignored, "almost everyone's got a swimming pool. Even the Giaccherinis are already digging."

"The Giaccherinis?" Vito leapt to his feet and at last "saw" the eldest son. "Where, may I ask, are they doing this? Under the house? Or where the toilet is? Their plot is four times smaller than ours! Has everyone gone mad, or what?"

"They've knocked down the garage, where the tractor used to be," interposed Massimo quietly.

"And they've put the tractor on the roof?"

"No, they've got rid of the tractor," said Alessandro excitedly. "What do they need a tractor for, dad? You can't take tourists out on them! And for the price of a swimming pool, even a small one like that, their income will grow, and I don't suppose they'll mourn the loss of the tractor."

"Rubbish! People who come to Montepulciano don't come here to swim. There's Monsummano for that." The old man waved his hand in the general direction of the spa resort with its hot springs to the north of Florence. "They come here to see the fortress!"

"It's good, father, that you've started to acknowledge that!" said Alessandro pointedly, now thoroughly browned off. He had begun to pace out the ground round the perimeter of the old demolished barn of which only a line of stones trampled into the ground now bore witness. They had probably not been removed when the building was taken down.

"What are you saying that about?" Now Vito had "forgotten" about the presence of Massimo, and had totally retreated into the field of conflict created by his elder son.

"About the fact, father, that five years ago, when we came to you with the idea of building a hotel, you said that no one would come and who needed this fortress! Or have you forgotten already?"

"Ah, so that's what you were talking about... Back then I was only talking about the fact that we couldn't risk everything: vineyards, olives and, finally, the restaurant, everything that fed us, for the sake of a vague idea."

"Well, and what do you think now? Was it worth it, father?" said Alessandro, already without malice, but somehow through inertia.

"Of course it was! But don't you forget at what cost all this was built and how much time went by before we began to get a return on the hotel! What we all ate while you were building it. Shall I remind you?"

"This is a pointless argument," said Alessandro with an angry dismissive gesture, turning and making to leave.

"So don't argue!" shouted Vito after him. "Of course, I didn't go to business college, but it's obvious even to me, a country bumpkin, that we can't go on investing in something that's only just begun to pay its way. We can't at present allow ourselves to bury several tens of thousands of euros in the ground. We haven't earned them yet."

"And we won't, father!" Alessandro had returned, and switched to the tone used with stubborn children who won't eat their nourishing kasha, "Because for the summer, tourists will choose Giaccherini's villa, where, after a day tramping round Montepulciano, they can chill out in the swimming pool."

"He hasn't even got a restaurant!" snapped their father uncertainly. "Some sort of misunderstanding. Better go to McDonalds. He won't see any tourists. Not ours at least."

"Dad," Massimo softly re-entered the discussion, trying to calm his elder brother down with a hand gesture unseen by the old man. "I've explained to you once that people book rooms through an internet search engine. Even tourists at that point don't know who has what restaurant. They simply put 'with swimming pool' into the search engine. And since we haven't got a swimming pool, the search engine gives them a list on which we, together with our splendid restaurant, simply don't figure. They won't know about us! And they'll go to Giaccherini, and even if they get diarrhoea from his horrible cooking, it won't do us any good. They simply won't know about us."

"Then they should do! People who know us will come!" The old man's voice betrayed more hope than certainty in what he'd said.

"Possibly," Massimo countered patiently. "If they don't want to try something new, something with a swimming pool for instance. There's no shortage of restaurants round here, so in forty-degree heat they won't be able to leap into the pool if you haven't got one in your hotel. What's more, I wouldn't count on all last year's clients – the majority of them will want a change of scene – the sea at La Spezia, Ravenna, or they'll simply want to stroll round Florence. People like new things, and there aren't many who come to Montepulciano several years running, even if they liked it here a lot."

"What are you driving at, Massimo?" The old man was tired and wanted to put an end to a conversation of which he'd had enough.

"At the fact that our struggle for custom in effect begins afresh every year. And every year we must again prove that we're the best round here. Every year we'll be compared with others."

"We can show them a thing or two…"

"Yes, of course we can, dad. But to do that we need to be noticed, need to be in the comparison."

"And you think a swimming pool is the most important thing. We build a swimming pool and all our business problems will be solved. Am I right?"

"We're not saying that. We're saying that making money will be more difficult without a swimming pool than with one."

"And I'm saying to you, dear boys, that it would be even easier to make money if we built Disneyland here! But we don't have that option. And it will be difficult to make money. But it's better to make heavy weather out of making money than to part with money we haven't earned by sinking it into another building! We haven't yet recouped all the money we put in and you're demanding I continue investing! Somehow I don't remember our talking from the outset about a swimming pool and its key role in this business."

"The situation was different then," said Alessandro, trying to get back into the discussion.

"So what do you want me to do? In a year's time the situation will change again and you'll say we'll get nowhere without a casino, that Giaccherini's put a roulette wheel in his cowshed and we haven't got one."

The sons said nothing. Vito, mistakenly imagining that he'd won the argument, went on calmly:

"So, Alessandro, what I say is…"

"The goalkeeper is half the team," said the elder son angrily, and went into his office. As he passed his father, he gave him a slight nod, indicating to his brother with his eyes that he expected him in the office for further discussion.

Vito merely swore.

Vito and Massimo, left alone, were tormented by the pause. Massimo picked up a bottle of wine which had fallen down and offered to top his father up. His father gave a deep sigh and held out his empty glass. At the same time as the glass was filling up, Massimo, reluctantly leaning towards his father, said:

"Don't draw a line under it, dad. I beg you. Think again."

Vito nodded, but did it somehow obliquely, indicating neither consent nor refusal. Massimo placed the bottle, which was still half-full, on the grass, tenderly clapped the old man on the shoulder by way of apology, and went after his elder brother.

Vito continued sighing deeply from time to time as he relived the quarrel with his children. The wine warmed him up, but the warmth stopped somewhere around his chest; his legs felt cold in the February wind. Vito pulled out a blanket from under him and tried to wrap it round him below his waist. During this manoeuvre the old man caught the glass which he had placed beside his chair and the wine disappeared into the ground in a trice.

Vito followed it with his eyes disappointedly. At that moment he felt himself to be just like an empty glass. After all he'd just been full of plans, like his glass had been full of wine. But time had so quickly overturned his vessel that all that was left to him was to watch his life slipping way into the fertile Tuscan earth.

Still with these thoughts, Vito was on the point of reaching for the bottle, but changed his mind: by force of long-established habit he made a bottle last all day – half for lunch and the rest after supper. Of course, no one would prevent him finishing the bottle he'd begun now and opening another one in the evening to compensate for his loss. He was briefly tempted by the thought but it was immediately rejected by the "protocol service" of consciousness, and Vito continued sitting stubbornly with an empty glass. This made his mood even worse.

Vito's relationship with his elder son had always been emotional; both father and son were equally responsible for this, and the only question was who would explode first. The amusing thing was that people around them always perceived both of them as calm, balanced individuals. And it's true that neither father nor son had ever manifested so much impatience and belligerence either with members of the family or with friends as they did with each other. One normally speaks of the "scythe striking the stone" but here it was simply a case of two scythes meeting. Sometimes it seemed there wasn't a single question over which they would have reached immediate agreement. To be more accurate, there never was agreement, only compromise – partial and temporary.

For all this, they each had one essential distinguishing feature: if Vito quickly froze after an argument and began to "hear" his opponent, Alessandro relived the conflicts for a long time, retreating into himself, chewing over the insults again and again and returning to the cause of the argument only with difficulty. Very often he didn't even return at all to such questions, doing everything in his own way, but, as a rule, in a very cunning way so he could not be accused of overt disobedience to his father.

The phrase "the goalkeeper is half the team" referred to the most obvious example of their longstanding feud – to their protracted argument about Alessandro's role in the school football team. Alessandro, like the majority of boys, of course wanted to be a striker and seek glory in his opponent's goalmouth. It would certainly have been strange if Vito had agreed with this: in his view the anthropological data of his tall twelve-year-old son, multiplied by good reactions, opened up good prospects for him to be a goalkeeper. Truth to tell, for a time Alessandro was delighted to have a little rest between the posts, the more so because he really found it easy, but as soon as their team floundered in its efforts to score a goal, the boy tore off his line without waiting for his coach's instructions.

The coach himself was pleased with Alessandro's all-round ability and took his time over making a choice. Unlike Vito, who felt they were wasting valuable time. It would not be too much to say that, as soon as his father suggested he start special goalkeeping training, it was the last straw for Alessandro: in all seriousness he wanted to give up football completely so as not to have to stand in goal. The argument reached the protracted stage, during which each side devised cunning strategic plans to achieve their aim. Vito bought some rather expensive goalkeeping gloves and gave running commentaries on the actions of goalkeepers during matches involving "I Viola",[4] each time never forgetting his crowning phrase "the goalkeeper is half the team", which made Alessandro sick. From that time onwards the phrase became a generalised term, denoting the abandonment by the son of what he regarded as a senseless argument with his father. After these words came – nothing, just the banging of doors and Vito's cursing.

The football story had a sequel: in reply to what the son was convinced were steps taken by Vito towards Alessandro's preordained role as a goalkeeper, the son reacted radically and effectively – he became the best striker in the team. The stimulus of his quarrel with his father was so strong that Alessandro simply held the ball, was greedy with his passes and propelled the ball into his opponents' goal with every allowable part of the body. Alessandro was possibly not the most skilful forward; he did not have a bullet-like shot or intricate dribbling skills, but with his vigour and expressiveness he regularly demolished the enemy's redoubts.

The coach could not have been more pleased with the performance of his trainee and gradually came round to the idea that the boy was correct in his self-definition. Instead of being pleased with the achievements of his eldest son, Vito flew into a rage and acted very sophisticatedly.

The success of the school team opened up the prospect of its taking part in the championship of Tuscany. For a rural team with a primitive selection policy, the highpoint of which was the luring of a defender, massive beyond his years, from a neighbouring village, who would win the ball from his opponents more by fear than skill; this was a big achievement. However, participation at this level required money – for strips, balls, refurbishing the school stadium, at which they had to receive teams from other towns, and, most importantly, funds were needed for away matches. The level of funding needed was beyond the means of the commune of Montepulciano, and required a sponsor.

....

[4] *The Purples*: a reference to the colours worn by Vito's favourite football team A.F.C. Fiorentina.

It should be noted that the word "sponsor" itself was by no means familiar to all the local inhabitants, whose acquaintances and trading relationships did not extend further than a radius of a few kilometres from the fortress wall. At that point there came the highpoint of Vito's life; he remembered his youthful commercial ventures.

The general delight in the new strip with the logo INOXRIV[5] in the middle was blighted for Alessandro by his name on the goalkeeper's jersey and the attempts of the coach to avoid looking him in the eye. To Vito's surprise, Alessandro did not voice his disgust at his father's low cunning. Although Vito was ready for this. More than that, he realised he'd overdone things and gone too far in his argument; he expressed this by ordering, at his own expense, a second outfielder strip for his son, about which he told nobody and which he kept in one of the kitchen cupboards. To everyone's surprise the boy put on his goalkeeping kit without a word and went to training, after which he was taken to hospital with a broken finger. And although the coach swore to Vito that the injury had been incurred in the course of play, as he had seen, and in no way could be the result of a malicious strategy on the part of the boy or his team mates, Vito was sure that this was his son's final argument.

And, it must be said, it worked: what was impossible for a keeper, to wit, play with a broken finger, was possible for an outfield player, and Vito had to admit defeat in this argument.

The team lost almost all its matches and came last, a fact which did not seem to upset Alessandro unduly; he had gained his main victory before the championship started. In spite of the fact that his son's stubbornness for the most part irritated him, Vito was proud of the character of his elder child, and more than once told the story of the broken figure when in company. Of course, if Alessandro wasn't around.

....

[5]   INOXRIV: name of a major Italian company, with factories all over Italy. The company was founded in 1941 by Aurora Rivadossi, hence its name INOXRIV (inox – stainless steel+ riv – the name of the founder). The crockery and tableware made by INOXRIV are made from high-quality stainless steel.

Their life under one roof would probably have been impossible but for Vito's wife, who always served as a buffer between them: she skilfully manipulated both of them, not allowing Alessandro to go beyond the bounds of traditional respect for his father, and reminding Vito of paternal feelings which, in their family, were always placed above everything else. Moreover she was able to do this in such a way that both parties remained convinced that they had, at the very least, not lost. Naturally, after the death of Vito's wife, Massimo attempted to take on these functions, although he did this in his own way: he focused not so much on nullifying the conflict as getting a result satisfactory to all.

Vito still did not understand whether he was more upset by the intransigence of his eldest son Alessandro, who took after Vito so much, the torment felt by the kind-hearted Massimo, who suffered from the conflict, or his own lack of confidence of being right. Stubbornness over conducting the business was not an old man's whim – over everything that concerned the house or the restaurant Vito was always extremely careful. There was nothing on which he placed more value; he could take whatever risk you like and, if he lost, would blame only himself, but with the restaurant he did not allow any speculative ventures. It was as if old man Genarro could come back and make him answerable.

4

1955. MONTEPULCIANO, ITALY

"Good morning, Angelo."

Angelo raised his head, heavy after a sleepless night, above the bar. Through the open door the morning sun, herald of a warm day, burst in to the still-shuttered bar. Angelo could not make out the face of the young woman – in the doorway he could only see the silhouette of her shapely body, around which was a suggestion of a light flowered dress which almost completely dissolved in the sunlight. He lowered eyes dazzled either by the sun, or by shame.

"Hello, Letizia," said the boy in welcoming fashion, his eyes fixed to the floor. To recognise visitors by their voice was the prerogative of the grandson of a bar owner in a village with a few dozen inhabitants.

"Is Genarro in?" asked the girl, herself turning back over a heavy chair which had stayed on the table after things had been cleared up the previous evening.

"No," came the voice of Genarro from the depths of the house, "and he won't be today."

Letizia sat down distractedly on the very edge of the chair.

"Genarro," the girl repeated, reproachfully.

"I'm telling you he's not here. At least the kind-hearted Genarro, whose welcoming, cheerful nature is known throughout the commune of Montepulciano, is definitely not here today. So unless you're an angel capable of relieving a headache, you'd better go."

"I've got business with you," said Letizia, trying to engage the interest of her interlocutor.

"Not an angel," muttered Genarro sadly.

"What?"

"I tell you, if it's business negotiations, you couldn't have chosen a more difficult time," announced a rather crumpled Genarro as he came into the bar. "Well, go on, speak, if you're still not scared to."

Letizia fidgeted on the chair, glancing sideways at Angelo, who was no less crumpled than his grandfather.

"Son, you might get our tablecloths from Sofia," commanded the old man, realising the reason for the young woman's indecision.

"Yes, but it's early. They're not dry yet – she only took them last evening." Angelo did not want to go, but the reason for the visit by his friend Vito's youngest aunt was of interest to him.

"Go and check then."

"Genarro, I've got a full set for today. I'll get the others this evening."

But Genarro, who had guessed what the business negotiations with Letizia were about, was implacable.

"Go."

Muttering discontentedly under his breath, Angelo went past Letizia, evading her hand, which tried guiltily to stroke his head.

Genarro had been prepared for the visit of twenty-two-year-old Letizia, although he'd been expecting not so much her as her vivacious elder sister Giulietta. "The girls have chosen another tactic" he told himself with a smile. Genarro realised that Vito's mother would definitely not come on such business; after the disappearance of Vito's father in the maelstrom of world war, she had added a certain abstractedness to her natural gentleness.

The father, whom Vito did not remember, had served in the "Ravenna" mountain infantry division,[6] famous for its traditions

....

[6]   3ª Divisione fanteria da montagna "Ravenna" – a unit of mountain infantry of the Royal Italian Army, in existence 1934–43. It took part in battles on the Western and Eastern fronts during the Second World War. It suffered major losses when Soviet forces counterattacked near Voroshilovgrad. The remnants of the division returned in April to man local defences in Tuscany as part of the Second Army Corps. They

and decimated at the beginning of 1943 somewhere on the steppes of Ukraine. The family heard nothing about him from the end of 1942, and only the homecoming of remnants of the division, who became part of the Tuscany homeland defence force, brought fragmentary information about him. All that was obvious from this information was that Vito's father had been killed. His fellow soldiers, among whom there was no one who had known him personally, relied on divisional lists where Vito senior was listed as "killed", and told the easy story to the relatives that he'd been killed instantly when a shell exploded in his trench.

Seeing the young widow, devastated by grief, the corporal could do no better than to add that her husband died in his sleep. The corporal had said this many times, and so the lie had become convincing, as if he himself had been sleeping in a neighbouring bunker which had survived intact. Hearing that her husband had not realised he was dying had consoled the widow; the corporal was aware of that. It had transported her to some limbo state, between grief and peace of mind, in which state she had remained permanently ever since.

In this situation the boys' education was taken care of by their father's three sisters, who, unlike his mother, were extremely forceful and energetic. At that time the aunts were a little older than Vito was today and transferred to their nephew their still unrealised maternal instincts and their sense of duty to their dead brother.

"Have your guests already gone?" the young woman asked politely and interestedly, surveying the still empty bar and taking her first steps to enter it.

"Yes, early this morning. An old friend dropped in," Genarro reported, unsurprised that this was well known, as things usually were in those parts.

"And I didn't think you had any friends outside Monte-pulciano."

"Still some old ones, Letizia."

"And new ones?"

....
remained there until Italy surrendered.

"You can only have old friends. New ones are comrades," observed the barman philosophically.

"Ah." Letizia had clearly exhausted the prepared topic of conversation. "So, in general, how's business?"

"Letizia…" After his nocturnal celebrations, Genarro was not disposed to engage in matitudinal chat, and slid under the bar counter.

"What?"

"I won't buy." Genarro pulled out a large wooden box with the INOXRIV logo in the middle, and placed it on the table. "You came on account of this?"

"Genarro." The girl blushed. "If you don't buy, no one will buy anything here any more."

"My dear girl, that's a very, very bad argument in trade."

"I'm not trading."

"So what are you doing?"

"I'm trying to solve a problem."

"Not your own, mind you."

"You know it's my own."

"Letizia." Genarro came out into the room and sat down opposite the young woman. "At sixteen, young people have the right to their personal problems. And their mistakes."

The young woman tried to interpose something, but with a gesture Genarro asked her not to interrupt.

"If I'd slept last night," he went on, squinting at the sun, "and hadn't drunk wine, I'd have been able to tell you a lot about what I did when I was sixteen, what responsibilities I bore and what problems I tried to solve. And believe me: of all the problems, money was the least."

With a gesture Genarro invited Letizia to reply.

"I won't even argue with you."

"Thank you, young lady."

"Yes, you're right – it's Vito's problem," Letizia began to get worked up. "From start to finish. He created it and he must solve it. And he's never refused to do so. Not once. You won't get anything out of him. He's fine and got everything under control."

"That's right. That means he's a good bloke and everything will work out for him."

"Genarro, he doesn't say anything, but I know this is his third attempt to earn some money. I also know that the first two went horribly wrong." Tears could be heard in the young woman's voice. "Vito's a very clever boy but he's bloody naïve. Those crafty swine from Siena easily dump any old junk on him which nobody else will take."

"Well, if my words will make you feel better, I can tell you that this time he brought some excellent goods."

Letizia straightened up abruptly and looked Genarro in the eye. He immediately realised that this conversation was difficult for her. "She's a proud girl. She'll give Giulietta a run for her money yet," he thought.

"Excellent goods?"

"My girl, I don't know much about this, but when my friend saw the crockery yesterday, he was very surprised."

"What by exactly?"

"By the fact that he saw them not in some Portofino fish restaurant, but in this remote neck of the woods."

"So you won't buy them nevertheless."

"No, Letizia. It would be like asking everyone, including old Uncle Cesare, to go into the bar in evening dress."

Unexpectedly, both burst out laughing, perhaps picturing to themselves Cesare in the bliss of old age and in evening dress.

"Well, Vito hasn't yet bought any dinner jackets," replied Letizia, picking up the jocular tone and thereby causing the pair a repeat access of hilarity.

"Just don't give him the idea."

"You find it funny, Genarro, but we don't know what to do with him."

"Well, why didn't you ask old man Genarro? I know exactly what young Vito needs."

"What?"

"Peace. Leave him in peace. Stop being his guardian."

Letizia said nothing.

"Let him make as many mistakes as he likes," replied the barman, as if reading Letizia's thoughts. "If he's as good as you say, the time will come when he'll pull himself up by his bootstraps. If he hasn't any talent for commerce, he'll soon try something else. Well, that's not terrible: we can't all be Agnellis."[7]

"Genarro, that's all true. There's just one thing you haven't taken into account: in order to understand whether he has entrepreneurial talent or not, it's got to be given the chance to manifest itself. But these murky dealings which he's been dragged into – I don't consider them a chance. He's simply been exploited on account of his youth and impetuousness. If he has no luck a third time, he won't persist with this any further. He needs one successful deal! I'm sure he'll sprout wings after that! I wouldn't have lifted a finger if he'd asked me for help."

Letizia was so sure she was right that her cheeks went red and her breathing became irregular. No trace of tears remained. Genarro poured a glass of water. Letizia was drinking eagerly when Genarro tried to come back at her. But the barman had not even managed to open his mouth when, without stopping drinking, the girl indicated with a gesture that she hadn't finished talking:

"And another thing, Genarro. The business passed to Agnelli from his grandfather. So we've all been helped at certain moments of our lives."

It was now Genarro's turn to say nothing. He already understood that he would be buying the tableware. And the crux of the matter lay not with Vito, about whom, for all his sympathy for the boy, his opinion had not changed, but with Letizia. Her faith in his nephew had suborned him.

The enthusiasm on the part of Vito was extremely strong, not least on account of the background against which he saw this whole story. His own daughter Sofia had not shown such interest in setting up Angelo, unloading him entirely onto her father. Of course, Genarro put this down to the young age at which she became a mother – it is difficult to expect responsibility from a

....

[7]   Giovanni Agnelli, better known as Gianni Agnelli (12 March 1921, Turin – 24 January 2003, Turin). Italian entrepreneur, chief shareholder and executive director of FIAT. Grandson of Giovanni Agnelli the elder, an industrialist in the first half of the twentieth century and founder of the car firm FIAT.

IGOR ZAVILINSKY

child. Although Genarro felt that at that very moment he was beginning to contradict himself – he had just been talking of sixteen-year-old Vito's sense of responsibility. Genarro was not a fully-fledged father, raising his daughter from birth, taking her to school and fending off her first boyfriends, but he indulged his own child and could only be objective towards the children of others.

Sofia went away to Milan immediately after the war, leaving her grandfather with her son. She left him there for several months, until she settled in her new place. These "several months" lasted ten years. At first she tried, from time to time, to find fresh excuses for the separation – the search for work, for a new place to live, a new marriage, a new flat and much, much else which, in her opinion, might prevent the boy from growing up in harmonious surroundings. But after a few years the theme of linking up with Angelo again was somehow imperceptibly removed from the agenda. Truth to tell, Genarro and Sofia acted more or less in sync in this situation: Sofia stopped promising to bring Angelo back at about the same time that Angelo stopped wanting to let him go. Angelo himself, who had grown up in Tuscany, could not imagine life in the big city and, unlike his old friend Vito, did not dream of leaving his village.

"I have one condition," said Genarro, breaking the silence, "or rather, two."

From the unexpectedly positive outcome of what had seemed like a losing ploy, Letizia took only a moment's thought before nodding happily. She had no misgivings about agreeing to a dozen conditions.

"I'm ready to buy this crockery, but only at cost price. I'll pay exactly what it cost Vito. If you want to show a profit for the boy – that's your prerogative and your money."

The girl continued to nod happily.

"Second. You release Vito for the whole summer to work for me. He'll live with me too. I need help for the time when Angelo is with his mother. However, even if he doesn't go to Milan, I've got enough work for everyone. I won't pay him much, but he'll eat with us. And in the autumn we'll see. Agreed?"

"Yes, yes," Letizia agreed hurriedly and quickly made to leave, as if afraid that Genarro would change his mind. She was already in the doorway when she turned and said: "Thank you! You'll see – you'll be proud of Vito yet!"

"Letizia! The important thing is for the boy to have something to be proud of."

Letizia's body showed shamelessly through her dress as she paused in the doorway before leaving. Genarro sat with his cup of coffee and smiled distractedly. Who knows what he was smiling about: his meeting with his French friend, or his part in deciding the fate of young Vito, or maybe, and this was the most likely explanation, Letizia's shapely legs which disappeared from the doorway rather quicker than they disappeared from his memory.

5

FEBRUARY 2015. NEW YORK, USA

"This isn't a stroke!" Without any dramatic pauses, Aaron blurted this out to Cristina, who had jumped up to meet him.

Cristina, who had stopped in the doctor's doorway, as if absorbing the relief of this news, turned away to the armchair and sat down heavily.

"Thank God!"

"This is the good part of the news…"

"What's the second part?" Angelo's daughter pricked up her ears.

"Cristina, this is 'the first bell', continued the old doctor, adjusting his glasses, – or more accurately – the last: all this is already too much for him. I, of course, will patch him up in a few days, but every new crisis could be the last."

"You know it's useless to talk to him about this."

"This means we must not talk; we must do!"

"Do what?"

"I don't know, Cristina." Aaron sat in the armchair opposite and nodded his head towards Angelo's daughter. "You know – I always play safe. But here's my opinion all the same – he's entered into the danger zone. What's happening with you at the firm? You're not able to sup from the same bowl?"

"What bowl?"

"So my grandmother said…"

"Yes, it's all about the purchase of this shop…"

"Angelo is opening a shop?! Finally, we get down to business…" Aaron approved like the good Jew he was.

"No, Aaron, they convinced him to buy the biggest internet store in the country. It's a very big and long-term business."

"So where's the problem?"

"Papa simply can't digest anything virtual. You wouldn't believe it, but a year ago he still had a fax in his study. He still hasn't got rid of it."

"Well, that's understandable. I'm used to writing everything longhand. When I write, I think. As soon as I start using the computer, all my thoughts are dissipated. Probably the glare from the screen has a bad effect on me."

"You've got a notebook. There's no glare," said Cristina reproachfully.

"Really? Well, that means there's something else…"

"All right. It's a matter of habit… But here it's a question of big money, Aaron. Very big money. But you know papa. If he digs in, no one can budge him."

"But you're a member of the board of directors."

"I can't oppose Angelo openly. Investors are like a flock of birds in the forest. A twig just has to snap and they all rise into the air and fly off. Although I agree with Steve on strategy – if we're only going to work in conservative markets there'll be no growth."

"Oh, my dear, I understand very little about such things. I know that you're a clever woman and I take you at your word, but my dear, forgive an old man, I'm with Angelo – I do not understand the value of a company in which, besides computers and long-haired wimps, there is nothing."

"That's what he said – word for word," Cristina summarized sadly.

"And you were not at the meeting?"

"I just flew in from Chicago," Angelo's daughter answered guiltily. "This quarrel bored me. And it was a shame to look at its convulsions. Aaron, you must understand: I'm as accustomed to my father as I am to simple truth. For many years he was a few steps ahead of the market, but now he lags behind."

"He understands that himself and so he goes out of his mind. But he won't give up."

"He's tired."

"Besides you no-one else will say that to him. They're afraid."

"Well, now for you there are arguments. They're very strong. I don't know how things will turn out. You must look into it."

"There's a more important question that worries me – he needs a rest."

"You're talking about a holiday?"

"Yes, not less than a month of complete rest."

"That's unrealistic," Cristina declared categorically.

"There are no choices in the matter," snapped Aaron.

"Dad will not leave the company now. Simply because the fragile advantage of votes on his side will be instantly destroyed. The balance rests exclusively on his authority and physical presence. If he were to miss even one board of directors meeting, the number of his supporters would decrease sharply. And he understands that."

"We need to think of something. We've got to speak with Steve. He's such a capable, intelligent man."

"Steve – he's an interested party. A month without Angelo and he'll jump at the chance to win over the board of directors and replace my father."

"My dear, in that case, Steve is our ally. We can solve two problems at once: It's impossible for Angelo to remain president of the company. It's usually against my rules to say this, but if you don't remove him from his job, death will do it for you."

Cristina shivered at the directness of the words. It seemed, that up to this moment, she, understanding in theory what might be threatened, had all the time avoided the word "death". All the conversations were around "health" and "risk", euphemisms, second-hand ideas, and no-one was prepared to say what was hidden behind these cautious assessments.

Cristina had known Aaron since her childhood, and he her from before that: from the moment Angelo's former wife became pregnant. Aaron was no longer the healthy fat guy he had been in his youth and in his mature years; when, entering their still not very big flat, he had seemed to fill the whole space. He filled it because of the physical parameters of the flat, and the sounds, and the smell of his eau de cologne, and the themes of the conversations. Aaron was big in every way. But as the years passed, he diminished, became less. In the end, only his professional cynicism and his eau-de-cologne were left.

Aaron fell into that category of fatalist doctors who think that the greatest harm to a person comes not from illness but from their perception of their own health. This was of particular relevance in the age of the internet, when every patient began to have a heart-felt, internet-informed opinion on any ailment, which inevitably was communicated to a doctor and a demand made, without fail, for his refutation or confirmation. Aaron would react aggressively, sending his home-grown medical experts to find treatment on Google, or sometimes even further away still… For this reason, despite his high level of qualification and indisputable talent as a doctor, opinion on him was varied. He was rumoured to be a rude cynic. However, beyond these criticisms no-one could say a word against him – from a professional point of view his practice was close to ideal.

As a result, Aaron abandoned his most hysterical and impressionable clients, and those who were left were faithful to him and there was no limit to the trust they had in him. Angelo was very much a part of this group. Perhaps Aaron was the only authority over Angelo, among either the living or the dead.

"Aaron, he will listen to you. You know he will," Cristina almost implored.

"My dear, as far as the medical part of this goes, I will impress upon him, I will even try to prove to him, that in those years when he had been dealt the very best hand, he did not have time to spend his money, helped in this parsimony by the small number of relatives he had, and so now he is suffering all this for the sake of ten or twelve bloodsuckers from charitable funds who look down on him like vultures, barely concealing their impatience. But this strategic planning I do without any hope that he will agree with me…"

"Then what's the point of saying all this?"

"The point is, my dear, that he will tell me and my life-affirming reasoning to go to hell, and I will be offended." The doctor narrowed his eyes cunningly.

"Really?"

"Oh, believe me, I can be offended," said Aaron, not without pride, "and Angelo will throw me a 'bone', a little gift so that I won't grumble. He will say to me: 'What have I got to do, you old fart, so that you relax and lay off me? I'm ready for anything, only don't ask me to take my pension!' And I'll ask him to take a holiday. And he won't be able to refuse me."

"You're a cunning devil," remarked Angelo's daughter, laughing rapturously.

"But this is only half the job. A holiday with an iPhone, an iPad, an iMac,, and other i-nonsense won't do him any good. In his case it might be even worse: a deficit of information, or an interpretation of information by his assistants, will excite him more than a complete absence of it. I need to 'cut him off' from everything... How to do this – I don't know. You'll have to go away and think about what hole to send him to. Even if you buy an uninhabited island – even if you drag him up Everest..."

At the mention of Everest, Cristina raised her eyebrows.

"I do have one idea," said Cristina thoughtfully, sunk in contemplation.

"My dear, that's great," Aaron wheezed as he got up from the low armchair, and, having taken a jelly-baby from a saucer that stood on the reception counter, he moved towards the exit, "I'm going now. Phone me when you think of something."

6

FEBRUARY 2015. MONTEPULCIANO, ITALY

When Massimo dropped into the office, which was in a new wing, Alessandro was measuring it by pacing from wall to wall. Catching sight of Massimo through the glass door, Alessandro hurried to open it for him.

"Well, has he said anything yet?"

"I think you're pressurising him too hard…"

"You always say that. What did father say?"

"Nothing." Massimo hurried to the water cooler. "All I got out of him was a promise to give it some more thought."

"There's no time to think!"

"Have you got a better suggestion?"

Alessandro did not answer, and continued walking to and fro. Then he stopped abruptly and asked:

"How much time do the workers need?"

"Well, their plans are ready. Bottom line: at a pinch, a month after we place the order we'll be able to say we've got our swimming pool."

"That means we've got a couple of weeks to make a decision."

"Why?"

"Because the first bookings start in April," muttered the elder brother, looking at his computer.

"Well, I wouldn't say that… Of course, I played along with you when we were talking to the old man, but all the same, I don't think we'll have a bad season without a swimming pool. We're getting bookings, even more than last year. It won't be easy, but…"

"It won't!" Alessandro interrupted sharply, while continuing to gaze at the computer.

"What?"

"We need a swimming pool by April!"

"Alessandro, there's something I don't understand… So far we haven't promised anyone anything." Suspicions had begun to take hold of Massimo and he sat down opposite his brother and tried to look him in the eye. In reply Alessandro did the opposite and walked away to the window. Massimo abruptly turned the computer screen towards himself, clicked the mouse a few times, and froze.

"What have you gone and done?"

"I'm doing something positive, Massimo. I'm taking bookings!"

"Alessandro! You can't! It's a scam! We won't get rid of it like that!" Massimo's gaze wandered distractedly over the screen.

"It's not a scam, Massimo." Alessandro spoke without turning round and kept looking out of the window. "There'll be a swimming pool."

"You shouldn't have done that! All right, so he didn't say so, but father won't stand for it!"

"Stop moaning!" Alessandro turned decisively towards his brother. "You know very well that 50% of bookings are made in winter. I had no choice. If I hadn't made an announcement about the pool a month ago, we wouldn't have any of the bookings which you're so pleased about! I'm sorry I didn't do it in December. God knows how many we've missed…"

"But you realise that if there's no pool, there'll be a scandal! We'll simply be dropped from all the hotel search engines and we'll have to compensate clients."

"No, we won't, Massimo! There will be a pool. Instead of preaching, think how we can talk father round. We've got two weeks!"

Alessandro again turned away to the window, looking towards the place where the pool would be, as if trying to construct it by the efforts of his own mind. In the centre of the lawn, which in their plans would be the location of the pool, stood Vito's armchair. In the absence of its owner, who had disappeared into the restaurant, the chair seemed to be saying to Alessandro: "Don't even think of it!"

"And if we can't talk him round?" Massimo, sensing an impending family row, was in despair.

"Massimo! We have no alternatives," replied Alessandro calmly. "On the internet we have a pool. That means we have one in the real world."

"Father will kill us."

"In the first place, he won't kill you. And secondly, for what? Massimo, we've got enough deposits on rooms for half a pool." The elder brother knocked the computer screen as if it was a money box.

"You know what I'm on about. You know him. He won't forgive us. You'll be right at least a hundred times, Alessandro, but this is too much."

Massimo, who in commercial matters was in full agreement with Alessandro in any argument with his father, was not so much angry with his brother as fearful of the upcoming show-down. His elder brother had always been bolder and more entre-preneurial than him, which in the end dictated the division of powers between them in the business. Alessandro was in charge of the marketing of their business and of all external contacts and links with tourist companies, whereas Massimo was in charge of the domestic arrangements and the guests. Buttering up guests was his forte, something which his character suited.

From his childhood, Massimo had been unable physically to stand conflicts. They simply made him sick. For the same reason he did not like sporting contests. He loved sport, but only training. He was a good, patient sportsman, and had shown promise in many disciplines. However, when it came to competitions, with their inevitable rivalries, the boy fell into a stupor. Even in such a competitive form, conflict killed any desire in him to get a result. Massimo had always suffered from this.

Of course, not only in sport, but in life as a whole, kind-heartedness begins to bring dividends, as a rule, in later years, but in childhood and adolescence it brings only suffering.

For many years, his father had supposed that he could be influential and make a "real man" of his son, meaning firmness of character and the ability to stand up for himself. It hardly needs saying that this merely added to Massimo's tribulations; he fell into a closed circle, unable to come into conflict with his father on account of his own dislike of conflict.

It was obvious to Vito that his son's character came from his mother; furthermore, what he had loved in Gabriella, in his son drove him mad. And he could not reconcile himself to it, worried as he was about the future of the boy who, in his opinion, would find life tough in this cruel world. It is not certain how long this "war for masculine character" would have gone on, had it not been for the illness which struck Massimo at fourteen.

It began with an ordinary attack of flu, to which no particular attention was paid in the house and which was simply allowed to run its course. The situation was so serious that Massimo spent three days in intensive care. Vito, like any concerned parent, heaped all the blame on himself for what had happened. Finding no other obvious cause for such a severe form of an ordinary illness, he saw in it a reaction by his son against his father's attempts to change his God-given character. For three nights Vito did not leave Massimo, who was thrashing about in a fever, and for all three days he begged forgiveness of him and swore he would accept his son as he had been when he was born. His father's pledges, or correct treatment, or, more likely, a strong youthful organism, gained the upper hand over the illness, and three days later Massimo was at home with practically no sign of his recent bout of ill health.

Such a rapid recovery produced an impression, not only on the doctors, who had literally been struggling to save the child's life, but also, of course, on Vito – for him it confirmed the accuracy of his explanation for his son's illness. Vito remained true to the pledges given at the sick boy's bedside; never again in his whole life did he reproach Massimo for his kind-heartedness and softness. Fate repaid him handsomely for solving this old problem by bombarding him with the successes of the high-flying Massimo.

Later it even seemed to Vito that the illness had strengthened his son's character, making him more decisive and competitive among his peers. However, frightened for the rest of his life, his father was afraid to discuss this question with himself, even in his thoughts, which he scotched in their infancy.

Whether Massimo had really become bolder, or whether he had simply adapted to the quirks of his own character, or had simply used it to maximum advantage, by the age of thirty Vito's younger son was in full charge of his father's household and had gently eased his father out. This was done so delicately, that to this day the old man was sure that he was in charge of everything in the hotel and restaurant. Moreover, Massimo was an ideal buffer between two likeminded people – father and elder son – whose business discussions seemed never to end peacefully. By and large, it was thanks to Massimo that the business existed and thrived; but for him Alessandro would have thrown everything up a long time ago and gone off, as he'd planned earlier, to the south of France, where he's been offered a job in tourism, while his conservative father would have stayed behind his old bar.

Massimo, retreating a little from this shocking revelation, began to think logically:

"One thing I can say for certain: as long as father's here, we won't see a pool. You realise, not a single local workman would dare to come to our house without Vito's permission."

"So what do you suggest? Send him off on leave?" came the taunt from the elder brother.

"I'd like to. But you realise that no force in the world could make father budge."

7

1955. MONTEPULCIANO, ITALY

"Vito, get behind the line!"

"I have!"

"No! Your foot has crept out beyond the limit of the table – look!"

"Stop it, Angelo! What does it matter if my toes have crept a bit further? I don't throw with my feet. My hands are no nearer the board because of this!"

"All the same!"

"Angelo, stop moaning!"

"I'm not moaning. Let's play fair!"

"Yes, let's, for heaven's sake!" So saying, Vito took a whole step back and got ready to throw the dart.

"No!" Once again the younger brother began to moan.

"What is it now?" said Vito irritably.

"Now you're well away from it."

"What's that to you? You should be pleased. It'll be more difficult for me to score!" said Vito angrily.

"When you lose, you'll say I didn't play fair," retorted Angelo without much conviction.

"You don't know what I'll say."

"You will say that."

"Have I ever said that, even once?" asked Vito with an affable smile.

"Well, no." Angelo began to fidget in his chair. "All right. If you lose like that. I'll think I haven't won fairly."

"Angelo, you're a pain."

"I just want to win fairly."

"If it was simply a matter of fairness, you would argue every time. As it is, you keep an eye on it only when there are loads of dishes. Admit it, Angelo, you're simply afraid of losing!"

"That's not true. When there are loads of dishes it's you who begins to cheat."

"All right. Calm down. All the same you won't beat me, and it doesn't matter to me where I won from." Vito got ready to throw.

"Vito!"

"All right. All the same, you're a pain."

Vito returned to the agreed spot, ostentatiously lining up the toes of his bare feet with the table and then, without pausing, threw the dart at the board. The dart flew so quickly that it seemed not to have flown at all. Angelo, who had thrown first, began to tot up feverishly Vito's three throws. Even before the dart hit the board, Vito seemed to understand the situation and moved off towards the washing up disappointedly.

American soldiers had given the darts to Genarro at the end of the war – they had been billeted here for more than a week in 1944. How the soldiers, who had spent several years in trenches, kept the game intact, was still a mystery. At that point Genarro had only recently moved to these parts and, until he sold the hotel in the Alps, did not have the resources to repair and refurbish the bar, but the rooms were fully habitable. To soldiers who had spent many months in field conditions, these modest arrangements seemed the height of luxury. Incidentally, the American sergeant who had lived here in 1944 subsequently put Genarro in touch with either his uncle or his aunt's husband, who owned a small business somewhere in Texas, and, dreaming of spending his old age in Europe, he eventually bought a five-room apartment on the Italy-Switzerland border.

At first it was visitors who played darts, but soon the majority of the darts were either lost or broken, and they became a kind of integral attribute of the building, like a picture on the wall, with two intact arrows blatantly stuck in the bull's eye, without having been thrown.

For Genarro these darts were one reminder, even if indirect, of his life in the north. At least nothing was sharper in his memory than the dart board and darts on the wall.

Like all their visitors, Vito and Angelo, having spent all day working behind the bar, practically never played darts. There was just one exception – if the boys needed to settle some argument. In that case the sum total of three throws was decisive in their decision-making. In this straightforward game the difference in their ages was unimportant and, taking account of their equal ability in throwing, one could say that the result was in many ways a matter of chance. Actually, that's what they needed.

Most commonly at stake in such quarrels was the choice of work at the end of the day: clearing up the bar plus Cesare or washing up. Angelo preferred the first, the parameters of which were stable: rearranging the furniture, washing the floors, and taking ninety-year-old Cesare home did not take much time.

Things could be different with the washing up: sometimes there wasn't much of it, but on feast days, or when there was a wake, washing up could be pure punishment. In such cases the motivation for playing increased dramatically, accompanied by emotions worthy of a Fiorentina match. Victory by either of the boys would turn into a spectacle full of sarcastic triumphalism, with the victor marching past the washing up, singing the national anthem, and a demonstration of very possible variant of passing the time idly, including lying on the bar.

Arguments about washing up were perhaps the only cause of rivalry between Vito and Angelo; having been friends for several years, they became even closer after Vito moved into Genarro's house. This was helped by their working together – Genarro tried to ensure that there was plenty such work – and especially by conversations in the long evening hours after the bar closed.

"I'll help you," Angelo would say, thus demonstrating his nobility, after he returned from walking old man Cesare home.

"It's all right, kid. Relax! I'm just finishing," Vito would reply magnanimously.

Angelo sat down on the bar and examined the photo of the mountaineers which, as he had promised Maurice, Genarro had hung on the end wall, where from a distance, it reminded one of an icon.

"Would you have been afraid?"

Vito looked up from the sink in order to understand what his friend was talking about, but delayed answering.

"I don't know. But I would certainly have been cold," the boy replied, with a touch of irony at his own expense.

"Do they pay for that?" said the younger boy thoughtfully.

"They do. And quite well," came the unexpected reply from Genarro who had slipped quietly into the bar.

"What for?" said Angelo in some puzzlement, having jumped down from the bar.

"For the possibility of doing it."

"Why?"

"What do you mean 'why'?"

"Why do they need it?"

"Well, why do sportsmen play football?"

"To win the *scudetto*!"

"They've got their own *scudetto*.[8] They've each got their own *scudetto*, Angelo," said the old man, sitting down in his armchair.

This armchair was the sole object which remained from the previous owners. Genarro liked to sit in it of an evening, drinking wine. For Angelo, the comparison with football was not convincing; the material and other benefits which celebrity brought to sportsmen were well understood. They might risk their legs, but not their lives.

"I don't know, Genarro," insisted his grandson. "For me, everything's much clearer with football: regardless of anything, just rake in the money and take your choice of the girls!"

"Do you think that when Julinho[9] is taking a penalty he's thinking about girls?"

"You can say one thing for certain: when he misses, he is," Vito put in, leaving the sink and holding in his still wet hands two bottles of red wine. Genarro nodded approvingly towards the proffered bottle.

....

[8]   Literally *Little shield*. The badge worn on the jerseys of the team which wins the Italian Serie A.

[9]   Brazilian footballer. Born Júlio Botelho in Sao Paulo 29 July 1929. Died in Sao Paulo 10 January 2003. Played right half-back. In 1992 was named best player in the history of the Italian club Fiorentina.

"Never mind the footballers." The barman settled in his armchair and changed the subject. "Vito, what would you like to get by way of your own personal *scudetto*?"

"I want to go away to Rome, or, maybe, Milan. Doesn't matter where," said Vito dreamily, wiping his hands on his apron.

"Good Lord, Vito, what don't you like about Montepulciano?" said Angelo in surprise.

"I like everything," replied Vito enthusiastically, straddling his chair with his bottle, "but I don't want to have this choice all my life – washing up or clearing up."

"What will you do in Rome?" asked Genarro, taking his first swig of the wine.

"Well, I'll think of something. But I certainly won't wash dishes."

"You wouldn't be washing them here if you played darts better," said Angelo pointedly.

"It's not a matter of dishes," said Vito, good-humouredly ignoring the barb.

"So what is it a matter of?" Angelo still did not understand his friend.

"You can't be satisfied with what you've got, even if everything's fine and you've got enough to eat and clothes to go out in." With a glance towards him, Vito asked permission from Genarro and, receiving a scarcely perceptible nod in reply, handed a half-empty glass to Angelo. "Angelo, what do you dream about?"

"In all honesty?" said Angelo, pleased at being allowed a taste of wine. "A motorbike!"

"My dear boy! You can't dream about a motorbike," said Genarro with a wry smile.

"Why not?"

"A motorbike can't be a dream." Genarro laughed good-naturedly. "It's too small."

"Ah, you speak like that, Genarro, as if you've got one," said his grandson excitedly.

"I'll get one, if I want one. But I don't want the purchase of a motorbike to represent the fulfilment of a dream for me. You can't plonk your backside on a dream! You can on a motorbike. Do you understand?"

"No. What's bad about my dream?!" Angelo complained, somewhat offended. "If it's too small, I'll try to dream about a more expensive model."

"Are you ready to die for a motorbike?" asked Genarro unexpectedly.

The question made the boys shudder. Angelo looked at Vito, as if he wanted to check whether he would give the right answer.

"Die? No, of course not!"

"There, you've answered the question yourself."

"All right. Who is prepared to die for a dream?"

"Well, them, for example." Genarro poked his finger at the photo of the mountaineers.

"They're mad."

"That's just it. Everyone with a real dream seems mad to other people. And all because the majority of people don't live by their dreams."

"What do they live by?"

"I don't know. Daily requirements probably. Every day God sends they think about what they need, not about what they want. And even if, all of a sudden, they cogitate about their own wants, they're gripped by a fear of wanting something bigger than they need. A motorbike, you say... A motorbike is not a good thing to dream about, but a good way of achieving it is to dream about travelling right round the world."

Angelo fell silent, trying to comprehend what his grandfather said. In purely theoretical terms he understood what Genarro had in mind, but could in no way reconcile himself to it – he desperately wanted a motorbike, and even if he made a big effort to find an object more worthy of a dream, he couldn't. It really did seem to him that if he had a motorbike, he wouldn't need anything else from life. It was here that the difference in ages between the boys showed itself most clearly – Angelo already lived in a time when the achievement of happiness was understood and specified down to the last detail of the longed-for motorbike, and such a state of mind did not brook substantial changes in view of the unlikelihood of its being realised in the foreseeable future. As he reached adolescence Vito was full of passion and ambition, doubts and plans, not always concrete ones but ones which excited him all the more because of that.

"And what's happened with your dream?" Vito took the bottle from his friend as he re-entered the conversation. "Have you still got it?"

"Well, I did have, of course. And more than one probably. And did your dreams come true?" replied Angelo.

"You know, it's an odd thing. Often something comes true which you hadn't dreamed about at all. That doesn't mean that you made a mistake, or that dreaming is useless. It's simply that life is wiser than we are and realises precisely those dreams which are most important to us. Even if you don't agree with this at first and see in this outcome some mistake made by fate and sometimes, more than that, your own defeat."

"This is like climbing the wrong mountain!" said Angelo, thus revealing his awareness of the nocturnal conversation with the Frenchman, for which he got a kick under the table from Vito.

"Well, something like that," said his grandfather with a wry smile, making it clear that he knew about the listeners.

"Which wrong mountain did you climb?" asked Vito.

"I didn't exactly climb." Genarro nodded vaguely towards the photo.

"Annapurna!?" the boys said together.

"Well, nothing quite so definite. Maurice and I planned an expedition to Nepal. Probably you wouldn't call it planning. We discussed the idea of climbing to eight thousand metres. Of course, that was our dream. For Maurice, by dint of his age at the time, it was a somewhat puerile dream, but for me it was quite deliberate – after all, I was a highly qualified mountaineer. I'd thought about it earlier, before the war, but only in Maurice did I see a partner. He was as big a nutcase as me." Genarro gave a wry smile, as if to say: "What, you didn't know you were living with a nutcase?"

"Then what?" Angelo was eager to know.

"Then what? Circumstances arose," Genarro tapped his grandson lightly on the nose, "which did not allow me to fulfil my dream."

"I spoiled everything," said Angelo sadly.

"Lads! I permit you to ignore what old Genarro is droning on about, but I do ask you to remember the main thing: every man must be able to choose his priority: preferably quickly, always responsibly and precisely – without regret."

"But you've refused your main dream!" Angelo was becoming sadder and sadder.

"Correct, but not quite. I tell you – life is wiser than us. Taking one dream, Life, like a card sharp, substitutes another. And when the trump card is taken from your hands and you're dealt another, face down, it's difficult to thank fate for it: you resist, you keep thinking how to get the lost trump card back, and when you realise that it's impossible, you get angry. You're angry until the new card is turned over. Sometimes a lot of time passes before you realise how much more important was the dream you've been gifted."

"Why have you never talked about this to us?"

"Well, Sofia is a woman, and male dreams are for men only!" Genarro's whole demeanour indicated the equality of his interlocutors in this male conversation. "And you, dear boy, were too little for such conversations. I suppose it's only now you can understand me."

"Why didn't you return to the dream about Nepal later?" put in Vito.

"How could I, Vito? Angelo was growing up, Sofia wanted to realise her own dreams, to which she had a complete right. But if I'm honest, I felt the time had passed – physically and emotionally. Do you know what my grandfather used to say?"

"What?"

"'The horse is a goner. Get off it.' I felt that however much I teased myself with this idea, my 'Nepalese horse' was already a goner and I had to move on."

A pause hung in the air. Everyone had their own thoughts. Or rather, they all had the same thought, but from his own point of view. Genarro poured himself the remainder of the wine, ignoring a second bottle and giving the boys to understand that the meeting was at an end. It was already rather late and they all realised that the conversation had to end, but no one, including the old man, knew how to do it: somehow too many lofty words had been spoken for an ordinary evening, even taking into account the recent arrival of the heroic mountaineer. Genarro finished the bottle, glanced once more at the photo, and, finding no better way of ending the conversation, simply walked out, patting his grandson's hair as he went.

"I'll climb it!" Angelo unexpectedly announced. He was a little tipsy and poked his finger at the photo.

"That's his dream, not yours," was Vito's reasoned reaction to this.

"He exchanged it for me. That means it's my dream now!" the young man said heatedly, impressed by the conversation.

"You can't even imagine how difficult it is," reasoned Vito.

"I'm not going tomorrow. Basically, it doesn't matter when. I'm simply obliged to do it in the course of my life. This will be my token of gratitude to the old man for what he's done for me."

Vito, whom the alcohol had barely affected, looked carefully at his friend, as if weighing the seriousness of his words.

"Hell! In that case I'll have to climb it too!" Vito said unhurriedly. "Someone must be alongside when you get hysterics on the summit."

"Uh-huh, if you don't run off because of the cold."

"We'll check it out!"

"Deal?"

"Deal."

8

MARCH 2015. NEW YORK, USA – MONTEPULCIANO, ITALY

In her forty years, having had the same number of years as an air passenger, Cristina had not ceased to be amazed at the speed at which "scenes" change with air travel. Just think of it: in so short a time to be at an evening reception in the house of an important client, then the journey and the tailback to JFK, the flight in the night sky, and in just a few hours the swiftness of the dawn.

Even though she could see it for herself, and flew regularly, every time Cristina saw in this a small wonder, accompanied by an utterly childish sense of joy. All his life Cristina's father had been frightened to fly, which was why he had rarely got out of New York. This played more than a minor role in her promotion to her father's business, because certain questions were so confidential in nature that Angelo was able to resolve them only himself, or through a person in whom he had near absolute trust. All this had begun immediately after university with trivial errands, but after a few years Cristina was representing her father in most of his negotiations outside New York. The consequence of this activity was, of course, Cristina's endless flights – at first around the country, and later around the world. Despite such regularity, the flights remained for her a source of joy.

Boarding the flight, Cristina switched on "flight mode", not only for her mobile phone, but also for herself. For her this mode meant the opportunity to be alone, to watch some sort of woman's film, hardly loaded with meaning, simply to gaze out at the endless varying clouds, to eat a little fresh bun (forbidden in her dietetically concerned New York life), having spread on it (Oh my God!) a tiny dob of butter. It meant the opportunity to ignore the twenty-four hour clock, to drink a bottle of champagne – i.e. everything that was almost inaccessible to her on earth. It was important because none of these actions would gnaw at her conscience either during or after the flight: everything that happened on board the plane was left on board the plane. This was so pleasant that to Cristina it seemed a pity to sleep during the long flights, not to prolong the pleasure. But besides physical pleasures Cristina derived satisfaction from the very aesthetics of aviation – every detail of the flight attendants' uniforms, the peaked caps of the pilots, the presentation of their meals, the almost ritualistic safety instructions, the glossy inflight magazines, the travel accessories, the clicking of the safety belts, even the sequences of the sounds of the plane; all this comprised for her a perfect world. Evidently a permanent life in such a world, as for the flight attendants, would gradually defeat its charm, but Cristina's time on the flight was so transient that she could preserve this idyllic picture. Regardless of her mood before the flight and of what Cristina expected at her destination, she always emerged from the plane in good spirits.

A little over two hours after dinner in Rome, Cristina saw the old walls on the horizon. The car left the autostrada, winding along a narrow road between endless vineyards and olive groves. The grey-haired driver pointed above the wheel through the windscreen, muttering:

"Montepulciano."

The speed of her displacement from New York; the putting on of her usual business suit today; the leather interior of an expensive car – none of this allowed Cristina to feel that there were any fundamental differences from her feelings in New York. Cristina was in a capsule, filled up to now with the comforts to which she was accustomed. She looked through the window of the car as if at a television. What was happening in the window, or more accurately, the absence of any signs of life in the February Tuscan landscape, presented her with a moving, silent picture. Probably for this reason Cristina did not feel any of the excitement she had expected to feel on arriving in her father's native country.

The satnav confidently informed them of their arrival at their destination. However, the appearance of the house in front of which the Mercedes stopped was quite different from the house she had seen on the internet. The driver, seeing the sign didn't correspond, also understood that they had arrived in the wrong place, and swore quietly in Italian. Cristina took the address of the villa from its website and put it into her phone, quickly discovering that they had stopped short of it by a little over a mile. Having compared maps, the driver drove on further, and soon they stopped outside a set of beautiful wrought-iron gates. On a stone wall, which was just big enough to indicate the entrance and to hold the gate, Cristina unexpectedly saw a familiar surname – Agriturismo De Rossi. Of course, she had learned the previous evening that the villa bore the surname of her grandfather Genarro, whom she had not known, but now, having seen these big, wrought iron letters, the consciousness of this touched her: even if it was a long time since she had used her father's surname, this did not change her feeling of ownership, which extended to everything connected to De Rossi.

Steadying herself as she was hit by a sudden surge of emotion, Cristina glanced around. A very big house in the traditional Tuscan style with a flat tiled roof stood on a small elevation. It was not even a hill, but she nevertheless sensed a superiority over the fields – between where Cristina stood and the fortress walls of Montepulciano, already distinctly visible several kilometres away, this was the highest point. The remainder of the elevation, some of it with buildings on it and some of it empty ground, could be seen in the distance. The villa itself was exactly as she had seen it in its photograph on the internet. From the side which faced Cristina could be seen an open first floor, under the arches of which was a small restaurant with ten or so tables. Evidently February was not the most popular time for tourists, and many of the tables had been cleared away and were resting along the wall, reminding her of big wheels from some sort of huge cart. Next to them rose up chairs, stacked one on top of another. A little further on could be seen a second, newer, building, built in the style of the main villa, its appearance suggesting that it served some sort of administrative purpose, and with a garage on its first floor. Because of the contour of the land, from the edge where Cristina stood it was difficult to see the other side of the hotel's grounds. The land between these two buildings was divided by immaculate gravel pathways and covered with neat lawns. In everything – in the house and in the courtyard – one could sense tidiness, bordering on pedantry. It wasn't that there was a lack of personality. The land was not "dead", did not geld the soul. Even in the absence of people one could feel life, and it seemed to Cristina as if at any moment children might run out on to the lawn catching a ball which risked rolling out into the road. However, Cristina could make no claim to objectivity, considering the mixture of feelings she had been experiencing for the last few minutes.

The driver, who had entered in search of one of the hotel staff, returned and indicated that Cristina should get back into the car. In answer to her perplexed look, he waved his hand towards the other side of the hotel, where it looked as if there was another entrance. Sure enough, after fifty metres Cristina saw a more modest gate, not bearing the family name, which had been already opened for them by a boy of about ten.

Cristina noted to herself that instead of the embarrassment that she would have expected from a boy of that age, there was a scarcely perceptible, dignified nod of the head. It seemed as if, had he had a hat, he would have used his other hand to tip it. The car's wheels spun with a satisfying crunch of gravel stones. The sound initiated some sort of chemical reaction in Cristina's spirit, freeing from her genetic memory a warm wave of fantastical memories. At that moment everything around her became familiar and homely, as if it was her who had chased after a ball on these lawns. Her good sense dryly pointed to the impossibility of the existence of such memories, but her heart happily acquiesced in the deception and continued to leaf through the pictures of a fictitious photo album. The Mercedes stopped. The driver opened the door and Cristina climbed out directly opposite the main entrance of the house. Straight towards them hurried a thickset man of about thirty. He was dressed in workman's overalls, but to judge from the confidence with which he walked, and the proprietorial look which he cast about him, it was clear that he was no gardener.

"I apologize for your wait, Signora Esposito. We don't use the central gates, in winter." The young man spoke clearly, although with a perceptible accent, as he moved towards her. His face was open and handsome.

"It doesn't matter. Call me Cristina, please."

"I am Massimo." The young man introduced himself, warmly shaking Cristina's extended hand. For a moment she wanted to keep hold of his hand. In it she could feel something genuine, masculine. His palm was not immaculately clean, but bore traces of fresh and recent wounds, which said something of its owner's lack of squeamishness when it came to manual work. Even so, the shape and neatness of his fingernails would have been the envy of any woman. Cristina, in examining Massimo's hands, had allowed an awkward pause, and, in an attempt to hurry the conversation along she blurted out:

"Are you the owner of this excellent hotel?"

"Some day I will be, if my father doesn't arbitrarily cut me out of my inheritance," answered Massimo with a laugh, inviting Cristina to follow him inside.

"Your father's capable of doing such a thing?"

"I really hope not," the young man replied, laughing quietly.

"It might not be worth taking the risk. Maybe you should be more dutiful?"

"I am dutiful. But if the old man decides to rewrite his will, he'll begin with Alessandro – my older brother." Again Massimo laughed, opening in front of Cristina the door to her room on the second floor. "Make yourself comfortable! This is a special room – it has an internal window to the restaurant. You're never going to miss breakfast and you can order room service without a telephone."

"What fun! It's the first time I've seen anything like this!" Cristina glanced through the small internal window, from which a panoramic view of the restaurant opened out.

"I'm sorry, all our rooms are small – the building is old and we try to create comfort from what we have at our disposal."

"I think you've done really well. I like it all. Thank you!"

"Then relax, dinner will be in about an hour." Massimo put Cristina's bags in the corner. Cristina automatically dipped into her purse in search of change, but her eyes met with Massimo's startled glance. Again, an awkward pause hung in the air. Cristina could not find a quick explanation to avoid offending the hotel's possible inheritor. Massimo deliberately held a mocking pause, curiously eyeing Cristina to see how she would disentangle herself. After a moment, he took pity and gave a good-natured laugh.

"Excuse me, it's a reflex I've developed over the years," Cristina confessed, laughing partly out of relief.

"It's a good reflex, I'll wait for you at dinner." Indicating the restaurant window, Massimo took his leave.

The room turned out to be a suite of two small rooms. On entering, visitors found themselves in the sitting-room, in which stood a sofa from which it was possible to look through the window at the bustle of the restaurant, or beyond the bustle to a television mounted on the far wall. Practically the whole of the bedroom was occupied by a big bed. The room, like the rest of the house, was "of the past", and anyone who did not know its history would have had little trouble inventing one for themselves. Every handle on a chest of drawers, every blind on a window or wooden beam on the ceiling was soaked in time. Yet it did not have the moth-balled smell of a museum. Cristina could not rid herself of the feeling that she had been in this room at a time when all these objects were new. It seemed as if the day's rapid spatial displacement had triggered an actual movement in time.

Between the sitting-room and the bedroom was the bathroom. A little weary from the emotions coursing through her, Cristina hurried in and settled herself into a hot bath. Through the window at her eye level she could see only the sky, and only in the very corner of that "picture", the top of the fortress walls of Montepulciano, already familiar to her. Lowering her gaze, Cristina saw with amazement a bottle of wine standing in ice in a wine cooler on the edge of the bath, its cork barely in. "It's true, they know how to create comfort," she thought, stretching out her hand towards the bottle.

After the hot water of the bath and two glasses of wine Cristina felt drastically shortened, as if compressed by the night's flight, travelling against the movement of the earth. Realising that the evening's plan was threatened with disruption, Cristina dressed, and sat down on the sofa with the firm intention of awaiting dinner. She wanted to satisfy not only her hunger, but her growing curiosity about this building and the people who lived here. The compromise with the sofa was terribly naive, and Cristina quickly fell asleep. The traveller's sleep was so deep that she did not hear Massimo's two timid attempts to knock on the door. At the third knock he gave up, realising that the American was sleeping off the rigours of her journey. At first Cristina did not even understand – she woke and immediately was frightened, or maybe it was the other way round. She would feel awkward in front of the owners and she hurried down to the restaurant.

Downstairs it was empty. The only light on was behind the bar. In the centre of the restaurant, as if in the ring of a circus, stood a solitary table, which had apparently been set out for the hotel's only guest. The table was covered with a snow-white cloth, and, despite the absence of any dinner, was still set up. It was evident that the hosts, up until the last moment, had been hoping that the guest would come down. In the centre of the table stood some wine – not in a bottle, but in an unusual thick glass decanter. Under a tea-towel, Cristina found a chopping board with a knife and bread. There was a big piece of cheese, with several smaller pieces which had already been sliced off, as if whoever had set the table was hinting at the correct way to cut cheese. Cristina guessed that originally there had been more food on the table, but that the rest of it had been cleared away. She was angry at herself now that she had been left hungry – New York time was stubbornly demanding a meal.

Cristina glanced round the room and then, trying not to make a noise, sat down at the table. She looked at the cheese as if bewitched. It was not so much the cheese itself which excited her, but the crumbs which had been scattered around the board as it was cut. These crumbs of various sizes were so appetizing in their chaos. If anyone had sliced the cheese without littering crumbs,

IGOR ZAVILINSKY

an experienced New York chef, standing at a little distance from the table, would have thought for a moment, twirling the lock of hair which poked out from under his chef's hat, before crushing one of the slices with strong fingers. Then, as a final flourish, he would have scattered them from a height across the board, trying to depict the essence of rural life. Cristina took a couple of crumbs, and before eating them, she smelled them. She did the same with the bread, and then the wine. Bliss flowed through her body, causing her to close her eyes. The red wine was like nothing she had tried before. She scarcely had had time alone with her thoughts to ask herself the question: "What is this?", when she received an answer from behind the bar:

"It's Montepulciano D'Abruzzo."[10]

Cristina shuddered and opened her eyes. Behind the bar, resting with his elbows on the countertop, stood an elderly man. He was dressed in a simple shirt with sleeves which had been rolled up, revealing strong, hairy arms. The man seemed to be somehow organically part of the interior of the bar, so much so that Cristina had no doubt that this was Vito himself – the owner of the hotel and her father's childhood friend.

Actually this was the limit of Cristina's knowledge of Vito. Angelo talked little about his childhood in Tuscany, a big part of which he had spent with his grandfather in this hotel.

"You can only try it here. Locals say the wine is too good to sell. They drink it all themselves."

"Cristina Esposito," the guest introduced herself.

"You didn't think about going back to De Rossi after the divorce?" The old man narrowed his eyes cunningly.

Cristina raised her eyebrows in surprise. "Nothing's secret any more," she laughed.

"Not these days, young lady. You'll have to ban Google, like the Chinese."

"Do you research all your guests so carefully?"

....

[10]   Montepulciano D'Abruzzo is an Italian Red wine made from the Montepulciano grape in the region of Abruzzo in east central Italy. It should not be confused with Nobile di Montepulciano, a Tuscan wine made from the Sangiovese and other grape varieties.

"No, only those who arrive in low season here in our backwater, for a couple of days from New York. Yes, it needs to be said – I've got nothing better to do. But the boys don't know anything."

"You've taken me unawares."

"So it wasn't the other way round," laughed Vito, leaving the bar and making towards Cristina's table with his wine glass, "so we're quits."

Cristina stood up and stretched her hand towards Vito. Vito ignored this gesture and embraced her, kissing her twice, and clearly taking pleasure from it.

"You're not like Angelo." Vito, still not releasing Cristina's hand, examined his guest.

"They say I'm more like mum."

"Just his look. The eyes. That's all. Nothing else."

"Do you remember him well?" asked Cristina, resuming her seat.

"Not well," the old man answered, sitting down opposite her. "The thing with age is that you can forget where you've put your glasses in the evening but remember precisely something from sixty years ago."

"That's nothing like Angelo! He remembers month-old quotations."

"Well, he's the younger man!"

"Oh yes!"

They both laughed. Vito poured wine for Cristina and himself.

"Let me feed you. What shall I make for you?"

"No, no Vito! There's no need! It's already late, and this excellent cheese is more than enough for me!"

"OK fine, but in New York it's only just gone dinnertime. And you missed it."

"Did you think of that yourself, or did you take it from my subconscious?"

"From your subconscious my dear."

Vito, in a well-practised movement, lit the stove and quickly began to prepare the food, glancing through the open door at Cristina.

"Vito, how come you're still behind the stove?" Cristina resolutely took a piece of sausage from a plate which had just been put on the table.

"In what sense?" Vito looked out of the kitchen.

"Why don't you hire a cook?"

Vito laughed to himself. "No, you mustn't think such a thing. This is the best Finocchiona I've ever had occasion to try. I swear!"

Cristina theatrically raised her fork with the sausage stuck onto it, as if she were swearing an oath. "However, is it possible that you don't want a little rest?"

"I am not able to sing."

"What's that got to do with it?" Cristina was surprised.

"And I am not able to write verse." The old man paid no attention to her question.

"So?"

"How can I express my feelings?" Vito answered without a drop of pathos, not for an instant ceasing to prepare the food. As Cristina watched him, she was bewitched by his gentle, but very precise movements.

"Angelo asked you to give me something?" Vito brought Cristina out of her reverie.

"He doesn't know I'm here."

Vito raised his eyebrows, but did not say anything. He was convinced that searching questions never helped you to learn more than the person wanted to say. Since Cristina had come such a long distance to see him, it was certain that she had some business and that she would not remain silent. Therefore, the old man continued to prepare the food, only from time to time glancing at the daughter of his childhood friend.

"And you will dine with me?" asked Cristina, when Vito put in front of her a plate with types of sausages on it that were familiar from her childhood.

"No. It's not that I've become a vegetarian in my old age. It's simply – before sleep I can't allow myself such food. I shall drink with you – that will never do me any harm, I hope." Vito moved his chair towards the table and filled two wine glasses.

Cristina realised that it was time to tell Vito why she had come, but she delayed. The Finocchiona helped, offering her the opportunity to concentrate solely on her food. From time to time Vito moistened his lips with wine, a cunning smile playing across his face.

"I need your help." Cristina came straight to the point.

"You do, or Angelo does?"

"I do. For the sake of my father."

"I'll do everything in my power, Cristina." Vito was serious. Cristina was silent again. Now, despite Vito's readiness to help, she did not know how to get to the crux of the matter. "Angelo is ill."

"What's up with him?" Vito asked with his eyes alone.

"Last week he lost consciousness at a meeting. It was a suspected stroke. But this time he was lucky."

"How can I be useful – once things have calmed down?"

"He needs a holiday."

"Excellent. I don't suppose Angelo needs a discounted rate for my modest abode, or indeed for any hotel in Italy."

"You're right about that. The problem's something else – how to convince him. He's never once been on holiday in his whole life."

"Well, here I'm a bad advisor – I've never had a break from my work. I understand Angelo: something you enjoy doing can't tire you."

"With all due respect Vito, I didn't come here to get your advice."

"Then what do you need from an old man like me, young lady?"

"I want to ask you to help me convince him!"

"Me? Cristina? I haven't seen Angelo in almost sixty years! Will he even remember me? Is it possible that in all these years there hasn't been a bigger authority than Vito?"

"It is precisely you I need. No one more able comes to mind."

"And what sort of a joy will it be for him to listen to old man Vito? Supposing he does remember me."

Cristina did not answer; she merely pointed with her hand towards an old photograph.

"What? What's that you're showing me?" asked Vito, tracing with his eyes the direction in which she was pointing.

"Annapurna," Cristina said simply.

"Yes, that's all very well, Cristina." Vito laughed. "That's a child's fantasy. That's exactly the same as offering you a Barbie for Christmas. How pleased would you be with that?"

"It's the only thing I know about my father's childhood. And about you, as it happens. I was five years old, maybe six. I was ill." Cristina pushed her plate aside, keeping just her wine glass. "Dad was rarely at home. But then I happened to get seriously ill and he spent one night with me. That was the only time he'd ever stayed lying beside me all night long. In fact by that time I was already a little better. Besides, I'd slept all day the day before and at night I didn't want to sleep. I was frightened that he'd leave if he found out I was better. I didn't want there to be any chance of that, so I tried to pretend. Thankfully my temperature stayed a little high. I only had to breathe heavily and groan from time to time."

Cristina reddened, as if she were still ashamed of the deception.

"Angelo just came to see me in the evening and didn't intend to stay in my room. But probably my pitiful appearance stopped him. Dad lay there beside me, in his shirt without a tie, his hands behind his head. Even now I fancy I can catch the scent of his eau-de-cologne. Seeing that I couldn't get to sleep, he stayed a while – the role of father was painfully unfamiliar to him. You know, Vito, he never fulfilled that role in an everyday way – I always felt that he cared for me, but at a distance. He never forgot about my needs, my desires, and especially not about birthdays, but it was more like the concern of a rich, but not very close, relative – an uncle or something."

"You know, Cristina, people are divided into two types: some say 'I love you' and others – 'You too'. The fact that he did not express his emotions with words doesn't mean that he didn't love you."

"Yes, I know. I never was deprived of love. I didn't know any other father, and to me it seemed that's just how it had to be. Which made that evening very unusual."

"And then Angelo told you about Annapurna?"

"I think he simply didn't know what to talk about. He never read me any fairy-tales. I suppose he didn't know any. To tell a child, let alone one with fever, about stock market quotes, would have been a no-no even for Dad. He somehow uncertainly, quietly began with the words 'you know in Nepal there's a mountain called Annapurna – the most dangerous mountain of all the Himalayas.'"

"But if I'm honest, Dad never was a constant feature – we always had complicated relations, which were tied to work. To his face I never called Dad anything other than 'Angelo' or 'boss'. When they called me from the hospital and it was still not clear how serious it all was, I understood that some sort of constant had been shaken, a rug had been pulled out from under my feet."

"Cristina, we'll depart this life anyway. You need to find out how to live without your father. May God grant him good health and long years!"

"That all makes good sense, Vito. But I'm talking about feelings. Somehow in one moment I understood that my whole life rests on my father – I don't mean that he's a big part of my life or that he's important, but that he is my life."

Both were silent. Cristina was belatedly embarrassed by her frankness in front of a virtual stranger, and Vito did not know how to add to what had been said. Neither could find anything better to do than to return to the wine. More precisely, Vito gave Cristina the opportunity to return to the wine independently.

"Why limit yourself when you don't have to? It's not doctors who've forbidden you to open a second bottle…You won't pour some for yourself?"

"I've had my drink for today."

"Is that your norm for the day?"

"No it's not norm, it's simply a rule: no more than a bottle in a day."

"Well, we drank it the two of us."

"I've already had half, with dinner." Vito laughed quietly

"A strange rule."

"Why?"

"No, it's not doctors – I sort of made a deal with myself."

"What's the point of such a deal?"

"The ability to achieve it, Cristina."

"Thank God, Vito, that you didn't agree with yourself not to drink at all."

"I'm glad too!" Vito laughed and stood up to take the plates from the table.

"You're going to help me?" Cristina threw the question after Vito as he retreated into the kitchen.

"Yes." Vito had switched on the dishwasher, and Cristina barely heard his answer above the noise.

Not a word was said for the next five minutes. Both were privately anxious about the results of the conversation: Cristina drank her wine, and Vito, with excessive meticulousness, washed up the several plates left from dinner. The old man finished the washing up and began to put the crockery in the kitchen's suspended drawers. His movements were overly precise, making him seem a little aloof.

"But how am I to do it?" asked Vito, finally emerging from behind the bar, wiping his strong hands. "I can't imagine what I'll say to a man I last saw when we were children. I can't imagine what I'll say in order to persuade him to do something he's never once done in his life before."

"I didn't say you'll have to persuade him."

Vito sank into the chair and his whole posture and expression seemed to say: "Now I really understand nothing."

"So what have we been talking about all this time?"

"Your help."

"Well, what?" the old man was perplexed

"I'll persuade Dad myself. You only need to play along and not betray me."

"In what way?"

"By saying that this was something dreamed up by me, and you yourself did not want to travel to Nepal."

"And why would I want to travel there at my age, my dear? Somehow this looks unlikely... forgive me."

"There's only one thing that Dad's not able to do – that's refuse you..."

On Cristina's face there was not a trace left of her recent emotion – she looked steadily into Vito's eyes. Angelo's daughter did not simply look, she was waiting for an answer.

Vito froze under her direct gaze. Smiling to himself, a little sadly he asked:

"Well, what do I have to do?"

Even Cristina's body, trained as it was by frequent changes of time zones, could not cope with this late-night session with Angelo, and, having fallen asleep only in the early hours, she woke up closer to midday. Cristina did not hurry to get up. She sat up in bed and observed the bustle of the hotel staff in the courtyard.

The preparation for the holiday season was in full swing. Massimo was explaining something to two workmen, who, by all appearances, were planning to change the line of the gravel paths. The owner's son walked along the proposed new route, explaining the direction guests would take. Stopping in front of a big empty lawn, Massimo began to conduct with his hands right and left, apparently explaining the advantage of a certain point for observing the fortress walls. However, there was something strange in his behaviour – he continually, mischievously, glanced in the direction of the house.

A little to the left, through the big windows of an office, Cristina saw the second heir – Alessandro. Despite the distance and the obstacle of the window, Cristina did not doubt that it was him, pounding energetically at a computer keyboard; the midday rays of the sun were falling directly onto his face, and it was not difficult to divine in his features the son of the man with whom she had spoken last night.

Local people would probably describe what she observed from her window on the second floor as bustle. For a person who had grown up in Manhattan, however, such a definition would clearly have been an exaggeration, and would have caused a sharp attack of irony. Probably it was precisely such an ironic smile that wandered across Cristina's face as she watched the daily routine of a Tuscan provincial hotel. Moreover, Cristina was torn between two mutually exclusive desires – to lie about in bed and to go downstairs and drink a cup of coffee.

Of course, it would have been possible to order breakfast in her room, but, having seen how the numerous employees of the hotel were occupied, Cristina would never have allowed herself to do that. She was a product of her father's school of business, according to the principles of which all the resources of the company should be directed to making a profit, not serving the people who receive it. For this reason, there were few secretaries and assistants in their office, a fact which new employees took a long time to grow accustomed to, and guests attending negotiations were at times shocked when their drinks were poured by one of the vice-presidents. Angelo himself did not acquire a domestic maid, and the appearance ten years ago of a personal assistant, in the form of the "universal soldier" Anna, arose from her father's pathological hatred of computers; she meticulously sorted and repeatedly thinned out incoming mail, and gave it to him in type-written form. Answers to letters he also dictated to Anna, reading through the type-written drafts and making corrections with a red pen.

Generally, Angelo trusted words that had been said more than words that had been written. This was, of course, eccentricity – old-fashioned, and, possibly, a tribute to his Italian origins: a look into the eyes of a partner was always more important for him than the intricate points of a contract. Lawyers who provided their services to her father went out of their minds from the number of contracts Angelo concluded verbally, scarcely having time to catch up with the paper aspect of the contract, to which the boss was always indifferent. But such an emotional manner of conducting business bore its own fruits, and, during thirty years of activity on the exchange, it had not led once to any significant mistakes. On the contrary, the speed and decisiveness of the taking of such intuitive decisions always gave an advantage to their company, allowing them always to be ahead of their analytically minded competitors.

Cristina was different. She may have taken her outward manner from her father, but not her psychology when it came to business. Her genes were down-to-earth, if not to say calculating; her mother could be seen in her character. Almost two decades of work with her father had taught Cristina to trust his actions, but even so, that did not change her own internal problem-processing algorithms. With each and every transaction that Cristina meticulously analysed and reckoned up, she was struck by the correctness of the instantly taken decisions of her boss. This matter of the purchase of an internet store, though. In six months of debate, no analytical conclusions or arguments had been able to convince her father of the soundness of such an acquisition. Even for such a trusted ally of Angelo as Cristina always had been, this was too much – all her innate analytical systems hit out against the baseless obstinacy of her father, justly supposing that in the present case the real issue was a trivial, senile whim.

Cristina suddenly became aware of her surroundings. She had not noticed how her thought had led her thousands of miles from the courtyard of the provincial hotel. She understood that this place had its own passions, and that by the light of their incandescence a discussion about a new flower-bed could not give way to debates around multi-million-pound deals, but nevertheless she was not able to detach herself from an envy of the simplicity of Tuscan life, although this was a somewhat high-minded idea of the town's inhabitants. Her body, which had been prepared by winter to huddle up as she crossed the boundary between the house and the courtyard, accepted with surprise and gratitude the warmth of the early Tuscan spring. Everyone was so occupied that they did not notice Cristina's appearance. This suited her completely, and allowed her to continue the observations she had begun from within the house. She cautiously trudged along the path beside the house, fearing that a crunch of gravel would draw attention to her.

Massimo, with his peripheral vision, did indeed notice this new character "on the stage" and moved in her direction, though he was stopped by a friendly but resolute gesture. The young man halted tactfully, asking with a nod: "How are you?" Cristina, in the manner of a television presenter for the Deaf, with her lips alone and with fastidious emphasis, mouthed "perfect" and indicated vaguely forward with her hand, as if saying that she would walk here for the present. Massimo answered in the same way – with his lips alone: "Enjoy!"

Passing around the building, Cristina drew closer to the "office", through the glass doors of which, as before, the preoccupied Alessandro was visible. Alessandro did not see his guest even when she knocked on the glass. Sure that this was one of his employees bringing the next set of questions, he kept his eyes down and went on trying to finish the sentence he was typing. Cristina opened the door and entered the small office. On the wall hung old photographs, in which, with difficulty, could be divined the outline of the hotel – and in the figures of the two lads who stood near the wall could be seen the present managers of the business. A little lower hung framed certificates of education in the names of Alessandro and Massimo, and also certificates which recorded high ratings from two of the biggest hotel finders. Cristina, who on principle never stayed in hotels with a rating lower than nine, looked in admiration at the high score of 9.4.

"How long did it take you to get your 9.4?"

Alessandro raised his eyes and, seeing his guest, gave a start of surprise:

"Five years, but if I stop noticing my guests, we'll quickly lose it," the young man joked apologetically, coming out from behind the table.

"Not bad, Alessandro!"

"Good morning, Miss Esposito!" he said, showing off the level of his management skill.

"Cristina, please."

"Cristina."

"I've always thought that such ratings aren't needed. After all, it's impossible to please everyone…"

"It's possible if Massimo's the one paying attention to the guests." He nodded in the direction of his younger brother, who, at that moment was in conversation with one of the maids, tenderly holding her hand in his.

"This how he reprimands the staff, you understand."

The idiosyncratic business qualities being demonstrated by Alessandro's brother amused Cristina. "He's splendid!" Cristina gazed tenderly, fascinated, unable to look away from the scene, which was rendered mute by the closed office door. What struck her was not so much the boss's gentle treatment of his subordinate – that quality in itself was not so rarely encountered – as the moment which followed, after the maid had scurried off to correct her mistakes. Usually after such "tenderness", a boss, relinquishing his role as "caring and understanding", and confident that no one is watching him, shows on his face his true attitude to his lower-ranking staff: he rolls his eyes, signifying "God, she's a fool!" or mouthing words very far from the "It's nothing, my dear, easily put right; off you go!" which was what Massimo had just said. There was not the slightest trace of a change in Massimo's expression.

Cristina was still thinking about this when she noticed that Alessandro had come to stand beside her, and also looking out of the window. His gaze could be traced far beyond his brother, however, and in it could be seen a long list of important problems.

"How have you settled in? Father talked to you yesterday?"

"Everything's excellent! Thanks! I'm still on New York time, so a night-time conversation for me is completely 'evening'."

"You've had breakfast?"

"Oh no. Breakfast – people always feel forced to have it. Even from childhood. To this day I cannot understand why people, without fail, must stuff 'at least something' into themselves."

"It's always been simpler for us."

"Probably with you everything is simpler."

"Possibly, Cristina. You know I began my career in the Marriott in Genoa. When I returned, it seemed that everything here really was simpler. But then I realised that it's not."

"Why not?"

"There, if a cleaner fails to rinse out a sink, they dismiss her. Here the cleaner lives three houses away, and we grew up together. I can't simply dismiss her – all of her relatives will come running to sort things out." Alessandro laughed to himself, but in this laugh there was no irritation, just an assertion of fact. "Although people here are hard-working. Here, in principle, everything is built not on fear, but on conscience. And on reputation of course. What the cleaner fears most of all is that people will talk badly about her. For her it would be shameful. She might not understand something correctly, but extremely rarely would she not try."

"But nevertheless she does not perceive you as the boss. Yes?"

"That is true. Here what we do is collaborate. No, not even that – we help. You know, that's precisely how the locals often perceive working for us – they're 'helping'. Wages for such services don't get rid of this feeling: besides the money, you must, without fail, thank them for their help and be prepared, when the opportunity arises, to render a reciprocal service. Most often it will be without pay, bearing in mind our status in the local community. Here money is somehow parallel with mutual relations."

"That's funny. People don't give any special orders."

"Out of the question," Alessandro laughed. "It would be like trying to give orders to a neighbour who's come to help you mend your roof. And here Massimo is irreplaceable. At times I don't have enough patience. He always has more than enough."

"And your father?"

Alessandro shrugged his shoulders vaguely.

"Father does not go into detail, and practically never emerges from his bar. There he is God and King. But, of course, as the owner, he controls all the principal matters."

A shadow passed across Alessandro's face, which did not go unnoticed by Cristina.

"To work with your Dad is complicated," said Cristina understandingly.

"With Vito?"

"With any father. I was together with mine almost every day for twenty years."

"Then you understand me!"

"I think… yes. That's everything! I'll let you get on." Cristina was embarrassed. "I'm going for breakfast."

"Enjoy your meal!"

"Thank you!"

Alessandro returned behind his desk, gave another look at a handwritten sheet of paper, and threw it into the basket. Then, with a shrug of the shoulders, as if casting away doubt, he resolutely began to tap at the keyboard.

9

MARCH 2015. NEW YORK, USA

The week spent in hospital did not pass without consequences for Angelo. Perhaps for the first time in his life, not counting the first three days of his honeymoon with Cristina's mother, he was isolated from the external world. His old friend Aaron tried to maximise the isolation by limiting the flow of visitors and Angelo's own access to information.

For the first few days Angelo experienced drug withdrawal symptoms, demanding, and later threatening, all the hospital staff with every imaginable unpleasantness if they would not guarantee him access to the internet, or at least to Bloomberg TV.[11] However, all the steps he took were predictable, and any possibility of "doing his own thing" were curtailed by strict instructions from the management.

But then his mood unexpectedly lightened. It was a quite new feeling. New feelings at seventy had cost him dear, and Angelo was in no hurry to rid himself of them, savouring all the shades of unknown emotions. He slept for a long time in the morning, watched a broadcast of Italian football, and read a book he'd pinched from a Puerto Rican nurse which turned out to be something between a detective story and a novel. The naivety and primitivism of the writing did not irritate him at all, and guessing whodunnit after five minutes of reading the detective story-cum-novel only evoked a self-satisfied smirk. Angelo could

....

[11]   A 24-hour international news channel, focusing on business and financial information. Founded in New York in 1994. Has a worldwide audience of 310 million.

not formulate a definition of his condition, although what he was doing was resting, a banal state, familiar to anyone. And although the old man continued to grumble at people and to demand access to means of communication, he realised, with a certain horror, that he was beginning to like his vegetable state.

After a five-day stay in hospital, Angelo greatly surprised Aaron by the ease with which he promised to arrange leave for himself after his release. At the time, Angelo was still convinced he would deceive his old friend and return to his business affairs as soon as he escaped hospital care. Aaron, who also had no doubt about the outcome, but had no serious grounds for keeping his friend on a leash, nevertheless released him to "house arrest".

Angelo went back to his big empty flat with mixed feelings. To his own surprise he did not immediately hurl himself into every serious error in production, although he did switch on the TV and watch the financial news. But he did this more mechanically than deliberately. The familiar strapline of the financial news brought bewilderment to Angelo's face; it was like a chance meeting in the street, after many years of separation, with the ageing face of a former lover – everything, down to the last wrinkle is familiar, but somehow different. The flood of stock market information, spewing out of the TV with its usual anxious tone, passed the old man by as he wandered round his room.

Absentmindedly taking a bottle of wine, which he had missed so much in the hospital, and throwing a sheet over his shoulders, Angelo went out onto the balcony. He sat down in his armchair and, for the first time, regretted that the construction of the balcony, which had been done to his specification, did not allow him to see what was going on below in the street. All that met his eyes were a few neighbouring roofs and a grey February sky. Somewhere up there he could hear the engine roar of a plane which had just taken off; it was as if it was making a big effort to escape the clutches of the clouds. Today, all its efforts in the leaden sky of New York were futile, and it rushed away empty-handed to where the sky was clearer.

From behind the closed door, the world of business was humming, trying to catch Angelo's attention. However, perhaps for the first time, this did not excite the old financier and did not arouse in him any desire to isolate separate intelligible words from the general torrent of noise. Those terms which did nevertheless get through to the old man's ears in articulated form caused him irritation. It was like the captain of an aircraft carrier being stricken with sea sickness. There's a touch of irony in this analogy when one remembers that when his company was flourishing, his financial empire was compared to an awesome warship by financial journalists.

Of course, there was an obvious explanation for all this: the last half year of conflicts within the company had completely exhausted Angelo. It's possible that this manifested itself externally to a lesser degree but, as things turned out, it poleaxed him in the form of the wretched fainting fit. And now his no longer young organism, being wiser than its owner and defending itself against more substantial unpleasantnesses, went into "economise" mode, and sent neurons of revulsion for the business of his whole life to all his nerve endings. In his "poisoned" state Angelo was bewildered, but could do nothing about it. All attempts to begin thinking about business evoked in him a feeling of contempt. What to do about it, he had, for the time being, no idea.

Alarmed by this development, Angelo poured himself some wine and mulled over who he could discuss it with. However, no one fitted the role of counsellor; he was sure that all existing potential interlocutors would take pleasure in such news and would merely support his departure – temporary or permanent. Each one would have their own reasons: Aaron from the medical point of view, Cristina from a humanitarian standpoint, while Steve would not pass up the chance of sitting in his armchair and investing in the internet store even if neither the store nor Steve were right. It was clear that Angelo would have to sort the situation out himself, and the best thing he could do right now, as he sat on the balcony of his flat on the Upper East Side, was to do nothing!

Angelo was delighted with this. After all, the decision to do nothing was still a Decision. Of course, people more often do nothing out of hopelessness or distraction, but not in his case. Angelo's inactivity was the responsible act of a wise man, or so he assured himself. It was like a pause in an actor's monologue; to some it might seem that he'd simply forgotten his lines, but everything falls into place when the artiste utters the next phrase, which has merely gained extra weight from the preceding silence and acquired hitherto unremarked meanings.

The decision he'd taken, together with the wine, spread pleasantly through the old man's weary body – after five days of immobility even the short journey from the hospital to his flat had exhausted him. The effect of the wine put him quickly back into circulation. "I must have something to eat," he thought without enthusiasm. He summoned the nurse Aaron had arranged for him, using the call button Aaron had also provided.

The lavishly proportioned Puerto Rican nurse took Angelo's order – to be taken to a neighbouring restaurant – and handed him several piles of paper which had been readied for him on his table. Angelo realised that he would have to wait some forty minutes for his meal, and to add variety to his recuperation, he decided to sort out the post which had accumulated during his week-long absence. In spite of the fact that the majority of letters automatically went into files which corresponded to large company projects which were on his radar, and in spite of the powerful filters which removed any spam from his attention, the file marked "miscellaneous" was still of impressive dimensions. This, even though Anna, his secretary of many years standing, cleared his drawer of any communications inconsistent with his pay grade, and only opened those which she had decided not to touch, not being competent to deal with the questions set out there.

Angelo skimmed through the headings of the first dozen letters, but quickly became bored. Then he turned his attention to several new files. The first of these was marked "wishes for your recovery", which contained sincere – both wholly and less so – expressions of concern for the state of his health. However, one must give credit: the majority of the letters were full of "heartfelt concern". This was not always the result of any great love on the part of the correspondents for old man Angelo, but rather a reflection of how much these people depended on the health of the financier. The second file was laconically marked

"Diagnosis", and was stuffed with the conclusions of a multitude of doctors, prescriptions, and detailed recommendations from Aaron.

Out of curiosity, Angelo was about to look at the doctors' scribblings, but at that moment he caught sight of another file, this one marked "Italy". Angelo had no dealings with his native country, so the appearance of this file was unexpected. In the file he found a single letter.

The letter was written on hotel notepaper. Angelo saw his surname there. He knew that Vito used the family surname in memory of Genarro, but all the same it jumped out at him.

The heading of the letter said "reference: Vito". When, at the age of seventy, a man gets a letter from an unknown address which mentions the name of a childhood friend, it almost always means that relatives are telling people about his death. Apart from death, there are no other reasons to remind people of your existence after almost six decades of silence. Nurturing no illusions about the contents of the missive, Angelo sighed "Vito, Vito" as he began to read the letter. The letter turned out to be longer than a normal obituary and was written in good English. The first sentences merely convinced Angelo of the accuracy of his surmises, since in them the author – apparently Vito's son – referred to his father's stories about childhood. But at the words "in sending you warm greetings, my father invites you..." Angelo became confused. Having re-read this part of the letter, he realised, with a sense of relief, that Vito was alive. After grieving so much at first on learning of his friend's death and then being delighted when his assumptions proved wrong, Angelo completely lost the thread of the letter.

Now calm, with no concerns about his childhood friend's life, Angelo was amazed at the concatenation of circumstances which had led to the letter's arrival at this precise moment. After all, even ten days ago he would have got Anna to write a tactful letter in his name in which a refusal would have been couched in polite terms. Angelo could not have found room in his timetable for a two-week trip to Nepal. And for all the sentiment of the situation and the nostalgia lodged in his Italian heart, it was still a foolish idea, and he would have found a good dozen reasons preventing him from even thinking about such a frivolous way of spending time. Now, however, as he finished a second bottle of wine, Angelo thought how well things had turned out. Of course, at that moment Angelo had unequivocally rejected the proposal, but his thoughts started to run against common sense and produce attractive points. Firstly, he would not have to dream up any explanations for his reluctance to plunge into work, and his unexpected enthusiasm for his idleness would have a sound basis, both for himself and for everyone else. Secondly, a trip to Nepal would not, please note, be a trip to Baden-Baden, and would tell everyone of the excellent state of the company President's health, a man who "despite problems with his knee has decided not to postpone a long-planned trip to Nepal with his childhood friend…" Thirdly, he would, at a stroke, rid himself of any hassling from Aaron and Cristina on the subject of leave. They wanted him take some leave: Here you are then!

Of course, Angelo was a long way from taking a positive decision, which at the moment was at the stage of "we must think about this", but, once lodged in his brain, the thought did not drop out of his play list.

Angelo read the letter to the end, once more said "Oh, Vito, Vito," and folded it up. He did this slowly, carefully, running his nail over every fold many times, as children do when they're making a paper plane the range of which depends on the accuracy of each "seam".

10

1955. MONTEPULCIANO, ITALY

In the back yard of Genarro's house stood a tumbledown cow shed, built, in its day, in typical Tuscan style. There was no point in repairing it, and it was used as a store for things of whose uselessness Genarro was convinced but which he couldn't bring himself to throw out on account of his innate thriftiness. Genarro himself and his close neighbours used the old walls of the barn as a source of materials for various basic outbuildings. The barn was fairly large, and even when it had covered all needs for building materials, it could still provide a large supply of stones. For a long time Genarro had wanted to clear this corner out and use it more rationally by installing a table and an awning. The more so because it was precisely from here that there was a sumptuous view over the surrounding area: Genarro's house stood on a small rise right in the middle of vineyards and olive groves, which stretched all the way to the walls of the fortress of Montepulciano, situated five kilometres away and looming ominously over the valley.

At the end of a hot day, before the locals began to flood into the bar for a quick glass, Genarro would often sit on one of these stones in the shadow of the longest wall. Leaning his back against the cold stone, he would hurriedly drink some white wine and ice and allow himself quarter of an hour of relaxation. Of course, given the help he had from Vito and Angelo, he could have allowed himself more – more time and more wine – but work in the bar, which had long since become more a habit than a chore, brought him to his feet at precisely the appointed time and chased him towards the regular customers, the roster of which was only altered by natural causes, the advent of which would also be noted there.

Everyone knew very well that Genarro could not be disturbed during these quarter hours at any price. In his day, when he was under instruction, Vito wondered, sarcastically, whether this rule extended to accidents and natural disasters – such as a fire in the bar. To which the barman answered firmly:

"Yes, that is an exception. In case of fire, I permit you to come to me and tell me how you've extinguished it. But in heaven's name don't run to me as if the fire is news and furthermore, don't come crawling to me with stupid questions about how to put it out."

The moment for this little siesta was determined by Genarro's biological clock, and changed depending on the time of year, but it was a permanent fixture on the border between day and evening, half an hour or an hour before sunset. In summer at this time the sun was still baking hot through force of inertia, like a frying pan taken off the hob which can still finish frying meat. The sinking sun lit up the rows of vines at a particular angle, illuminating the clouds of dust raised by the peasants and gleaming in a dozen of shades of green. Genarro loved this moment, and day in, day out never tired of it. In life there are few phenomena and, indeed, few people, capable of delighting us every day.

It was just such a moment, on one such day, that Angelo decided to disturb his grandfather. Fearful of incurring the old man's displeasure, the boy waited until Genarro finished his séance of meditation, and caught him just at the moment when he was on the point of quitting his beloved spot.

"What do you want?" said Genarro, anticipating his request.

"Vito and I have a proposal," the young man rattled off in business-like fashion.

"A proposal…" said the old man, savouring the word ironically. "Judging by your cheerful appearance, you plan to hit the jackpot with it."

"Well, not the jackpot…"

"So, what do you want from the old man? Advice? Start-up capital? A blessing?"

"None of those. We need that." Angelo indicated the wall of the barn.

"The barn? I can't even imagine what it can be any good for."

"For nothing. So Vito and I want to sell it," said the boy, screwing his eyes up slyly.

"A brilliant idea in its originality, but it does raise in me fully justified doubts. Who needs this rubbish?"

"That's just the point," blurted Angelo, who was pleased with the way the conversation had started.

"Tell me more!"

"Vito's auntie…"

"Which one?"

"Giulietta. She sometimes helps produce documents for the Montepulciano town council."

"Well I never. I didn't know she could type."

"There you are then. She told us once that the decision had been taken to restore the Eastern wall."

"Where Giuseppe's bar is?"

"Exactly. Funds are being allocated for the work. By the town itself, and some will come from Siena."

"Who'll benefit from it?"

"I don't know. Maybe holidaymakers will come here on excursions from the coast."

"They want to turn Montepulciano into a tourist attraction? I think that's a stupid idea. I can't imagine who would take it into their heads to come a hundred kilometres to look at those walls…"

"Well, I don't know about that."

"All right. It's not important. So what will you get out of this reconstruction?"

"Academics from Siena have asked for the wall to be restored using only old materials. They said that otherwise the wall would lose its historical value."

"I'm beginning to understand your idea. But are you sure these stones are old enough?"

"I am – since yesterday. We weren't going to bother you until we were sure that they'd be suitable. We showed both the stones and the barn itself to a representative of the commission."

"And?"

"They approved them. Unfortunately, the stones are no good for the exterior work – there they need even older ones – but for the interior work, they're fine. It's not quite the price we were counting on, but all the same – we've got a lot of stones."

"And how much will they pay?"

"A hundred lire for ten."

"A hundred? Not much."

"But they're prepared to take two thousand!" the boy hastened to say.

"You must remember that you've got to pay the workman for dismantling the garage, and for transport. I think not less than fifty lire per ten will go on that. Although, considering I didn't know how to give them away for nothing, it doesn't sound bad."

"Vito and I would like to discuss with you how to split the profits," said the grandson seriously, plainly embarrassed by the delicacy of the subject.

"With pleasure," agreed Genarro with marked seriousness. "It's a good idea, and due consideration of it gives me grounds for offering you with a clear conscience..."

Angelo had no doubt that his enterprise had succeeded.

"A deserved..."

Genarro even screwed up his eyes in anticipation.

"Fifty per cent," Genarro concluded.

For a moment Angelo thought he'd misheard. This was so far removed from his expectations that all the arguments he'd prepared about the deal were instantly dissipated. That was understandable since Angelo had been ready to argue Genarro down from fifteen to ten per cent, and what he had proposed to say on that basis lost all meaning against the background of his grandfather's proposal. His brain tried feverishly to find not arguments, but just words, anything but shameful silence. However, the shock was so big that no words came. Instead, a flood of tears, which he tried desperately to restrain, welled up in his eyes. This new problem was so important that the child's entire psyche was involved in solving it. Angelo could not allow himself to be humiliated in front of his grandfather. It was difficult to imagine a more nightmarish scenario. But Angelo felt so sorry – for himself, for his efforts, for Vito's and his splendid idea, for the time spent on working out all the details, and most of all for their hopes of making a profit. The more so because this project contributed towards their goal – perhaps not much, but all the same it was a substantial part of the budget for the trip to Nepal. Much bigger than the daily contributions which the boys had made from their pocket money and tips in the month that had passed since they had decided on the expedition. The worst thing for Angelo was the pathetically small size of the steps which the friends could now take en route for their Dream. Unlike Vito, the younger of the two friends was unable to see in every lira thrown into an old jam jar a link with the forthcoming expedition. Though he talked in these terms, seeking inspiration from the jar as it filled up, in his heart of hearts he realised that their efforts, unless kick-started, would get them to Annapurna by the eighties. Angelo tried to talk to Vito about this, but Vito merely got angry. He was certain that every lira put into the kitty would do its job and that the main thing was not to stand still but to add a little, however small, every day. This did not mean that Vito did not share his friend's fears, that he didn't realise that in a month they had managed to collect enough money to buy one mountain boot, maximum. However, the older boy believed that their income would change for the better and they would get the chance to make a dramatic improvement in it. This occurred with the appearance of the idea of selling off the stones from the old barn. As this idea developed, Angelo's belief in the practicality of their plans grew. It wasn't even so much a matter of the estimated amount of their profit, which although significant when set against their other money-raising attempts, nevertheless kept the boys nearer to the start than to the finish of their project. Angelo needed a precedent to show that they were capable of something substantial. This nurtured his faith in the reality of their dream, making a bridge between the abstract and the real. And, now, when reality was almost upon them, the obstacle was not just anyone, but the person who was closest to them. Everything happened so unexpectedly that Angelo didn't have time to get angry with Genarro. It seemed he still hoped that this was merely a temporary misunderstanding, miscommunication or some such. It was with these thoughts and with repressed tears in his eyes that the young man stood before his grandfather. As for Genarro, he, as if not understanding what was going on in his grandson's heart, was expecting what was for him the boy's logical agreement to the extremely generous terms he offered. The pause dragged on and Genarro nudged Angelo:

"Well, what do you say, partner?"

In the word "partner" Angelo detected mockery and clammed up even more, merely forcing himself to say:

"I must talk to Vito."

"Do. If you agree in principle, let's sit down the three of us and discuss details."

At that the boy said no more and ran off, leaving his grandfather with a satisfied smile on his face. Genarro did not hurry back to the bar; contrary to his usual habit, he went on with his siesta, contemplating his empty bottle in somewhat disappointed fashion.

11

APRIL 2015. ROME, ITALY – KATHMANDU, NEPAL

Even at a fairly venerable age, Vito had only flown a few times. For the last twenty years or so he'd been a permanent fixture in Tuscany, visiting his old friend Luigi in his little house near Grosseto just once a year. However, even then he didn't leave Tuscany. These week-long visits had a certain ritualistic character: the old men would meet, and reminisce about old times when they had relaxed in this house with their late wives.

Vito was not badly affected by these reminiscences, which could not be said of his friend, who had lost his wife some eight years previously and was still mourning her. Vito, who had been a widower for nigh on twenty years, was reconciled to his loss. Moreover, his solitude was relative – in his house there was always a horde of the hotel's regulars, restaurant customers, his own children, their wives and their girlfriends; additional noise was supplied by his grandsons and their noisy friends. Admittedly, visits by the latter were strictly regulated by Alessandro, and the boys were only allowed onto the premises in low season, when they couldn't get in anyone's way.

It was getting to the point where Vito was rather envious of Luigi's quiet life, filled as it was with bright sadness. Vito dismissed these feelings, seeing very clearly that it wasn't a matter of envy – there was no particular point in being envious – but a desire to be on his own, if only for a short time. He was deprived of this luxury. In any case, Vito did not much like these trips, mainly because of the endless conversations along the lines: "do you remember this?" and "do you remember that?", of which he's got fed up by the evening of his arrival. Poor Luigi did not want to discuss any other topic, and ignored the selection of news items, meagre but certain, taken from the life of Vito since they'd last met.

Vito disliked the house even more. A fine house ten years ago, with a small lawn and a distant but high-profile sea shore. After the death of his wife, Luigi made efforts to turn the house into a mausoleum. Vito had genuinely respected Luigi's late wife, but today she looked at Vito from practically everywhere – every little patch of wall had been turned into an iconostasis. Vito went to sleep, woke up, had supper and even did his business under the watchful, and somewhat stern, eye of the poor woman. Two days into his visit and Vito indeed began to feel that he detected a mute reproach in her look: why, she was saying, are you staying around here. In fairness to her, it must be said that in her lifetime Luigi's wife had been an extremely cordial hostess. It was only death which had ruined her character.

Thus it was that Vito's only journey in a year had been the obligatory trip to the Ligurian coast, which had taken several unhurried hours of travel along dusty Tuscan roads. The flight from Rome to Kathmandu, and the change of planes at Doha, of whose existence Vito had not been hitherto aware, were therefore more than ordinary events.

Despite all Cristina's efforts at persuasion, Vito set one strict condition: each of the old friends paid his own way, and, as far as finances went, acted as they saw fit. Vito made just one concession: bearing in mind Angelo's health problems, for the ascent to Annapurna base camp, from where professional mountaineers set out for the summit, they would use a helicopter hired by Angelo's company. Angelo's daughter was extremely persuasive, saying that it wouldn't be right for Vito to incur great expense through Angelo's fault. With some misgivings, Vito concurred with these arguments, but as for the rest, he was adamant. At his request an economy class ticket was purchased for him, and Alessandro reserved a modest, but highly rated, hotel in Kathmandu, where the helicopter would be waiting for them.

Vito was sent instructions, the detail of which somewhat offended him with its hint of senile weakmindedness. The old man quickly turned the offence into irony, but nevertheless decided to adhere to the timetable set out in them.

After a brief farewell to his family, during which, to Vito's surprise, the most emotional was Alessandro, Massimo took him to Rome airport.

Despite his self-confident and calm aspect, as he entered the airport terminal, Vito began to panic somewhat and began to think more kindly of Cristina's instructions. Vito was grateful that Massimo remained with him right up to security. Even though he kept bombarding Vito with extra details of the plan which he already knew, he nevertheless helped his father cope with his access of fear.

As he crossed air side, Vito felt like the fish in a cartoon he'd seen several times with his grandson, who had swum away from a coral reef and got lost. He could barely keep himself from turning back towards Massimo, who hadn't moved from the spot. Forcing himself to adopt an impressive gait, and even whistling, Vito moved into the terminal. Having gone a few yards, he nevertheless decided to have a quick look round and, to his surprise saw Massimo enthusiastically waving his arms and trying to shout something to him through the thick glass. With a nod of his head Vito asked what he wanted and got an immediate answer in the shape of a clear gesture from his son indicating the opposite direction to the one Vito had chosen. "If I've already gone the wrong way here, what will happen in the mountains? Better not to think about that," the old man muttered to himself, indicating with a gesture to his younger son that he didn't need him to tell him which way to go. "You go home."

Vito plunged into the duty-free innards of the airport, somewhat amazed to see the hustle and bustle and the urge to buy anything at all before take-off even if it was only a little cheaper than in an ordinary shop. The prices on alcohol produced no impression on him, taking into account that the basic selection at his bar consisted of local wine which he obtained at different prices from those charged to the tourists who leapt out of their coaches for two hours to look round the walls of Montepulciano. Having gone right through two such shops, Vito grew bored and began to look for his gate. He had calmed down a little after his initial nervousness, and was beginning to understand how the airport was set out and to find his way about the place.

The flight passed without any untoward events. Vito desperately wanted to sleep, but as soon as he began to nod off, some announcement would be made to passengers, mostly concerning expected turbulence. Vito cursed inwardly, said the pilot was hysterical, and again tried to sleep.

His neighbour, who had stuffed his ears with the earplugs that were handed out to everybody, was sleeping soundly, barely distinguishable from the huge double bass which he had placed on an adjoining seat. Never in its life had the double bass been so close to taking on the essence of a human being: it had its own ticket and, like all the human passengers, was strapped in with a safety belt. Vito, from whose elderly ears the earplugs kept treacherously falling, was forced to spend half the night thinking about two equally daft questions: does a double bass get offered food on board and what would his neighbour do with this huge double bass in Kathmandu.

Short of sleep as he was, Vito could not work out how to find an Italian film in the computer in the head rest in front of him; as a result, the only entertainment available was to watch the plane moving across the map of the world on a screen. In addition, the flight of a real plane and a little picture plane on a monitor did not in any way correspond with each other in his consciousness, and evoked thoughts of the inferiority of modern travel: in a few hours Vito had almost travelled further than Alexander the Great did in a lifetime.

Vito was so carried away with watching the dynamic map of the aircraft's flight that for a moment his imagination transferred him to the prototype Boeing and bore him off into sleep. Fortunately, over India the plane stopped shaking, and Vito slept until the announcement that the pilot was preparing to land at Kathmandu.

When Vito left the plane, he was extremely hungry – he had not touched the packed meals which had been brought through the cabin several times; eating reheated food was beyond him. It was too early to claim his room in the hotel and so, leaving his rucksack at registration, he set off in search of a bite to eat.

Quickly realising that he had no criteria whereby to choose an eating establishment, the old man went into the first restaurant he came across and spent a long time examining the menu. He decided not to order a pizza or pasta, thus sparing the reputation of the local chef, but in the part of the menu which listed local dishes he didn't recognise anything.

Vito was already on the point of leaving when a familiar word suddenly caught his eye: "momo". Still uncertain how he knew such an exotic word, he ordered two different portions of these "momos", assuming that nothing bad would have lodged itself in his ageing grey cells.

And indeed, he was quickly served with two varieties of puff pastry dumplings – six with chicken and six with greens. When he raised a momo with greens to his lips Vito smelt a familiar smell which, like a missing element in an electrical connection, completed a closed circuit of memory: that was it: momo!

The funny thing was he had never actually eaten momo, but among the spices in the kitchen of his childhood which Genarro used constantly in his cooking was a packet of Nepalese spices Maurice had given him. On the packet, in large letters, was written MOMO. All the spices were used regularly, being renewed and replenished the whole time. Only the packet of MOMO remained unclaimed in the midst of this fragrant melange. Vito and Angelo sometimes took the packet and sniffed the specific smell of the spice which, as it turned out, became firmly attached to their childish picture of Nepal.

Once Vito asked Genarro when he used exotic seasoning but he merely shrugged his shoulders vaguely, mumbling about the need to know the exact recipe. He didn't know it, so the seasoning stayed put and did not move. Many years later, during a regular clear-out, it was thrown out accidentally. Who knows, if the name of the dish had been more complicated, Vito might not have recalled it as he struggled with the familiar smell. But MOMO had swum to the surface of his mind the moment he put the first dumpling to his mouth. The old man was delighted that it turned out to be really tasty. Although a genuine carnivore, in his confusion Vito was ready to acknowledge that he liked the vegetarian alternative even more.

12

APRIL 2015, NEW YORK, USA – PARIS, FRANCE

Angelo had been through many stages and many methods to cure him of his fear of heights and, bearing in mind his financial independence, there had been a huge number of these. All the same he readily understood that some of these methods were dreamed up by quirky psychologists on the back of an envelope as they tried to hang on to an as yet uncured client who was capable of paying and, furthermore, wanted to pay. To this problem, dozens of hours of, as it turned out, useless therapy had been devoted, of which Angelo, as he closed in on forty, grew tired. Realising the uselessness of correcting himself, Angelo had started to correct the world about him.

His position and his purse ensured that he could do that, the more so because he did not encounter the problem directly very often; it was enough to avoid panoramic lifts, not to fit floor-to-ceiling windows in his flat, and not to go to the rooftop receptions so beloved of his former wife. Despite all this, there was a paradoxical exception to these rules: the huge window in his study on the 45th floor. Perhaps Angelo perceived the view onto Central Park as an illustration, like the posters of Niagara Falls in his flat in the eighties. Be that as it may, Angelo could stand for a long time right by the window and, despite the fact that he was separated from the "stone chasm" by only a few inches of thick glass, he would feel a remarkable sense of peace.

However, his main difficulty was caused by his fear of flying. In this case, his fear of heights was augmented by an unwanted feeling of powerlessness – the feeling that he could not control his own safety or his own life infuriated him much more than the vertiginous height itself. Cristina supported him by handling the majority of meetings outside New York on her own authority, but a couple of times a year she was not able to stand in for Angelo, and he was obliged to fly. His only cure was whisky – which would have horrified all the psychologists who made money out of him. Raised on the best wine-making traditions of Tuscany, and extremely sparing in his use of strong drink in his normal life Angelo in a plane was like a Russian tourist on a charter flight. At the same time, he was fortunate in possessing an organism with two startling characteristics: firstly, alcohol in large quantities reduced him to a state of something like anabiosis – the rather emotional and, in the Italian manner, voluble, Angelo, at the first signs of intoxication, quietened down, sought solitude and tried, without bothering anyone, to adopt a horizontal position; secondly – for some unknown reason, irrespective of his level of intoxication, Angelo sobered up the minute the undercarriage of the aircraft touched town on the runway, as if an intoxication circuit breaker in his body cut out.

Through a process of trial and error, Angelo had, over a period of many years, worked out and honed an "aerowhisky" algorithm which allowed him to deal with his phobia, if not in principle, then at least on an *ad hoc* basis during the flight, in such a way that it was not evident to others.

He drank the first glass hurriedly in anticipation of his plane's arrival, which was absolutely normal for users of the airport business lounge. The first shot made him feel mildly and pleasantly tipsy, removing any nervousness about upcoming stress while allowing him to conduct business conversations on the phone. The second glass had no aesthetic component – it was simply a technical matter: it was important to drink up before entering the tunnel or the car which was taking him to the aircraft. His calculations were precise, designed to bring the alcohol from the second glass into play just as Angelo took his seat in the aircraft. This was very important as the dose contained in the second glass already affected his coordination, prompting Angelo to run quickly through the cabin and take his seat in first class without delay. For some technical reason, as they left Atlanta the passengers were brought back to the terminal, and it cost Angelo no little effort and maximum concentration to maintain an easy, unforced gait.

The third stage, came as the plane taxied to the runway. Here, the third glass would be drunk, inducing mild oblivion in Angelo which would relegate departure from the earth to a barely discernible background. Whisky, like Manet, replaced stark reality with splendid vagueness, raising questions where there were none before, finding beauty in hitherto banal objects, and an enchanted Angelo would look through the plane window at the big city, dwindling and seemingly afloat, and smile blissfully, hastily taking his fourth glass of whisky, which would plunge him into a happy world bereft of the terrors of sleep.

However, what worked over relatively short distances, could not be used on long flights – Angelo simply wasn't able to put way the amount of alcohol which would sustain his marginal state for many hours, The plane had barely reached the mid-Atlantic when a sobered-up Angelo, unable to force himself to sleep, was sitting mulling over in his head phrases from a press release about the death of the founder of DRI group in a plane crash over the ocean. Even in this state, however, Angelo, who always insisted on correct formulations, agonized over the arrangement of words, trying to give the document a tone which, despite the tragic nature of the event, would instil optimism in the company's shareholders and prevent their panicking; in addition, he expected from his loyal partners in the company solidarity in these dramatic times and a demonstration of their loyalty. Despite the fact that Angelo's head was occupied with the substance of an obituary, the cerebral activity was a great help in deflecting him from his actual fears. But at the same time the improbably massive aircraft on the monitor screen had hit northern France and was unambiguously signalling its intention to fly as far as Paris in the immediate future.

Angelo had specially requested this stopover, and the onward flight to Kathmandu would await him only the following day. He so rarely ventured into Europe that he took advantage of any opportunity to be on his native continent. Of course, he could, if he had so wished, have filled the intervening time with meetings with French colleagues, which would have been beneficial for business, but to his own considerable surprise, Angelo had requested that his presence in France should not be advertised.

Having taken another hundred grams of "landing" whisky, Angelo put on his headset, trying not to look out of the window, through which the lights of the Paris suburbs were already visible. Shutting his eyes, Angelo immersed himself in the rhythm of loud music, trying to visualise the moment when the plane would touch down softly on the damp runway, its undercarriage throwing out clouds of sparks and his fears. A flight attendant asked him to remove his headset, which he indeed did just before the woman sat down and put on her seat belt. Ignoring the ritual safety instructions, which he sometimes found incomprehensible, Angelo put his headset back on and continued to exorcise his fear with its bass notes.

Despite all this, Angelo knew very well that the coming evening would be remarkably pleasant and life-affirming. He had even thought up his own term for this condition – EPS – Euphoria of the Passenger who Survived. This condition would last until bedtime, and dwindle to nothing by breakfast time: a hotel omelette would return him to reality, rendering the fears of the previous day comical, but his happiness, the cause of which was simply that he, like thousands of other passengers, had that evening safely come down the aircraft steps, was ill-founded.

He had almost a whole day before the evening flight to Kathmandu and, unencumbered as he was by business affairs, Angelo wandered round the city. He had trouble remembering when he'd last been in Paris, and it was ages since he'd walked its streets with nothing to do. Idleness took him so much by surprise that he imagined passers-by were turning to look at him.

Angelo did not hurry, turning at random from one street to another and only vaguely aware what part of the city he was in, although from the numbers of noisy young people he deduced that his route had taken him to the heart of the student Latin quarter. He had scarcely taken that in when he saw the entrance to the Jardin de Luxembourg – almost the only place in Paris known to Angelo from previous walks. He walked towards the familiar fence and, out of the corner of his eye, spotted a wine merchant's shop. He went in and, without paying any attention to the names and brands, started to look for the cheapest wine. This was not difficult because right opposite the entrance was a whole stand of promotional wines at 5 euros, one of which Angelo immediately took, using only one criterion for his choice – it was dry and red. Thus had he embarked on his student days during his first visit to Paris. The nineteen-year-old Angelo had been encouraged by his stepfather to further his education by a trip to Europe and found the choice difficult – fantastic Paris or nostalgic Tuscany.

His stepfather who, for reasons which Angelo did not understand, was jealous of his homeland, although he himself was Italian, did not even consider a visit to Tuscany as an alternative. As an adult, Angelo realised that, despite his position in the financial world, his stepfather had a complex about his roots in the Apennines and became "American" as fast as he could; he did not go to Italian restaurants, did not like Italian films and in general tried to avoid anything that reminded him of his homeland. His relationship with his wife's son was, if not chilly, then neutral, and he wanted to "recast" his stepson as an American teenager not so much with the boy's future in mind as for his own reputation as an "American", or at least as far as his business circle saw it. A visit to Paris by a top-class young student was very much in the American style.

But at this point Angelo's mother unexpectedly intervened, showing, to general surprise, uncharacteristic persistence. With a sinking feeling, the brilliant student was informed by his stepfather that there was a possibility of choice. Angelo did not reply immediately and took several days to think about it.

While the young man thought about it, his stepfather did not waste time and, in order to increase the attractiveness of his variant, rang a banker friend in Paris and asked him to help put together an interesting programme for the young man.

As soon as the following day, Angelo became the possessor of a ticket for a concert at the Paris Olympia by the Beatles, whose popularity in Europe was growing, and was given a guide in the shape of the banker's daughter, whose name he had now completely forgotten.

Angelo knew nothing of the hysteria circulating in Europe but yet to reach the American continent, for which a new name – beatlemania – had been dreamed up. Even without this bonus, the young man inclined to the Parisian variant, and when his stepfather "made his day" with the news about the concert tickets, he did not disappoint his parent, who was proud of his own inventiveness and proudly announced the results of the internal family tendering.

The girl who had been given the job of accompanying Angelo was, it seems, a year older than him and was at first less than delighted to go with her father's idea of looking after an American contemporary of hers. To make matters worse, the idle, and somewhat spoiled French girl knew neither Italian, which Angelo still remembered, nor English, which he already knew very well. It was precisely this fact that later, in Angelo's opinion, accelerated the transition of the young people to a more universal means of communication – sex; yet again, not knowing what to say, the girl, whose name completely escaped him, answered his question with a kiss. This happened in the Jardin de Luxembourg, where the young people were whiling away time over a bottle of cheap red wine which, at that time, you didn't have to wrap guiltily in paper and hide from the police. Wine and a baguette were an excellent lunch for two young people somewhat chilled by the Parisian winter's day. After lunch they dropped round to her flat, which was in a prestigious area nearby, in order to warm up. Silence was the most romantic part of their romance; after all, who knows what faults and contradictions they would have found in each other if conversation had been an option.

The concert itself made no impression on the young man, who had been brought up on Italian melody. The sound was horrible, and the appearance and behaviour of the musicians strange. Songs made popular by American groups, now covered by an English group, sounded odd to Angelo, and the Liverpudlians' own songs made no impression. This did not prevent Angelo from telling his stepfather of his dream come true and about the universal happiness to be had in Paris.

The romance between the young people ended as easily as it had begun. They parted, and "more kissing was pointless".

IGOR ZAVILINSKY

They didn't promise to write – there was no sense in it given the wordless nature of their love. They said goodbye in the same Jardin de Luxembourg with a light and awkward kiss: her lips pecked the air and his, foolishly, met her ear. As if clearing a space for more important information, Angelo's memory deleted the name of the Paris banker's daughter, as if with an eraser.

The assistant obligingly packed the bottle in a plain wrapper, and when Angelo asked where he could get a fresh baguette, pointed mutely down the street.

April sunshine was making the square in front of the palace agreeably warm, and Angelo sat down augustly on a numbered metal chair. He placed a second, heavy chair under his feet. There were few people around, but from time to time health-conscious Frenchmen would run past, while a large number of mothers and children strolled by.

The crisp baguette tempted Angelo far more than the wine, and he quickly broke off the end. The taste of the still warm bread did the impossible: after the first bite Angelo recalled the name of his French girlfriend – Sophie. That was it! It was as if there was a note with a prompt in it in the baguette. This trivial fact, which clinched nothing, lifted his mood, and he set about the baguette with enthusiasm, surreptitiously taking sips from the neck of the bottle which was poking out of its wrapping. The sun warmed him up a little, and Angelo even unbuttoned his sports shirt, letting in the carefree atmosphere of the park.

Sophie... She could not be called beautiful, but there was something awfully attractive, evocatively sexual, about her. Or perhaps it was simply youthfulness. And not so much Sophie's youthfulness as his own: for a young man of twenty the sexuality of girls depends on them to a lesser degree.

It was only now that Angelo thought that this five-day romance was, perhaps, the most successful of his life. In all subsequent relationships there were too many words, emotions, accusations, and claims. But that was not the main thing. Sophie treated him selflessly, unlike her American contemporaries, who viewed him as the child of a successful banker. This image, created through his stepfather's efforts, formed a corresponding barrier around the young man, through the stakes of which normal romantic relationships were practically out of the question. With the years, the status of the adult Angelo changed, but his early career pattern left unchanged his suitability as a potential marriage partner. This naturally led to his early cynicism and a high degree of sexual irresponsibility. Well aware that girls tried to exploit him, he "got his retaliation in first" and actively exploited them himself.

It should be noted that for all this Angelo was well content and did not suffer from a lack of love, being fully satisfied with pseudo-romantic and infinitely varied sex. Only once, when he was over thirty, did he feel that he was loved. Somewhat later he realised that even on this occasion he had encountered calculation – although not financial calculation – from a girl from a rich family who was actively seeking an equal and saw one in him. This, somewhat later, was sufficient time for little Cristina to appear.

Angelo's total commitment to work and the financial independence of his wife made their marriage practically unclouded. They both raced through life at top speed, and even did so in one direction, though on parallel lines, meeting occasionally in "wayside cafés" and very soon ceasing to spend the night together in motorway motels. And on one such day his wife's path veered sharply to one side. This happened painlessly, albeit unexpectedly, for all concerned, including the then adolescent Cristina. Angelo remembered his grandfather, and gradually came to the conclusion that he was genetically predisposed to solitude. He found total satisfaction in business, money aside, which gave him the full gamut of emotions.

To his disappointment, Angelo quickly grew tired of the baguette, half of which still remained. Continuing to suck wine through the aperture of his package, he gave the remains of his bread to the local pigeons, among the crowd of which two gulls stood out by their colour, size, and boldness. Angelo did not care for them, and deliberately threw pieces of bread beyond them. The gulls were unaware of what they were doing wrong, and rushed feverishly from side to side, scaring their grey confrères out of the way in their attempts to get a bigger piece. Angelo grew tired of amusing himself with the birds and, carefully placing the unfinished bottle by a rubbish bin, quickly tore the remnants of the bread into large pieces and threw them into the thick of the throng of birds, who went crazy with such generosity.

13

1955. MONTEPULCIANO, ITALY

"I didn't expect anything like that from the old man." Vito angrily ran a cloth over a plate in the sink, risking breaking it in his hands. Angelo, feeling utterly depressed, did not reply. Vito continued with the washing up. With time this activity had come to resemble meditation: as he made his way through washing up a mountain of plates, his thoughts achieved great purity, and as he sorted the crockery, he would put his thoughts, cleansed of other emotions, in their appropriate places. Genarro's proposal was so unfair that it evoked not only displeasure in the friends but also righteous anger against their mentor. It was this anger that Vito was carefully taking out on the plate, risking its destruction before the destruction of his own wrath. Some fifteen minutes later the washing up was done, though there was still a little more work to be done. Vito silently and methodically sorted the different kinds of plates, glasses and forks, stowing them in their accustomed places.

Throughout all this, Angelo had been simply picking at the table, glancing at his friend now and then hoping for enlightenment in the form of a moment of genius on Vito's part. At last Vito finished his work and sat down, straddling a chair opposite Angelo. The younger partner realised that the decision had been taken. If Vito had sat down normally on the chair, crossing his legs, it would have meant that they would discuss something, but the back of the chair facing him excluded all discussion. Angelo experienced contradictory feelings: on the one hand, he was stung by the fact that, for all the formal equality of their partnership, Vito had taken the decision himself; on the other hand, torn apart by emotions as he was, he wasn't ready to take decisions.

"So that's how it is," said Vito calmly.

"That is to say, we refuse the deal?" asked Angelo fearfully.

"On the contrary – we agree to Genarro's conditions."

"Vito! We agree to peanuts?" Freed from the necessity of making a decision, Angelo gave full rein to his emotions.

"Not peanuts, Angelo. We'll earn money."

"Except our money has shrunk, if you hadn't noticed."

"Not all is lost, my friend…"

"I merely think that Genarro does not deserve half the profits. They're simply his stones. He's been giving them away left and right for nothing. It was only us who thought of a way of making a profit out of it," said the younger boy with righteous indignation.

"But the key words are 'they're his stones'. And you don't dispute that. Anyway, the deal is essentially already done. If we refuse, all he needs to do is hire a vehicle and some workmen and go ahead without us. Our share will just go with the transport and the old man will keep his money in any case."

"How quickly he worked everything out!"

"And you thought…"

"Crafty old bugger!" Angelo was still furious.

"Didn't you know it?"

"Of course I did."

"Do you know why you are so cross?"

"Yes, I do!"

"No you don't. You're cross because for the first time, Genarro didn't give in to you. He just acted as he would have done with anyone else. He's teaching us."

"But it seems to me he simply decided to make a killing. Sheer greed!"

"Angelo, I don't remember his being tight-fisted. Do you? Give me one example."

Angelo said nothing.

"I don't remember any. He can be cunning and calculating; he won't concede an advantage, but he's not greedy. I'm sure of that."

Angelo gradually came round to his friend's view, but still could not cope with his anger. It was easier to think of his grandfather's greed than about the fact that he was teaching them.

"What does that change?" Angelo turned his chair with its back towards Vito, thus lowering the intensity of their discussion.

"A lot. If we understand the motives for his actions, we'll be able to get the better of him. If it's not greed, then he's ready to negotiate. He's simply waiting for proposals from us – he wants us to bargain with him."

"How so? Vito, this is a very simple deal. Here are the stones; here's the money. What else is there to say?"

"You're forgetting one thing."

"What's that?"

"Delivering the stones to Montepulciano."

"We can't do it any cheaper. The old man's right about that – no one will take less than fifty lire per ten. You and I have talked to everyone about that."

"No, not with everyone." Vito smiled enigmatically. He liked to tease Angelo by saying he had an idea which the other could not guess at.

"Well, go on," said Angelo angrily.

"Look," said Vito soothingly. "The old man wants a fifty-fifty split. All right. We agree. But that relates to splitting the pure profit more than anything else."

"Vito, why are you going round in circles?"

"OK. We dismantle the barn ourselves and deliver the stones to Montepulciano!"

"What?"

"And we take fifty lire for labour and transport. Taking that into account, we end up with seventy-five lire for every ten bricks. As against the less than perfect fifty we'd reckoned on."

"Brilliant!" exclaimed Angelo sarcastically. "And you intend to cart the barn there yourself?"

"Not just me." Vito continued calmly. "Of course, not just me. With you. Angelo!"

Angelo merely spread his arms in disappointment, thus suggesting to his friend that he expound his brilliant plan.

"Angelo, calm down and listen." Vito got up from his chair and turned it to face Angelo. "Work on the wall will begin next spring. I reckon we've got to deliver about ten tonnes, that is, ten thousand kilograms."

"And," mumbled Angelo without enthusiasm.

"Each of us can take twenty-five kilograms on our back, so together we can take fifty each time."

"Isn't that rather a lot?"

"Angelo, remember how last spring we lugged the wine from the town? That was heavier."

"I really did almost flake out then. All right. Let's assume we can."

"That means we can shift ten tonnes in two hundred trips. If we do it every day, we'll easily manage to get it done before spring comes."

"Six kilometres every day with twenty-five kilos on our back? Vito, do you think that's on?"

"Absolutely," said the young man confidently. "I'll tell you what – in Nepal there'll be more – kilometres and kilos. If we can't do this work there's no sense in going such a distance. After everything we've done for this project, to go there in order to understand our own feebleness. It would be stupid, Angelo."

"I don't know, Vito…"

"So regard this as training, and not badly paid training at that!"

14

APRIL 2015. KATHMANDU, NEPAL

It was after two o'clock in the morning when Vito finally managed to fall asleep, having first done something he had last done at school – set his alarm. He wasn't going to rely on an organism not yet acclimatised to local time. And it was as well he did so – his telephone alarm caught him completely unawares. For some moments Vito tried to grasp where he was.

The friends were to meet in Angelo's hotel at eight in the morning. The helicopter flight to base camp was planned for nine. The weather outside the window gave grounds for optimism. Cristina's plan envisaged that the old men would return to Kathmandu in the afternoon, so in his small rucksack Vito put only his documents, his purse, and a bottle of water. Lunch would be at the base camp, after which the old men would have a couple of hours to explore the vicinity without going into the mountains further than tourists were allowed.

Angelo had been due to fly into Kathmandu late the previous evening. It was no more than ten minutes' leisurely walk to his hotel. It was quite warm in the street, so Vito put his jumper in his rucksack, assuming that he'd need it at higher levels. They were due to be taken by car to the airport, where the helicopter awaited them.

When he got to the hotel, Vito settled himself comfortably on a soft sofa in the foyer. Probably for the first time in all recent days, Vito felt excited by the forthcoming meeting. He realised that whatever scenario he chose for the meeting, he couldn't avoid banal phrases like: "Long time-no see." And "You've scarcely changed in the last sixty years!"

Until this morning, Vito had not experienced any special emotions at the forthcoming meeting with his childhood friend. This worried him somehow – this was his best friend, and the old man had expectations, but all the same he didn't have any sentimental feelings. Probably the fact was that for him Angelo had remained in his memory as the young boy with whom he played darts to decide who would do the washing up, and the old man whom he would see in a few minutes was unconnected with him. Having accepted this explanation of his own indifference, Vito relaxed a little. But now, when every opening of the lift doors could deliver Angelo to him, the old man's pulse betrayed him and wound up the tempo, while his memory leafed through, as if they were the pages of a photo album, the most vivid moments of their life in Genarro's house.

"But don't cry! Don't cry!" Vito kept saying to himself, afraid he might give way to his feelings when his friend appeared.

However, his friend was obviously not hurrying to so momentous a meeting; he didn't appear either at eight or five minutes later. After another ten minutes, Vito began to get anxious – they had chartered the helicopter, of course, and it wouldn't leave without its only two passengers, but the old man's punctiliousness gave him no peace, and pushed his excitement into the background.

Finally, Vito could stand it no longer. He went to reception and spoke the forename and surname of his friend as clearly as he could. A pleasant girl replied, equally clearly, that Angelo was having breakfast in his room and, to reinforce his understanding, pointed upwards. Vito, continuing the game of mime, put his hand to his ear like a telephone, as if to say: "Ring him." The girl dialled a number and listened to the ringing tone for a long time without taking her large eyes off Vito. As she was on the point of hanging up, the phone was answered. She quickly scribbled something in English, nodding to Vito as she did so. She hung up and pointed Vito to the lift, as if to say: "That way." The old man shrugged his shoulders to convey to her the fact that he didn't know his friend's room number. She "okayed" his signal, and with her left hand quickly wrote the number "504" on a piece of paper.

The door was open, and Vito went in. The room was on the top floor of the hotel. Most of it was taken up by a huge bed, made up hotel-style, which at such an early hour of the morning indicated that it had not been slept in. Finding no one in the room, the old man moved towards the balcony. The balcony, or rather, a terrace of massive proportions, so impressed Vito that he momentarily forgot why he had come. On a small rise in the middle of the terrace, a lawn was laid out. On the lush green grass stood a table and two wrought-iron chairs. On one of them sat Angelo, with his feet, clad in hotel slippers, on the other.

Vito was about to hail his friend, but at that moment he looked away from the table and saw… the mountains. There was a 180-degree panoramic view of the Himalayas. Neither from the street, nor from the heights of his hotel, had Vito ever seen anything like it. From time to time, as traffic moved along the streets of the city, he had seen the mountains, but like this – the whole horizon with snow-capped summits all at once – never! For a moment, Vito gazed entranced at the view, and then, collecting himself, turned his attention to his friend.

It was, without doubt, Angelo. Vito realised clearly at once that had they met in a crowd, he would not have had a second's doubt. It was not a matter of his resemblance to Genarro, which had come with the years, but of the similarity between Angelo as a child and as an old man. It was his Angelo, whom someone had made up as an old man for a joke and had put imitation grey in his hair.

"Why on earth have you climbed this high?" Vito surprised himself by asking a question different from all the other conversational gambits he had been running through all morning.

Angelo raised his eyebrows, not understanding immediately what he was being asked, or maybe who was asking it.

"Vito, when did you manage to get old?" Angelo asked after a second's pause, getting up to greet his friend.

"That'll do! In our village I'm still considered young," laughed Vito, embracing his friend. "At least that's what my aunties say!"

"They're still with us?!" said Angelo in some surprise, seating his friend on the chair opposite.

IGOR ZAVILINSKY

"All three, just imagine!" laughed Vito, not letting go of his friend's hand.

"Amazing! Now tell me that Cesare is still sitting in the bar of an evening!"

"You know he went on sitting there for a long time, and in a couple of months would have been starting his second century."

"Favoured spots!"

"You must come. The aunties will be glad to see you. Well, all except Giulietta."

"She won't be glad?"

"No, it's simply that she can hardly see anything. But you'll certainly get the traditional whack on the bottom!"

"Oh yes!" laughed Angelo. "Good Lord, Vito! I'd almost forgotten all that…"

The friends fell silent. The number of memories flooding in no doubt prevented them from latching on to any one in particular and talking about it. Both said nothing.

Vito became worried not so much by the pause as by thoughts of the helicopter waiting for them at the airport.

"Listen, we'll have plenty of time to talk – let's get on our way to the airport…"

"I'm going back to New York!" said Angelo calmly.

"When?" asked Vito, for a moment not understanding the drama of the situation and finding himself somewhere between memories and reality.

"Today, Vito. There's a plane at five o'clock," Angelo continued calmly.

For some time Vito sat in silence, digesting this information. Then, realising that it was a matter of cancelling the expedition to the mountain, he slowly turned round, as if afraid of scaring Angelo. On Angelo's face, apart from the traces of a sleepless night, was a fleeting, foolish smile. Vito could not make out whether it was apologetic or sickly.

It was only now that Vito noticed how oddly Angelo was dressed: by the layers he had on it was clear that they'd been added as the night grew colder. Underneath was a tracksuit, followed by a while hotel dressing gown. Round his waist was a blanket. It was only now, too, that Vito cast his eye over the table. Despite the fact that the space around it had been carefully cleared away, one could deduce that the night had been tumultuous – the staff had been afraid to remove an almost empty bottle of whisky and several packets of cigarettes, each one of which for some reason lacked several cigarettes. It was only now that Vito noticed a closed laptop, a small printer and a stack of printouts.

Vito was on the point of asking what had happened when there was a timid knock on the balcony door. Angelo did not even turn round. After an awkward pause, Vito himself had to react and, with a nod of the head, to invite onto the terrace a girl who was timidly shuffling from foot to foot in the expectation of receiving permission. The girl made for the table and asked permission to take back the computer and printer. Angelo merely nodded and said she could. The girl nervously collected the bits of kit together, and hastened to leave.

Vito again opened his mouth in order to ask a question, but Angelo pre-empted him by reaching for the bottle.

"Will you have a drink?"

"No, of course not. It's eight in the morning!" said Vito in a shocked voice, and, glancing at his watch, he corrected himself – it was eight thirty.

This correction by thirty minutes should, in Vito's opinion, have reminded Angelo of their plans, reminded him about the helicopter, and salvaged the situation. However, Angelo interpreted it in his own way, as if Vito, without exception, didn't drink before eight but at half past eight there was no problem. The result of this misunderstanding was a glass, in which ice cubes barely covered the whisky, having been spirited by Angelo from under the table, where he had no doubt concealed the ice bucket, in the manner of a fakir. Vito, not wanting to waste time on arguments, took the glass in formal fashion, and with a gentle movement of his hand shifted Angelo's feet off the chair and sat down on it opposite him.

"Is everything all right?"

"Everything's all right. All-right!" said Angelo, lingering over the words.

"But why do you repeat yourself?"

"Well, to cut a long story short... I've been sacked!"

IGOR ZAVILINSKY

"How do you mean, sacked?"

"Just that!" Angelo nodded at the stack of printouts.

"Can they really sack you? I was told you owned the company…"

"Well, I'm still the owner." Angelo was obviously irritated by the need to elucidate elementary details. "No one can sack me from being owner. Except me."

Vito said nothing, making it clear that he'd got no further in understanding the problem.

"Good Lord, Vito. I was President of my own company for thirty years! And they've sacked me in a day!"

"Is that legal?" asked Vito timidly.

"Oh yes! Absolutely! They called a meeting of the directors, depicted me as senile and got a majority for my retirement." Angelo spread his arms, which made the blanket look like wings.

Vito, who still did not realise the depth of his friend's tragedy, was on the point of making a joke to the effect that the board of directors were not that far from the truth, given how Angelo now looked, but, seeing his friend's desperation, he broke off. Instead, he directed all his energy into at least partially understanding the situation and not looking like a complete idiot.

"Will you lose a lot of money?"

"What? Money? My dear chap, what do you mean? They're prepared to lash out more than I can spend for the rest of my days, even if I live as long as Cesare. Money doesn't come into it."

At which point Vito came out with a stupid remark:

"So, maybe, good riddance to being President."

Angelo did not bother to reply. He simply began to look past Vito and towards the mountains. Vito remembered this habit very well from childhood days. It meant: "That is the end of the conversation." Vito swallowed his whisky mechanically, as if it were coffee, and even began coughing in surprise; it seemed he really had forgotten what he was holding in his hands.

To avoid another blunder, Vito decided to say nothing. He quickly realised that no argument would shift Angelo from his position, and that they could forget about the helicopter. Turning his chair towards the mountains, Vito sat down beside his friend. Of course, this gave him no chance of looking at him, but with Angelo in this mood there wasn't anything to look at. The friends said nothing. Vito was looking at the range of mountains, and his mood was worsening. Now, as never before, he wanted to get to Annapurna.

Vito was thinking that the most important events in his life had happened without his willing them. Moreover, Vito had, since childhood, been more than self-reliant, owing, probably, to his long-standing struggle for independence with the aunts who looked after him. And now, just as he felt that he was running his own life, that he was capable of taking decisions which bore on his fate, at that very moment that same fate, as if in mockery, had come up with something that turned his life upside down.

That's how it had been, beginning with the tableware Genarro had bought off him at the insistence of the aunts, a fact which Vito had only recently learned about; that's how it had been with the restaurant, which had come to him without his either wanting or willing it; that's how it had been when his grown-up sons had been getting ready to leave home and he and his wife had been thinking what to do with their newly acquired freedom, thoughts which her illness had put an end to. With the death of his wife had died all attempts to leave the bounds of Tuscany. It sometimes seemed to Vito that the very earth on which he had grown up would not release him, and that as soon as he had the prospect of leaving, it held on to him and would not assign him the means of doing so.

But when Vito had calmed down and reconciled himself to the fact that the longest journey of his life would end on the Ligurian coast, Cristina had appeared and suggested he accompany Angelo to Nepal, once again confirming the dependence of Vito's fate on other people and events. But that wasn't the least of it, and now this journey was being cancelled with mocking predictability one step away from completion.

"Angelo, I'm sorry it's turned out like this," said Vito pensively, not turning to his friend. "But I want to go up. And I'll do it. If necessary, I'll do it myself."

Angelo shuddered and looked at his friend.

"Is that all you can say to me – 'I'm sorry'?" There was a ring of steel in Angelo's voice.

"Angelo, don't unload all your disappointment on me," said Vito angrily. "Although if it makes you feel better, go ahead!"

"Thanks!" Angelo leapt to his feet. "That's just what I wanted to do!"

"I'll be glad to be of service." Vito was mollified and, getting up from his chair, went up to his friend apologetically.

"To hell with it, Vito… I don't blame you… It's simply turned out that your idea for a trip hasn't fitted the bill."

As he said this, Angelo tried to avoid looking his friend in the eye.

"It wasn't my idea," muttered Vito, in his turn averting his eyes from Angelo.

"What are you saying?"

"You heard – it wasn't my idea!"

"What are you talking about?"

"About the fact that Cristina came to me and asked me to write you a letter." Vito spoke the words, and only then realised how horrible they sounded.

"Cristina? My Cristina?"

Vito did not reply; he merely looked into Angelo's eyes. After a momentary pause, those eyes quickly filled with tears. Before the tears began to pour down his cheeks, Angelo turned away hurriedly.

"She said you needed a rest. A holiday. That it was a matter of life or death. I couldn't refuse her. Dammit! I couldn't have known it would turn out badly for you."

Angelo said nothing. Looking at his friend's back, Vito could not make out whether he was trying to cope with tears or was already thinking about something else. Notwithstanding the evidence, Vito could not believe that Angelo's daughter had been devious. And it wasn't that he was very fond of her or that he had been naïve. Vito simply knew that strange things happen in life: evidence does not always accord with reality.

Vito sat down again. Angelo stayed put, with his back to his friend.

"Do you remember how one night you ate one of the decorations off a cake left the kitchen the day before a wedding?"

"Where are you going with that?" asked Angelo, spluttering.

"Do you remember?"

"You bet I do! It was the most delicious decoration I ever had in my life." The memory of the taste of that cream seemed about to disperse the gloom of Angelo's thoughts on the spot. "And you gave me a right tongue lashing."

"After you were asleep, I realised they'd flay you alive. Even though you'd carefully smeared over the place on the cake."

"Why?" The inappropriate reminiscences of his friend were beginning to annoy Angelo, and he turned round.

"Because the symmetry was destroyed. As soon as the cake was on the table and visible from all sides, it would have been obvious. When I realised that, I sneaked back down and put everything to rights."

"How?"

"I had to remove an identical decoration from the opposite side."

"Very touching, but what's the point of these reminiscences, Vito?"

"Hear me out – you've got another five hours."

Angelo merely nodded, as if to say: "Go on, tell the story." And slumped wearily in his chair.

"At the very moment I was removing the surplus decoration from the cake with a knife, Genarro came into the kitchen."

Angelo looked up at his friend.

"Angelo, what was he to think of a child, at night, holding a cream decoration cut from a wedding cake on a knife? Not that I intended to eat it – if you recall I don't have much of a sweet tooth. I simply wanted to throw it away and save my friend from punishment."

"What did Genarro say?"

"He believed me when I said I didn't intend to eat it and only wanted to make the cake look right."

"What are you driving at?"

"Don't jump to conclusions about Cristina. Look carefully into everything."

Angelo shrugged his shoulders mistrustfully.

"Angelo, I know nothing about your stock market affairs and I don't claim to. The one thing I learnt in the bar was – analyse people a bit. I'm sure that despite all the evidence, there's another version. Or at least explanation."

Angelo did not react at all to his friend's words and remained silent. Vito again sat down beside him. An observer might have thought that the two old men were blissfully carefree and serenely surveying the mountains.

"So everything's all right with you?" Angelo broke the silence.

"With me? Absolutely."

"That's good news."

"Why news?" Vito did not fully grasp what his friend was talking about.

"I'm talking about your illness." Angelo again began to get irritated.

"What illness?" asked Vito in turn, with no less irritation.

"The one you wrote about in your letter."

"What letter?"

"Vito! The letter which invited me to Nepal."

"Yes, I read it through before it was sent. That's why I'm asking what illness you're talking about."

Angelo stood up and went into his room He rooted about in his things for a time, quietly cursing that he couldn't find it.

"Found it!" Angelo came out again onto the balcony with a piece of a piece of paper folded in three.

"Yes, that's the letter." Vito ran his eyes over the sheet of paper. "Why on earth are you carrying it around with you?"

"Your phone number was on the bottom of it and I simply threw it into my bag in case we got lost."

"I see," whispered Vito, not letting go of the letter.

When he'd finished reading, Vito, in some bewilderment, gave the letter back to his friend. Now it was his turn to say nothing.

"Did Cristina ask you to write about the illness? To be on the safe side?"

"No," replied Vito pensively, adding, "that wasn't in the letter."

"So?"

"In the letter there was only the proposal for the trip. Without any additional dramatics," said Vito, perplexed. "Did the letter come to your home address?"

"Yes, it's my home address, not my business address. Who posted it?"

"Alessandro. My elder son."

"What sense was there in adding something about your illness," said Angelo uncomprehendingly.

"Well, for instance, so that the trip would definitely happen," stated Vito sadly. "You couldn't have denied your old friend his last wish!"

"Why did they think that necessary?"

"Have you got your phone on you?"

Angelo rummaged among the papers on the table and offered Vito his iPhone. Vito shook his head.

"What?"

"Dial this number, please." Vito indicated a number on the hotel notepaper on which the letter had been written.

"What am I to say?"

"Ask…"

"What?"

"Say you were here with your family a couple of years back and are thinking of a return visit."

"Why?"

"And ask, among other things, what's new with them."

"Good Lord, Vito, what sort of a conspiracy is this? Would you care to explain?"

"Yes, and if they don't tell you, ask whether their swimming pool has appeared."

"Swimming pool?" said Angelo in surprise.

"Yes, yes, swimming pool. Ring them!"

Angelo dialled the number and left the balcony. Vito tried to eavesdrop on the conversation but could only catch the occasional word. That was enough, though; everything was perfectly clear to him, and the phone call was, by and large, simply formal confirmation of his guess.

After a few minutes Angelo returned and slumped wearily into an armchair. Vito's concern about a swimming pool was distracting him from his own much more significant problems. Although strangely, Angelo found himself properly side-tracked, and he genuinely tried to grasp the essence of his friend's anxieties.

"They said there'd be a swimming pool by May."

"That's so."

"Now you're going to tell me that something's amiss with this swimming pool."

"They got me out of the house so I didn't stop them excavating the pool."

"Well that's all right. A pool's a good thing for a hotel," said Angelo, immediately realising that he'd just repeated his friend's mistake by essentially siding with his opponents.

Vito did not react. It was now his turn to plunge into weighty thoughts. Nine o'clock was approaching, and the two men were sitting in silence on the balcony and simply looking at the range of snow-covered summits and realising they weren't a step closer to them. They were looking at the Himalayas as if on TV; the reality of their actual presence was being gradually eroded by unhappy thoughts about what had happened back home. Vito finished off a glass of whisky without realising, but tipsiness did not bring relief. Neither Angelo nor Vito had any desire to discuss their problems further. Everything was so obvious that silence was the best way to discuss them.

"I'm going home," mumbled Vito.

"What'll you do?"

"With what?"

"Well, with the swimming pool."

"Well, not dig it… It's time I moved out."

"Where will you go?"

"To the sea. I'll buy a little flat. I'll feed pigeons on the seashore. I should have done it a long time ago. What about you?"

"Well, something similar. I have a house in Sarasota."

"Is there sea there?"

"Yes. The Gulf of Mexico."

"Gulf?" said Vito disappointedly.

"Vito, the Gulf of Mexico is bigger than the Mediterranean."

"Ah," Vito drawled, in apparent comprehension, although it was clear that he found his friend's words unconvincing, "that's all right then."

The exchange of plans for life by the two old men had gone gloomily. Thoughts of relaxing by the sea did not delight either of them. The only way Vito knew of countering depression was – activity. Any activity, unconnected, as a rule, with the problem. The more monotonous, the better. The harder it was, the quicker it distracted from gloomy thoughts.

"Goodbye, Angelo!" Vito headed determinedly for the door.

"Where are you going, Vito?"

"I'm going to collect my things and try to buy a new ticket." Vito found the farewell difficult and wanted to get it over with as quickly as possible.

"Goodbye, Vito! Take care of yourself!" said Angelo, as if they were saying goodbye till the next day.

15

1955. MONTEPULCIANO, ITALY

Autumn was coming in slowly. Not that in these parts it was ever any different, but this year everything was especially drawn out. The days felt no different from summer days; it was as warm as ever, there was almost no rain, and nothing but dust between the vines. From the heights of Montepulciano the land was like the sky around Milan airport, except that, instead of vapour trails, it bore grey tracks of dust from passing tractors and grazing sheep. Dusty plumes, bent uniformly in one direction, hung over the land. For a long time turbid traces continued to hover in the air, existing independently from their origins. Genarro, who was drinking a glass of wine on top of the town wall, surveyed this evening landscape and found in it a similarity with human nature: we often live through experiences, not letting go of them even when they become almost a fog and when the link with the events which gave rise to them is, to all intents and purposes, lost.

Genarro might have seen many such dusty plumes, but the years spent in the mountains had taught him to value the present. His father often used to repeat "on an unlucky day the mountaineer dies", accustoming Genarro to the idea that all other unpleasantnesses are not worth dwelling on for a long time. Genarro was always considered an eternal optimist, although his optimism was of a special kind, at the basis of which lay the mountain guide's habit of relying entirely on himself. In the mountains one did not have to rely on a random tourist about whom you knew nothing. For this reason Genarro, who throughout his life had viewed many circumstances with scepticism, never, in any circumstances, viewed himself sceptically. Probably this was self-confidence. However, it was the self-confidence of a strong man. He had every right and every reason to feel it. Throughout his complex life he had never overstepped the mark of this confidence.

On Saturday Genarro traditionally went to the town, leaving the boys to look after the bar. This was his personal time and his personal walk. There were several obligatory ritual features to this walk: meeting a couple of friends, an ice-cream cornet, a phone call from the post office to his daughter, and some small purchases – not for the bar but for himself. And to round things off, a glass of good wine in his old friend's bar on the wall. However, on this occasion the sequence, built up and verified with the years, was changed: after his conversation with Sofia, Genarro bypassed the familiar shops and went straight to Giuseppe's bar. After drinking his first glass at the bar, it was only with his second glass that Genarro sat down at his table and surveyed the late-evening countryside. Giuseppe, who had known Genarro since he first came to Tuscany, became anxious.

"Is everything all right with you?"

"Yes, Giuseppe, everything's all right. Everything is all – right."

"If it was, you wouldn't say that twice," said his observant friend.

"I tell you – nothing out of the ordinary."

"All right, if you say so." Giuseppe moved away, knowing that if Genarro didn't want to say anything, it was pointless trying to drag it out of him.

The wine in the second glass was coming to its end. So too was the day. By evening, a wind got up, its coolness bringing everyone back to autumnal reality. Genarro remembered the jacket he'd left at home and regretted the fact that he'd have to make the considerable walk from the town in his shirt sleeves.

"Another one?"

"Angelo's going."

Giuseppe interpreted this as a positive reply, and filled his friend's glass.

"To his mother?"

"With his mother."

"Meaning?"

"Her husband, this Milan banker," – there was mild irritation in the old man's voice – "is being transferred to the New York branch. Sofia's going with him. She wants to take Angelo to America."

"What about schools?"

"Giuseppe! They tell me there are schools in America!"

"I understand. But they're all in English, no doubt."

"They'll sort things out. Some of them studied German there."

"No doubt it'll be good for the boy." Giuseppe had not yet worked out his friend's mood, and kept the conversation going in a neutral tone.

"Yes."

"Are they going for long?"

"Three years, for now. Then, how things turn out. Sofia wants Angelo to go to university there."

"That's great!"

"Yes."

"You're upset?"

"Why should I be upset? She's taking responsibility for him at last," grumbled the old man quite unconvincingly, and, as if realising this, he threw in a new argument. "A boy needs a mother more than he does a grandfather."

"All the same, you've got used to the lad... so many years..."

"There's nothing for him to do here, Giuseppe. Let him go, let him study." These last words were closest to what Genarro felt in his innermost being.

"Does Angelo himself want to?"

"He's still a child. He doesn't understand yet what's best for him. His mother will decide."

Genarro contemplated the fields near Montepulciano, which had grown tired in a day. The peasants had gone home, the dust had settled, and it was getting cooler. Somewhere in the distance, towards his bar, Genarro saw a belated tractor moving along. The tractor had thrown up a fresh plume of dust across the whole picture.

Genarro poured himself a third glass from a bottle which Massimo had kindly brought him. The old man loved wine. For him, wine was like an antiseptic of the soul which obliterated the regrets or, heaven help him, the self-pity which had appeared on the surface of his life.

"It'll be better that way," Genarro told himself. It was difficult to tell what predominated in this sentence: confidence that the step was right, or an attempt to persuade himself that it was. Moreover, for Genarro, the gap between these two positions was so small that he couldn't always tell them apart. Finishing his glass and leaving a third of a bottle for the bewildered Giuseppe, Genarro marched quickly out of the bar.

16

APRIL 2015. KATHMANDU, NEPAL

Towards evening, whether from burdensome thoughts or from the whisky which, since morning, through Angelo's efforts, had been infiltrating his organism, Vito began to feel ill. His head, accustomed to a strictly limited amount of the best Tuscan wines, was splitting with the effects of the raw Scottish drink. And in general, Vito now felt something which he felt extremely rarely, the last occasion being some three years earlier during an epidemic of a rare strain of flu: Vito felt himself to be a helpless old man. No doubt in order to counterbalance this, Vito went up to a mirror but, finding in it only confirmation of his feelings, he gave a disappointed sigh.

The approach of the Nepalese evening, which corresponds to the Italian day, brought sleep no closer to him. Vito went down into the vestibule and tried to find a broadcast of that day's Fiorentina versus Roma match. He had lost all hope of managing to watch a match involving his favourite team when a young man of about thirty with a computer came down to the vestibule. A minute later Vito heard, from the workings of the computer, the voice of the dreaded Carlo Giampa[12] yelling every time Roma attacked. But in current circumstances he had no option, and to ask his fellow countryman if he could watch the match with the sound muted would have been stupid even for such a devoted fan of the *Purples* as the old man.

....

[12]   Carlo Giampa: one of the most emotional Italian commentators. A devoted fan of Roma FC.

"Hello." The old man raised a bottle containing the dregs of his beer in welcome.

"Oh, greetings!" The young man jumped, clearly not expecting to hear Italian spoken this evening.

"You don't object to having a *Violets* fan for company?"

"Certainly not, especially as I'm a Milano fan." The young man laughed. He seemed younger than Vito had first thought.

And indeed, Luigi was a twenty-eight-year-old bank clerk from Milan who had just today returned from a trip to Annapurna with his wife. The match was drawing to a close, Fiorentina were losing, and the conversation between the two compatriots quickly switched from football to mountains. Luigi willingly shared his newly minted impressions.

"Were your rucksacks heavy?" Vito kept up the conversation out of sheer curiosity.

"No, they weren't. Mine weighed about ten kilos, my wife's less – about seven."

"And how long did the trek take?"

"Five days up." Luigi thought for a while, mentally counting the days. "And just under three down."

"You didn't go up too quickly?" asked the old man interestedly, having some knowledge of the matter.

"You mean the sixty metre a day limit on climbs? We only once exceeded it – on the last leg. We couldn't wait to get to Annapurna," the young man replied guiltily, sensing that his interlocutor was an experienced mountaineer. "How many days have you planned for?"

"About the same," replied Vito casually, clearly not wanting to discuss his plans in detail.

Luigi, taking this to be a manifestation of a kind of professional hauteur, did not insist on details, and continued to share the purely emotional side of his ascent. Vito took leave of his compatriot and went up to his room with the clear intention of sleeping.

At that moment the door of his room shuddered from blows, which from their violence, might be assumed to have been delivered by a foot. Even before the old man heard a drunken "Vito!", he somehow had no doubt that the visitor was the second "lucky beggar" of the day – Angelo. Whatever his friend's appearance, Vito was glad to see him – nothing could be worse than solitude today.

Vito managed to open the flimsy door before Angelo had had time to set about it again, to do which he'd already swung back a foot clad in a new boot. Only now did Vito notice behind his friend's back two huge rucksacks, apparently newly purchased, with a heap of tourist clobber sticking out of them.

In a state of high excitement, Angelo tumbled into the room and, in lordly fashion, threw the lot onto Vito's bed, apparently counting on an exuberant reaction from his friend. Without waiting for it, he asked Vito:

"What do you think, do we need self-heating insoles in our boots?"

"Do you think they won't give them out in the old people's home?" countered Vito without enthusiasm.

"You'll know better – they bombard you with promotional leaflets!" replied Angelo, pleased with his joke.

"Angelo, what the hell are you doing?"

"I'm going with you!" Angelo was busily shaking the contents of the two rucksacks onto the bed.

"I've got a flight to Milan in the morning."

"Do you remember how as boys we used to study magazines in Giuseppe's bar?" Angelo gave himself over to reminiscence and paid no attention to his friend's words. "Well let me tell you – it was all rubbish. We wasted our time. Here in one shop there are more things than in a year's magazine subscription."

"You are trying to compare the incomparable," Vito realised that it was pointless saying anything now to Angelo, who was in a hysterical state.

"Yes... There were times," said Angelo thoughtfully. "All right. What does our age matter? I've bought everything for the two of us."

"Angelo!"

"What?"

"I've got a flight tomorrow. Did you hear me?"

"Yes, of course. But you aren't going to leave me here on my own?"

"Angelo!"

"Listen! You yourself said – let's go up ourselves. Just you and me."

"Yes, I said that. I simply wanted to talk you round after your bad news."

"That's it! And you succeeded! You talked me round!"

"Angelo! I feel bloody awful today. Honestly."

"'Don't die'," said Angelo with facetious pathos. "In a word, rubbish. After all, it's not as if we're leaving now. It's just the whisky. Tomorrow you'll be as right as rain."

"Why do we need all this?"

Angelo stopped bustling about and looked at Vito. At that moment, Vito realised that his friend was completely sober.

"Vito! What else do we need?"

"A lot. And there's the added issue that we haven't got long." Vito laughed, but not very cheerfully.

"Screw it... We're alive! We, my friend, are in Nepal!!!" Angelo threw himself at Vito and rolled him onto the bed.

"You've gone mad," croaked the old man. "Let me go!"

"We're in Nepal!" Angelo straddled his friend and grasped his hands in his own. "You remember everything, Vito! You must remember! How we dreamed of this. How many stones we lugged for the sake of this!"

Angelo got off Vito and lay down alongside him. The old men lay on the bed, silently contemplating the ceiling of the modest hotel room. Both realised they were thinking about one and the same thing and that there was no sense in voicing their thoughts. Angelo was the first to break the silence:

"Why didn't we do this earlier?"

"What exactly?"

"Come here."

"We were busy."

"Yes, I have been pretty busy for the last fifty years," said Angelo thoughtfully.

"Don't those numbers terrify you?" laughed Vito.

"I've stopped trying to get my head round them. Fifty, sixty..."

"You're not flying to New York?"

"No. That wouldn't change anything. And I still don't know what to make of it. Honestly. I still haven't understood… I still can't – how can I put it…"

"What can't you do?"

"Localize my anger, or something… I realise that if I went home tomorrow, I'd be on the warpath. And possibly I'd have a chance of winning something back… not everything, of course, but certainly…"

"Getting a better deal for yourself?"

"Unkind!"

"Forgive me."

"Unkind, but essentially correct. But the thing is, I don't want more. Yes, and knowing my colleagues, they'll be ready for me. I taught them myself. They'll have Plans B and C ready which they would put to me depending how much noise I make. But now it's like offering a man who comes to town for a day a monthly instead of a weekly pass."

Vito gave a wry smile.

"But I don't know how far they're prepared to go," Angelo continued.

"To the point where Angelo Rossi shuts up."

"Exactly."

"They probably haven't seen you do that," Vito laughed.

"If I'm honest, I don't remember myself," said Angelo sardonically. "The only thing worse than execution is waiting for it."

"Especially if you haven't been told about the reprieve…"

"That would be better, my friend. That would be better."

The two men fell silent, imagining the bewilderment in the New York office. Angelo himself put faces to them, but Vito, who had not had that opportunity, probably imagined them more clearly – in depersonalized form.

"You know what, Angelo?" said Vito thoughtfully after a moment's pause. "Despite all the difference in our situations, we have one thing in common – we've been written off."

"Looks that way, Vito…"

"We're a hindrance. We are in the way. And, of course, they might be right in everything they did. And we should not think badly of them. Furthermore…"

"What?"

"You know, for the first time in our lives we can think about ourselves instead of them."

"You're an egoist, Vito!"

"Not yet, but I'm learning," laughed the old man, extracting the sim card from his phone not without difficulty and flicking it in the direction of the waste paper basket.

"When are we leaving?" asked Angelo, doing the same with his phone.

In the morning no trace remained of Angelo's determination of the previous day. Vito noticed this at once when he met him over a modest breakfast. Angelo had not wanted to return to his luxury hotel for just one night and had contented himself with a modest apartment, classed as "de luxe" here, a fact which had evoked a burst of sarcasm in him. When Vito arrived for breakfast, Angelo was picking fastidiously at a fresh omelette with a cheap stainless-steel fork, and met his friend's gaze with a lack of enthusiasm.

"How do you feel?" Vito had originally wanted to gauge his friend's mood, but in view of the latter's appearance adopted a more concrete approach

"Don't forget to ask me this evening," mumbled Angelo irritably, thus reinforcing Vito's suspicions about his state of mind, as he cautiously forked a piece of omelette into his mouth.

Vito, who the previous evening had swapped his traditional supper for a hefty drinking session, was very hungry. Nevertheless, by long-established habit, he could not take any food before having a cup of coffee. He poured himself a cup from the pot on the table and, raising his eyes to his friend, saw that he was shaking his head.

"What?"

"Don't drink."

"Why not?"

"Believe me. You mustn't drink it."

"It's all right. I had some yesterday."

Angelo shrugged his shoulders in disappointment, as if to say: "You know best." Vito took a sip and quickly transferred his gaze to his friend, who was merely waiting with a fixed expression on his face denoting "I told you". A realisation that something was wrong with the coffee hit Vito together with the realisation that the previous day he had had a coffee not here but in the neighbouring café. His hotel restaurant had been closed when the early-rising Vito had come down to breakfast. The subsequent emotions of the previous day had wiped his memory clean of this trivial episode, but the old man did not want to go into explanations for fear of encountering mockery from Angelo at the expense of his forgetfulness. Vito forced himself to take another sip to spite Angelo, and turned his attention to the food, trying to kill the oppressive after-taste with his omelette.

The friends dealt fairly quickly with the modest fare, and went out into the foyer, where the things they had collected for the journey were waiting for them.

Vito looked at the two identical rucksacks which Angelo had bought the previous day, and the two pairs of identical trekking poles. Then he shifted his gaze downwards to their feet, shod in yellow boots, and sighed.

"People will look at us and think we came from the same care home," said Vito with a helpless gesture.

"That's fine: we'll pretend we've broken away from the peloton and mad oldies will come after us," said Angelo in uncertain self-justification. Only now did he realise that the day before, in concentrating on choosing models and sizes, he had not worried about variety and had simply taken two of all essentials. Vito's remark prompted Angelo to refrain for the time being from presenting two orange waterproofs big enough for a person carrying a rucksack to put on. Instead, he asked:

"Vito! Have you got money?"

"In what sense?" Vito asked in his turn, in some surprise.

"I spent all my cash yesterday and I don't want to use my credit card."

"Why not?"

"It makes me easy to track down."

"We're really free if we've got cash!" Vito announced feelingly, adding "that's why I only use cash."

"You only use cash because you're too old for the ATM!" Angelo countered wickedly. "But now we've got it you can bail me out as we go!"

"You don't understand – you'll have to reconcile yourself to my innate parsimoniousness."

"Innate greed." Angelo corrected him

Vito was about to reply, but the manager of the hotel came up, a metal tag with the name "Nava" on the lapel of his jacket.

"Gentlemen, I see you're ready for the trek?"

Angelo caught a note of sarcasm in his words, but seeing the sincere and open smile of the young man, the old man realised that most likely he was just afraid of hearing sarcasm. What was more, one could surmise that even at this early stage of his career, as evidenced by his youth, Nava had never seen tourists like this.

"Yes, we were just looking for you to ask for help organising transport to Pokhara," said Angelo, relenting.

"And possibly, for some words of advice from you." Vito hastened to interpolate. "The fact is, originally we didn't plan an ascent. We were thinking we'd simply look round these beautiful spots, like the old things we are. But yesterday…"

Vito could not choose the right words.

"Yesterday we felt a sharp access of strength." Angelo came to the rescue of his faltering friend.

"Yes, so my friend and I decided to shake off the past," Vito concluded, not entirely convincingly.

"What do you want to know?" said Nava with interest and without a trace of surprise.

The friends exchanged looks. With Vito's tacit consent, Angelo began cautiously:

"What would be your estimation of the difficulty of the route to the Annapurna base camp, from the physical point of view?" Without exchanging a look with Vito, he added: "Are there any restrictions on age?"

"Well, I'd begin by saying there are two basic routes. The first is the so-called 'Annapurna Ring'. There are several variants of this route lasting from ten to twenty days."

The friends exchanged looks of alarm.

"And the second?" Vito hastened to ask.

"The second is the so-called ABC – Annapurna Base camp. It's one of the most popular routes in the country. It takes the inexperienced traveller about six to seven days. Of course, this depends on their speed of movement."

The old men nodded approvingly.

"As regards its difficulty," the young man went on, "what can I say? Imagine a multi-storey block."

"Splendid. Done!" Angelo became animated at the thought of an analogy which he understood.

"In that case you would have to go up the staircase in this block for four to five hours a day on average," Nava explained, hastening to add, "of course, with an unlimited number of pauses."

The old men exchanged looks as if each were checking what impression these words had made on the other.

"O-k-ay." Angelo dragged out the word pensively. "But what about the risks on the path itself? Will we encounter great heights? Can one get lost on it?"

"Imagine the multi-storey block again," smiled the young man, feeling that he had found the right form of description. "You've got to climb the staircase of this place, but there aren't any banisters. In other words, if you're sober and watch where you're going, nothing terrible will happen to you. Actually, you've as much chance of getting lost as you have on the staircase of your imagined block."

Nava's information clarified the situation, although it didn't add to the confidence of the old men, Vito especially, who was contemplating the rucksack as if measuring it against himself and against the trek which lay ahead. He found it difficult to evaluate his physical preparedness: on the one hand, having lived to a ripe old age, Vito had never experienced problems in carrying out his daily work – usually more than five hours of it – in the countryside. On the other hand, he realised full well that his workload in the vineyard or his household duties had nothing in common with a climb of several days into the mountains. He could not compare these activities, and the analogy with the multi-storey block was no help. He had difficulty remembering when he'd last been in such a building – in Milan he thought – and even then, he'd used the lift.

"One last question," sighed a dejected Vito, "but I fear you won't avoid using your analogy with the multi-storey block. Is it cold there?"

"It'll only be cold when you're near base camp, and, basically, at night. The loggias where you'll overnight are essentially plywood buildings with no heating, and the temperature in the last stops before Annapurna can fall to ten below. But there are always warm blankets there which will supplement your sleeping bags very well."

Despite the manager's optimistic message, Vito cringed.

"It's warm in the daytime there," added Nava, seeing his guests' doubts, "and on the first few days it'll be hot in the sun. But I would recommend you take thin gloves and a pair of warm socks."

"Two pairs," put in Angelo, thinking.

"Sorry, sir?" said Nava, not understanding.

"Two pairs of warm socks. You must always take two pairs, my friend."

"Yes, of course. Two pairs are always better than one," the manager agreed.

"And how much will this cost?" Vito steered the conversation into a more practical channel with forced cheerfulness.

"Well, gentlemen, at the moment no one apart from a helicopter will take you to base camp. It won't be too expensive as far as Pokhara. I'll have a word now with the driver who often takes our guests and get back to you at once."

Contented with the outcome of the conversation, the friends leapt from their places and made to leave. Vito paused a little for thought.

"Nava!"

"Yes, sir!"

"What do we owe you for such detailed guidance?"

"If on the way back you stay in our hotel, that will be thanks enough for me!"

"Excellent, Nava! We'll do that!" Angelo clapped the young man lightly on the shoulder.

"When do you plan to come back?" Nava opened his notebook.

Vito and Angelo looked at each other.

"Well, bearing in mind what you've said, plus one spare day, I think we'll be back on the 24th, and we'll fly out of Nepal on the 25th."

"Splendid! Then, if you've no objection, I'll keep the same room for you."

"Splendid, Nava! And we'd like to use the local mobile network if possible." Angelo waved an expensive phone.

"Yes, I'm very happy to help you with that!"

17

APRIL 2015. POKHARA, NEPAL

Pokhara[13] is a town of happy tourists and one street. One might even say "a town of happy tourists on one street". However, whichever way you put it, its essence is unchanged: all the temporary inhabitants of this little town circulate exclusively on Lakeside Road, which goes from the airport and runs right through Pokhara along the lake side. Hence why many tourists, especially in Nepal's two high seasons – autumn and spring – don't go more than a hundred metres from this main road. Above it, everything is crammed with small hotels; below it, between the road and the lake, are dozens of restaurants side by side, and Lakeside Road itself is like an international exhibition of tourist and mountaineering equipment, Naturally, there is more to the town than this, but it is a rare tourist who finds either the strength or the need to go further: Lakeside Road greets them, shelters them, feeds them, sells them essentials, foists light beads on those going up and heavy Tibetan bells on those coming down, and sees them off to their plane or the bus to Kathmandu.

The people you meet on Lakeside Road can easily be classified into two approximately equal groups: those who come for a day and will go to the mountains tomorrow, and those who will stay here for a couple of days after going up. Apart from the different choice of souvenirs, chronicled above, the first go about in well-

....

[13]   Pokhara: town in central Nepal on Lake Phewa, well known as the starting point for popular routes to Annapurna. The Lakeside region is on the eastern side of the lake and has restaurants and yoga centres.

ironed shorts and T-shirts, with characteristic creases from being kept in suitcases, and spend the whole evening carefully sipping a single can of beer and enthusiastically buying up trekking poles. The second group have freshly washed bodies and an outdoor tan and wear grubby T-shirts (they have no other), and allow themselves much more alcohol, changing drinking establishments several times in an evening.

Despite all the outward differences in these two groups, they do have one thing in common or something that even unites them. Everyone staying in Pokhara is happy: those arriving from Kathmandu in cheerful anticipation of adventure, and those who have completed the trek back with the feeling of a mission accomplished. To complete the overall pleasant picture, in Pokhara even the local population gets a great deal of pleasure from the presence of both groups with all their money and their naivety about spending it. Taking these circumstances into account, it is no surprise that many are convinced of the sacredness of these places, something which is actively supported (from self-interest) by the Nepalese, and through naivety (but disinterestedly) by the tourists. One way or another, irrespective of the root cause, tranquillity, almost blissfulness, reigns in Pokhara, and there is an unhurriedness that matches the waters of the local lake, Lake Plewa.

The first thirty or so minutes of the journey from Kathmandu to Pokhara were very nerve-wracking for the friends. There was complete chaos on the roads, with no clear indication of the direction of traffic, numerous mopeds loaded with goods, chickens and children and, most importantly, constant travel on the opposite carriageway. Old Vito could not relax, and filtered every situation through himself, reacting to potentially dangerous manoeuvres by his car and oncoming cars by pressing a non-existent brake pedal and turning a virtual steering wheel. It may be that Italians are not the most disciplined drivers in the world, but what the Nepali drivers did rendered him speechless.

Angelo, by contrast, was completely indifferent to what was happening en route, and as he looked out of the window, as if out of the window of his New York limousine, he thought his own thoughts. Bearing in mind the events of the previous day, it was not difficult to guess at the direction his thoughts were taking. This reverie turned the fairly variegated picture seen through the window into a nondescript background, and Angelo's expression would not have altered even if he'd unexpectedly seen the usual hustle and bustle of Manhattan through the window. In actual fact, morning in the outskirts of Kathmandu and the centre of New York are essentially much the same: the early-morning crowd of adults hurrying to work and children hurrying to school, the clamorous opening of cafés, the shifting of rubbish, the hooting of cars. When you look at it, there are more similarities than differences in these two pictures: only the smells are different, and they don't always penetrate the air-conditioned cars; the clothes are different – something New Yorkers don't pay much attention to – and the buildings have more storeys, which is unimportant unless you lean your head back.

Used to provincial unhurriedness, Vito should have noticed more differences, but he was too preoccupied with the road. This was probably a good thing, since the traffic chaos prevented him from thinking about the day before.

However, Vito soon began to "get the picture", and he ob-served a definite logic in the behaviour of drivers and pedestri-ans, a logic based on the profound courtesy shown by people to one another. As soon as he understood this, the shambolic cacophony of sounds resolved itself into by no means random signals: not once did drivers overtake pedestrians on the hard shoulder without warning them of their approach, not one crossroads was taken without a signal, and not one bend of the winding mountain road was taken by the bus in silence. And although right to the end of the three-hour journey Vito con-tinued to close his eyes when an oncoming vehicle dived back into its lane at the last moment, this was more a reaction of his subconscious mind than of fear.

On the whole, the road to Pokhara provided the friends with few reminders of what country they were in: the snow-capped peaks could be glimpsed only occasionally in the distance, and the way in which people swarmed along the road, mainly at its edge, was very different from the picture of these places they had had in their mind since childhood.

For Vito this was not a disappointment, more a surprise. Although not even that. Vito had not been surprised for many years: he probably accepted as his due the picture as it was, conscious of the difference between it and how he had imagined Nepal in his distant childhood. There was still some surprise, but it related to a high degree to the vividness of his childish stereotypes. The image, formed from meagre information about the country and exuberant child's fantasies of some sixty years ago, was so clear that at times Vito felt it was not an old man travelling in the bus but a youth of fourteen dreaming about a snow-covered country. Almost nothing proved otherwise, unless it was the lined hand which came into the frame, gripping the handle of the front seat.

Reality turned out to be faster-moving than Vito's flow of memories, and they arrived in Pokhara before he could restore all his childhood pictures. As they drew nearer to the lake, the composition of the population changed, and in the centre of the town Europeans outnumbered locals.

It had not yet dawned on the old men that their journey was drawing to a close, when the bus stopped in front of a hotel. It was a perfectly ordinary three-storey building, with a small parking area in front and a typical roof terrace above. Inwardly Vito feared for his satiated friend's reaction to the modest conditions provided for their overnight stay, and was relieved to note Angelo's total indifference to the external appearance of the hotel. Vito seized one of the identical rucksacks, while his friend stomped about beside the bus waiting for the driver to get his luggage for him.

The whole of the small parking area was crammed with identical rucksacks. It even occurred to him that, thank heavens, at least they were different from their two. Some dozen local boys swarmed round this heap of luggage. At first Vito did not understand the purpose of their activity: they moved, lifted, transferred and tied up the baggage, and it was only some time later that he began to realise that the result of all these operations were piles of two or three rucksacks, tied together, one on top of another. At the same time all the basic and supplementary harnesses, designed to lighten the load on tourists' shoulders, were put in with the non-essentials, turning new-fangled and apparently fairly expensive tourist equipment into primitive sacks. The piles were put in a row on the parapet by the hotel entrance. When the whole mass of luggage had been packed in this way, the young lads presented their backs and tied a tape in a ring under themselves. When the load was clear of the ground, the porters pulled on the other side of the ring and fastened it on their forehead. From the speed and ease of these movements, it was obvious to Vito that these youngsters did this operation every day. Within a few minutes all the luggage had been loaded into a large bus which did not come into the hotel yard but remained in the street. The last bundle was different from the others – it was a wicker basket of large dimensions into which had been put, so it seemed, a large red suitcase which occupied most of the space. The eldest of the baggage handlers went up to this basket and heaved it up onto his back, though not without a groan. Having dealt with this rather odd task, the handlers got into the bus.

Angelo watched with an ironic smile the process of degradation of the ultracontemporary tourist equipment to primitive bagginess and could not refrain from a commentary addressed either to Vito, or to himself:

"There's nothing more reliable than the old way!"

Without waiting for Vito's reply – the phrase appeared to have been addressed to his friend – he turned to his partner and asked sarcastically:

"Is there a swimming pool in this hotel?"

"Angelo, you're a pain!" muttered Vito and was the first to head for the entrance.

At that moment the hotel doors opened and an organised group of about twenty trooped out onto the street. They appeared to be of Chinese origin. They all had trekking poles and moved rather awkwardly, their feet newly shod, so it appeared, in massive trekking boots. This last fact seemed to enthuse them, and the whole crowd were discussing their new acquisitions, laughingly demonstrating to one another their motor skills, which reminded Angelo of film of the first moon landing by the Americans. The behaviour of inhabitants of Celestial Empire was so typical of Chinese tourists that it even seemed to Vito that he'd seen precisely this group in Montepulciano. Chinese visitors were brought there from time to time from the Ligurian coast or from Florence.

Headed by a business-like leader, the delegation was loaded noisily onto the bus, which was already leaving. But it had not yet reached the hotel gateway when it halted suddenly. Vito, who was about to enter the hotel, stopped. The only member of the group in ordinary shoes, the leader, leapt out of the bus and ran back into the hotel as fast as he could. He had reached the door when he bumped into a Chinese woman who was just coming out, and launched a torrent of curses at her. The woman, who was not in the first flush of youth, gave as good as she got, offering an emotional rebuff to the group leader. He immediately fell silent in surprise. The bus left the hotel. Vito waited a few more seconds to see if anything else would happen with the Chinese visitors, and then, persuaded that they really had left for good, went into the hotel.

At the sound of the opening door the young man behind the desk shuddered, apparently thinking that the saga with the Chinese was not yet over. Seeing two old men of European appearance, he could scarcely suppress a sigh of relief, and replaced it with a joyful "Namaste". Vito smiled understandingly at the young man, but in view of his limited command of English, could add no further words of encouragement as he handed over his printed booking slip, and indicated by his manner that there would definitely be no problems with them.

18

1955. MONTEPULCIANO, ITALY

The first few weeks were really difficult. Despite being a partner in their joint project, Genarro made no concessions in the bar, and generally gave the impression that transporting the stones to the fortress was purely a matter for the lads. It was especially difficult on days when something was on in the bar requiring the boys' presence from straight after school until late evening. Genarro would tactfully give the boys advance warning of such days, which would allow Vito and Angelo to move the delivery time for the stones from the usual evening time to early morning. The only positive thing about this was that the boys could do it on their way to school, thus saving evening time in so doing. However, bearing in mind the unearthly hour at which they had to get up in order to have time to pick the stones out of the barn, put them in sacks, and get to the spot allocated by the local municipality for storage, neither of them, especially young Angelo, was pleased with the saving. What's more, Angelo was embarrassed carrying stones in the morning when he met people from the same village and, nearer to Montepulciano, classmates. It was a different matter in the evening: without outsiders looking on, one could get to the wall quickly. But Angelo particularly liked the return trip, when he and Vito could travel light and a little downhill, with a feeling of duty done and half a cigarette for each of them.

It was comical, but their conversations during these walks were always devoted to Nepal. At other times they never talked about it, as if they strictly regulated the place and circumstances for these discussions. That said, they did not simply chatter

　　　　　　　　　　　　　IGOR ZAVILINSKY

childishly, but tried to analyse seriously all the details of the forthcoming expedition. They shared the scraps of information they had gleaned, set themselves tasks, and posed numerous questions to themselves. Answers were difficult. Genarro was not included in their plans, so they couldn't ask him anything, and they didn't know anyone within a radius of a hundred kilometres who would know what Annapurna was. Given the absence of television and the exclusively political and topical nature of local newspapers, the situation was close to a dead end.

Everything was sorted out unexpectedly and surprisingly easily. As the wall of the barn gradually melted away, a junk heap was revealed inside. It had been a fixture in this ramshackle building for many years. It basically consisted of pre-war items belonging to the former owners which, by some miracle, had been preserved; the remains of materials which Genarro had used when building the restaurant; objects of some quite unknown provenance; and a lot of half-decayed rags for which the household had no further use once they had served as bed linen. It was under one such pile that Angelo found several files of German-language magazines which, to judge by the illustrations, were clearly about mountaineering. They turned out to be copies of "Bulletin of the Austro-German mountaineering union" for several post-war years, the file of which was carefully bound with string and liberally spattered with dust. The magazines contained many professional articles – on equipment, on altitude sickness, on trial ascents. And although there was not a word there about the Himalayas – the magazine was aimed at those visiting the Alps – at the stage of preparation that the boys were at, this was more than enough to put their preparations on the right lines. There remained the problem of translating the texts from the German, since there was a shortage of illustrations.

Help came from an unexpected quarter. Giuseppe, the owner of the bar on the wall beside which the boys stored stones every evening, once happened to see the boys relaxing after another delivery of stones and attempting to read a German magazine. It turned out that Giuseppe was from Bolzano, in the German-speaking part of Italy and had known German from childhood. Furthermore, young Giuseppe had been placed in a German-language school, where he studied for three years; this had drilled the language into his head for the rest of his life. What worried the boys, of course, was that Giuseppe was a close friend of Genarro and might divulge all their secret plans. But they had no choice, and had to rely on the old barman's word, particularly because he undertook to help them entirely from disinterested motives, having decided in his old age to get some practice in his half-forgotten German.

As a result, their evening activity began to include, in addition to physical stone-shifting and decision-making about the expedition, a fifteen-minute theoretical part during which Giuseppe, furrowing his brow tremendously with effort, tried to interpret difficult mountaineering terms for them. The old man's knowledge covered, perhaps, two thirds of the material, and the remainder had to be guessed at. This turned these evening sessions into interesting games, sometimes resulting in heated quarrels about the meaning of the text, in which all three took part with equal fervour. Everything ended as a rule with a stormy argument and Giuseppe swearing he would never again help these ungrateful lads and would chase them out of the bar. The boys were not particularly worried by the old man's threats, and the next day, as if nothing had happened, would be standing on the open terrace of the bar with the next issue of the magazine in their hands and angelic expressions on their faces.

This was the time when the Tuscan autumn was at its height, muting the bright summer colours with shades of dull green, clothing itself with mysterious morning mists and exuding the lush taste of everything that had matured in the fields during the long hot days. Vito and Angelo had long got used to the daily expeditions to the town wall of Montepulciano and had even begun to increase the weight of their loads without any idea of speeding up the process. They simply threw first one, then another additional brick into their already full sacks. Probably, from a physical point of view, they could have carried an even heavier load, but this would have required a change of packaging, for which they had neither time nor particular desire. Angelo observed the barn wall gradually melting away.

IGOR ZAVILINSKY

He even found himself thinking that he didn't want this saga to end; he did not miss those idle evenings when, apart from the work in Genarro's bar, there was nothing to occupy him.

The German magazines ran out a month after the regular sessions with Giuseppe began. For another week the boys brought a few numbers for a second time, focusing on those passages which had been rejected because of their difficulty or because of the dead ends into which the participants' arguments led. When these were finished with, the boys continued to frequent Giuseppe's bar out of a sense of gratitude, but without the magazines. They simply sat with the old man and talked about this and that, not always sticking to the theme of mountains. Justifying himself with the thought that the cool evenings had arrived, Giuseppe would pour out some wine for them for the return journey: a bit more for Vito, half as much for Angelo. But while the old man was distracted by a hunk of cheese, Vito would restore parity with a quick movement, and thus evoke a wave of amicable feelings in his friend.

Vito's calculations concerning the transporting of the stones to the town walls of Montepulciano were spot on, and by the middle of winter the boys were even a little ahead with their plans. Their young constitutions had quickly grown used to their loads, and soon they were not reminded of their evening forays by sore legs or backs. Although the old barn was melting away before their eyes, it resisted as best it could, leaving behind one last bastion in the shape of a very strong end wall. Of a morning, this obelisk-like structure, the end wall, gazed reproachfully at everything surrounding it and took petty revenge as it tried to keep the rays of the winter sun off them. But the path of the sun, like the fate of the barn, was predestined, especially towards the end of this whole undertaking, when the boys realised that, even if they cleared all the stones away, to achieve their goal they would still have to take down this last wall. It was also obvious that simply picking the bricks out of the wall was no good, and they would have to forego their regular foray into town one day and devote their time exclusively to taking down the wall. To this end, the boys got hold of some tools from Genarro, among which, to their surprise, there was even a genuine ice-axe. They decided not to return it, and to store it for future use in Angelo's room.

At last came the inevitable demolition day. The delivery timetable for the stones allowed the partners to avoid worrying over one lost day, and they set to work with a calm mind. In addition to solving a purely technological problem – the acquisition of the requisite number of stones – there was in this action a moment of purely psychological importance: the end wall was for them a symbol of the last obstacle to their plan. It seemed that once this was done, everything would be all right. Such thoughts induced a certain euphoria in Angelo, and he bustled frantically about the stone wall, pushing it and trying to knock the end bricks out by kicking them, which was equally futile.

The decisive assault was set for a cool Saturday evening. Through long force of habit, Genarro was spending time with his friend Giuseppe, the bar was closed, and there was no one around. Vito, as usual, was suffering from the cold, and wanted to get the heavy work done as quickly as possible and to get back into a warm house. Angelo was given the role of assistant, who would make his appearance when the wall collapsed, or at least partly gave way, and it was possible to get individual stones out of it. In his heart of hearts, Vito was hoping that the wall would be completely demolished, thus simplifying the task of dismantling it over the following few days. It was precisely with this aim in view that Vito took a heavy sledgehammer and began to strike at the very foundations of the wall.

Vito soon realised that the evening would be a long one – his efforts remained practically unnoticeable and his blows were producing more noise than sense. Vito's sledgehammer broke off fragments of the concrete bricks on which it landed, but on the whole, it did no visible damage to the wall. Vito's teeth were set on edge by the vibrations of the metal sledgehammer caused by every blow, and his hands were treacherously painful from incipient blisters. After about twenty minutes of continuous wielding of the sledgehammer, Vito began to be gripped by panicky thoughts that destruction of the wretched wall would prove impossible, although that was not yet evident from the frequency of the blows. Angelo, who up until that moment had been leaping around in carefree fashion, felt the tension in the air, and calmed down and sat to one side, watching his friend's efforts and wincing in response each time the sledgehammer hit the wall.

"Have a rest," Angelo managed to say between blows. Vito, who could not make his mind up to stop of his own accord, was waiting for this, as if unloading all responsibility for the pause in the work onto the shoulders of whoever proposed the break. However, so as not to show it, before he stopped, Vito delivered five more blows and then put the sledgehammer down. He sat down heavily on a heap of rubble and began to examine the state of his palms. As if trying to check how hard the work was for his friend, Angelo picked up the abandoned sledgehammer and tried it against the wall. His blow was crooked and made with the corner of the sledgehammer head, which almost made Angelo drop the thing. He threw a glance full of respect and sympathy at Vito.

"Can you get hold of something to drink?" said Vito protectively in response to the glance.

"Right away," replied Angelo running off in the direction of the bar without further delay.

Left alone, Vito gave vent to his emotions, and booted the sledgehammer lying nearby, as if it was responsible for the wall's unyielding nature. There were exactly seven days left before the deadline for handing over the materials to a special commission consisting of representatives of the municipality, staff of the local museum, and a famous archaeologist from Florence. In order to get everything done without undue hassle, they needed to transport the remnants of the stubborn wall to the town the following day. Belief in the feasibility of these plans diminished with every blow of the sledgehammer. Vito understood the simplicity of the problem: here was the sledgehammer and here was the wall, but nevertheless he couldn't help thinking that there was a simpler solution. Although it was, above all, the powerlessness of a boy before a seemingly monolithic lump of wall which lobbied strongly for this thought. Vito was desperately keen for Angelo not to return quickly; he didn't want to look important again and create the illusion that he had everything under control. However, his friend was already back, carrying a glass filled to the top with water. Vito drank the water in one gulp and, in order to spin out the time before restarting work, he began carefully examining the wall, which was barely visible in the gloom. At the very moment when he was ready to resume work, his attention was drawn to a crack just to the side of the spot where he had been aiming his blows all this time. Vito's eyes ran along this crack and, to his surprise, he found it went in a circle. Summing up the whole situation at a glance, Vito noted with satisfaction that a huge block in the base of the wall was separated from the bulk of the bricks as it leaned slightly inwards. Vito didn't know whether this was the result of his previous blows or an original flaw. What did that matter – Vito again had hope. The boy took the sledgehammer and delivered several blows to the spot he had discovered. The noise of these blows was different from anything he'd heard earlier. Even without the crack, the different nature of the wall at this spot was evident. After several more blows, the circular crack became even clearer.

"We're away!" Vito told his friend excitedly. "Look from that side. Is it moving?"

Vito waited until Angelo had moved to the other side, then struck the base of the wall as hard as he could.

"Yes!" replied Angelo joyfully. "I can already see the corner of a brick."

Vito continued to deliver blows round the perimeter of the crack, trying to force the whole block out of the wall. After each blow, Angelo reported on changes. Part of the wall had half fallen through, and above it a vertical crack had appeared. Vito decided to take a break before the final push, and sat down on the same heap of rubble. The sun had already gone, and the boy looked forward to the moment when the wall would fall: he realised that nothing would change on a universal scale; nothing would even change on the scale of the commune of Montepulciano. The moment when he would sit on the remains of this wall would not be any different from the present moment, except in the matter of his own personal triumph, but for some reason it was precisely

IGOR ZAVILINSKY

this heap of old bricks which had become a matter of principle. And indeed, for some reason he did not understand, for Vito this wall not only made up the number of stones, hitherto insufficient for them to receive their fee; he had also decided that that if the wall fell today, everything would work out for him – as if behind this wall was hidden a secret door which concealed from him the path to his dreams, one of which was Annapurna. This was the biggest and clearest at the present time, but not the only one. Vito's ambitions stretched beyond the snow-capped peaks of the notorious mountain, and even if the direction of these ambitions was not entirely comprehensible, even to himself, this in no way reduced his confidence in its validity.

19

APRIL 2015. ROUTE ABC: START, NEPAL

"Well, what do you think? The holiday is beginning?!" Angelo tried to say happily, throwing his rucksack into the boot of a vehicle that looked like a jeep.

Vito did not share his friend's enthusiasm, and sat silently in his seat, holding his rucksack in his arms. The young driver kindly, but as though slightly teasing him, took his load, and silently placed it behind him.

Vito scarcely had time to close his door before the jeep jolted sharply forward. The driver said not a word in any except his own language, but he knew English – although that was completely irrelevant, as all his attention was devoted to the young student who sat alongside him. The girl was apparently returning home to a mountain village for the weekend, and her clothes and demeanour reflected a huge desire to look, albeit by Nepalese standards, like a city dweller.

The young man did not benefit from his position as a person providing an invaluable service because, it seemed, the student was travelling free of charge – or at the expense of the old men who had hired the jeep and the driver. Vito would have been calmed by the presence of the student were it not for the insane traffic on the road, where cars in the oncoming lane, as on the evening before, were scarcely fewer than in their own. The presence of the student led to the driver sitting turned fully around and talking ceaselessly, hardly looking at the road. After twenty minutes, the girl, who had for some reason identified the two old men as French, mumbled an embarrassed "merci" in their direction, and climbed out.

Vito sighed with relief, although quite quickly he understood that his happiness was premature. Having been left without female attention, the driver picked up speed and began some sort of inexplicable manipulation of small packets lying in abundance in the glove compartment. The young man would take out one of the packets and open it, not without difficulty and sometimes resorting to using his teeth to help him, and pour the contents into his mouth. Then he fell to chewing and spitting profusely through the open window of the driver's door. Once he'd chewed his fill, he took out a new packet and repeated everything again. All this commotion with the packets distracted him from the road no less than the student had, and infuriated the old Italian. Tired of all the bother, Vito turned to his friend, seeking his support. Angelo looked phlegmatically at his comrade and calmly said:

"It's tobacco. He's chewing tobacco."

As if once Vito knew this, things would immediately become easier for him. Of course it was good that it wasn't hashish, although the traffic might have been easier to deal with under the influence of narcotics. Still, their arrival at the start of the trek soon brought Vito's suffering to an end.

The friends climbed out of the car at the side of the road and, somewhat dismayed, looked around. It was not that they had been expecting to see the Arc de Triomphe, but what was in essence a dusty roadside, with scattered bits of packaging, disappointed them a trifle. The entire civilization of this place was limited to a few nearby primitive food stalls offering a simple choice of water and snacks. The old men did not even immediately understand where to go on further, until their driver, smiling, indicated with his finger in the direction of a small stand with a map.

The map, which was drawn onto a wooden base, was fairly worn: the figures for height and distance were faded, and the line denoting a path connecting population centres was barely visible. Of course this map, in modern conditions, was of no practical use, and was only an illustration of what lay ahead for the traveller in the coming days. That explained why no one had made any special effort to keep it in good condition. Nevertheless, the map made an impression on Vito – now for the first time he recognized the adventure into which he had been plunged. The end point, drawn in the top left-hand corner of the map, even in this primitive sketch, looked impossibly far away. Most likely for the greater intimidation of the inexperienced tourist, the top third of the map was painted on to a dirty white background, which, according to the conception of the creator of this masterpiece, must signify snow. The warmth-loving Vito shuddered even from thoughts of the cold, in which here, in the warm valley, he did not want to believe.

"Vito!" Vito heard the voice of his friend. "Frightened of getting lost?"

"Why do you say that?" the old man answered without turning round.

"You're clinging on to that map as if you want to take it with you!"

"I'm simply looking... There's no nearby path..." Vito's voice reflected his lack of confidence in his own strength.

"Leave it, old man." Angelo began to pity Vito, and approaching from behind, put his hand on his shoulder. "This is a tourist attraction. Like walking round Central Park."

"I haven't been to Central Park."

"Let's go there straight after Nepal!"

Vito finally tore himself away from the map and looked at his friend.

"Why not?... The last thing I want to do right now is to go home."

"And the last thing I want now is to be left on my own... if I'm honest..."

The friends were silent, each lost in their own thoughts.

"We're on our way!" Vito interrupted the silence and moved resolutely to the place where the beginning of a path could be seen. More accurately, they did not have a view of a path, but of fairly wide stone steps which zig-zagged away, high up in to the thickest part of the wood.

The civilized view at the start of the climb rather amazed Vito, and increasingly he began to believe Angelo's words – the trek was an "attraction".

But after forty minutes of the ascent, the old man's entire organism was already panicking, and he began to pant. He was horribly ashamed that his body had so rapidly capitulated. He tried desperately to hide it from Angelo, making unsuccessful attempts to normalize his breathing. Making his way up yet another "flight" of the steps, Vito, who was walking in front, stopped, and turned guiltily to his younger and more athletic friend.

To his amazement he could not see Angelo behind him.

"Angelo!" wheezed the old man.

There was no answer.

"You haven't died there?" asked Vito, trying not to betray his breathlessness.

"Everything's fine…" his friend, whose location Vito determined only by his voice, wheezed in answer. Angelo had stopped at the previous turn of the steps, and was currently hidden behind a large boulder. Judging by his voice, he was concerned about the same thing as his friend – his breathing.

At length, Angelo appeared from behind the stone, and unhurriedly, but quite assuredly, began to move on upwards. As he approached, Vito was able to see his unnaturally red face, the confidence on which was clearly forced.

"My shoelace was undone," lied Angelo, drawing level with his friend. "What about you?"

"Both…"

"What do you mean 'both'?"

"If I'm taking my lead from you, then both my shoelaces were undone." Vito looked into Angelo's eyes, and both men laughed and sat down heavily on a stone bench, in the back of which, very presciently, was carved a niche for a rucksack. This allowed them to sit on it without removing their loads from their shoulders. Exactly opposite the bench, whether by accident or design, there was a big aperture in the crown of the trees, through which a view opened out onto the valley from which they had climbed. The beginning of the path could not be seen, but the height to which they had climbed could be judged by the little river winding its way along beside the road and visible far below.

"How long have we been going?" asked Angelo, unable to tear his eyes from the valley, and probably trying to measure their height by reference to the time they had spent climbing.

"Less than an hour…"

"What do you think, will there be level bits?"

"I can't see any on the map…"

"Well it doesn't matter, we'll go gently… we won't hurry… we'll always have time to turn back…"

To every word from his friend, Vito obediently nodded his head, all his body language conveying his agreement – and the lack of any fanatical resolve to reach the end.

After another ten minutes, the steps came to an end, changing into a gently sloping path, along both sides of which, from time to time, they encountered the modest dwellings of the local inhabitants. It was difficult to call it a village, because in essence they were houses standing separately along the path, but on the map which they had taken with them, it was designated as a population centre. The landscape was completely European, in which trees alternated with fields and market gardens. The climb was significantly easier than in the first half an hour of their route, and the friends became a little happier. The bodies of the old men began to adapt, although the process was not instant: it added nothing to their speed, but allowed them to cope with their panicked breathing.

"In the last resort… Vito… we've got time… heaps of it… and we… we ourselves… decide… when… and where… to spend the night." In short bursts Angelo repeated the mantra, although it wasn't clear who he was trying to reassure – his old friend or himself. Vito, fearing that conversation would impede his breathing, merely nodded his agreement.

"Sweets!" Vito heard directly in front of him. He stopped, and reluctantly tore his gaze from the ground. On a narrow section, higher up the path, hand-in-hand blocking their way, stood two bare-footed young lads of about four and six. They looked resolute. The greatest resoluteness was concentrated in the stare of the older boy, while his brother, who, by all appearances, was acting exclusively on the orders of his elder sibling, had the air of having undertaken a serious mission, and of wanting to get it finished with quickly. Angelo was walking behind and did not see the children or notice his friend stop, causing him to bump his head against Vito's rucksack.

IGOR ZAVILINSKY

"Vito!" Angelo furiously reproached him, "Go on! It's still too early to rest!"

"Sweets!" repeated the older boy in English.

Angelo looked out from behind his friend, and finally understood what was happening.

"And we thought that the road was safe." Vito laughed, and went to remove his rucksack, in the top pocket of which he had half a chocolate bar.

"Stop, Vito!" Angelo also hurried to remove his rucksack, but he did not reach into the pocket where he had a store of fruit drops. He put his load down in front of the children. The older boy was amazed at the ease with which he had taken his prey, and having released his brother, stepped impudently towards the old man. Angelo waited until the boy reached him, and then with very clear gestures indicated first his rucksack, and then a lone tree which stood some two hundred metres higher up a flight of stone steps.

"Angelo! You're out of your mind." Vito was indignant. "There's a fifteen-kilo load in your rucksack!"

"Well, there's two of them," Angelo reasoned to his friend.

"Leave it, they're just kids!" Vito pleaded.

The lad well understood the essence of the argument the two foreigners were having. He waited patiently, hoping for the victory to go to Vito. All the while, one of the boys glanced warily towards a dilapidated building that lay just beyond a fence. This did not pass unnoticed by Angelo and, cunningly narrowing his eyes, he nodded in the direction of the house. The boy became agitated, but did not move from where he stood.

"Give him the chocolate!" commanded Angelo, and Vito, thinking that his friend had taken pity on the alpine-extortioners, readily offered the half of the chocolate bar which remained from their previous stop.

But it was not to be. Angelo mockingly unwrapped the chocolate, put it on top of the rucksack, and repeatedly pointed to the tree. The boy's glance moved between the chocolate, the old man, and the house, which, as it was already clear, represented a direct threat to the enterprise. Angelo, seeing the child's indecision, took a small, broken-off piece of the chocolate bar and put it in his mouth, at the same time licking clean his fingers which were covered in melted chocolate. "Ok!" The child forced out the word furiously, and grabbed at the straps of the rucksack. Angelo wrapped the chocolate bar and demonstratively put it in the top pocket of his bag, slapping it with his palm as if to say: "it's waiting for you." Vito, understanding the whole educative purpose of his friend's actions, was nevertheless unable to agree with it, and continued to wheeze with an air of indignation. Meanwhile the older boy deftly fitted the rucksack onto his back, and surprisingly easily stood up with it. It was immediately clear that he'd had to lug such loads before, and that the profession of forest robber was not the main thing in his curriculum vitae.

Vito transferred his glance to the younger boy, and discovered with surprise that the lad was laughing mockingly at his brother, who had counted on easy loot and had probably long agitated for an escapade for which he was now having to pay.

The older brother hissed a few words, eliciting an instant reaction from the small boy, who immediately threw himself behind his brother to prop up his rucksack. It didn't take much to guess that the talk had been about the exclusion of the younger partner from a number of shareholder schemes. This made Angelo more than a little happy, and he cried cheerfully "Forward friends!"

However, at that moment the whole enterprise found itself on the verge of collapse – between the loaded-up children and the longed-for tree stood a young woman. Throughout the exchange, Vito never understood whether this was the mother of the children or an older sister, but it didn't matter – her face was severe, and this severity was directed towards the elder child, finding expression in a long monologue. Although the old men did not understand a word, the general sense was clear – after all parents give these talks in all countries, and they sound roughly the same: "How many times have I told you not to do this!", "You've made me ashamed again!", "You even took your brother with you!", "The sweets in the house are not enough for you!" and so on. Between these angry phrases, the young woman had time to throw a glance at the tourists, and several times to insert an English "excuse me".

The older boy turned to the old men as if doomed, and began to lift the rucksack. However, Angelo stopped him with a wave of his hand, and turned to the young woman, trying to choose the simplest words and accompanying them with explanatory gestures.

"'We need help', 'old man'" (for some reason he indicated Vito), "'I asked the boys to help'!"

Angelo winked at the young woman and she, laughing with embarrassment, moved aside. The older boy did not understand a word of what had been said, but quickly grasped that the road was clear. Not waiting for his younger co-worker, he ran quickly up the stone steps. The younger boy was not able to keep pace with him, but, understanding that half a bar of chocolate was at stake, he tried not to lag behind, although his participation in the project had turned into a simple formality. The old men thanked the young woman for her understanding, and set off behind the boys, who in that time had already covered more than half the distance to the tree.

"'The old man needs help', you said…" grumbled Vito.

"Sorry, but for the sake of the children – I couldn't risk it. And you were looking so miserable that the girl might well have grabbed your rucksack herself." Angelo mocked.

"But they're carrying your rucksack!"

"A mere trifle. Besides you, no one's paying any attention."

"Of course they're not paying any attention. Besides me, no one's carrying their own bag!"

Angelo, who was becoming quite cheerful, slapped his friend on the shoulder and, unencumbered, passed Vito. In the time it took the friends to reach the tree, the children had managed not only to get their load to it, but to eat the entire fee. The old men said goodbye to the "forest robbers", and Vito stealthily slipped each of them a few fruit drops from his rucksack.

The contractually important tree, as it turned out, marked the completion of the uphill stretch. The friends found themselves on the crest of a ridge, and as the path wound further on, it was practically level. After a certain time the path turned into a dirt road, on which could clearly be discerned the tracks of a car. This development encouraged the friends; to go on the level after several hours of climbing made the whole business seem straightforward.

Probably for the first time in the whole day Vito began to look around him, and to note to himself that his ideas about Nepal were somewhat mistaken. More precisely, he began to give himself an account which had it that those "pictures" to which he was accustomed, and which provided a stereotyped representation of everything else – severe, snowy summits and the aesthetically perfect stony approaches to them, – still awaited them higher up. At this lesser altitude the environment was coloured with the hues of tropical spring, and struck a powerfully discordant note with the sharp peaks already visible on the horizon. Vito caught himself with a paradoxical thought – the more clearly he saw the mountains, the more clearly he understood that they were still far away.

Meanwhile the road became quite decent, and they began to encounter people passing by, a large number of whom were school children returning home to remote villages. The children walked in small groups, and outwardly there was little to distinguish them from children of the same age in Italy or New York. One thing which preyed on Vito's nerves was that the path for the children passed near steep slopes. In Vito's plainsman's imagination, any prank near such a slope could lead to serious consequences. Angelo caught Vito's anxious glance.

"Don't be silly. These children walk here several times every day." And for greater clarity he added, "Or do you think that walking along Fifth Avenue is less dangerous?"

20
APRIL 2015. ABC ROUTE, LANDRUK, NEPAL

It took Vito some time to realise that he'd woken up. He'd slept so soundly that it even seemed to him that he was in the same pose in the morning that he'd been in when he got into his sleeping bag the day before. His body ached. Vito could not work out which part ached – everything hurt. Well, maybe not his head. The old man tried to stretch, hoping that by so doing he would take the pain from his calves, but instead of that he got a spasm in his right leg. Vito frantically tried to unfasten the sleeping bag and jump out onto the floor, but the zip treacherously stuck and the old man continued to writhe in pain. Realising that he would not free himself quickly, Vito stood up in the sleeping bag and began to stamp his feet as hard as he could to relieve the spasm.

The spasm passed, but Vito was afraid to sit down, and, finally sorting the zip out, he crawled out. Angelo went on sleeping. The old man opened the door as quietly as he could, and went outside.

It had been light for an hour, and things were lively in the little mountain village of Landruk. In essence the whole village was a row of identical buildings built along one side of the path. They included the houses of the local inhabitants and loggias for tourists. Vito was not sure what had come first here: the villages between which the path had been laid, or the path, which was the centre of "life". Taking into account that the settlements stood approximately equidistant one from another, a few hours' walking apart, the Italian inclined to the second variant. Landruk was the last village which could be reached by car, albeit with difficulty. There was no road beyond it, and all loads were delivered by porters, which had an effect on the cost of goods higher along the path.

Because of this, Landruk was the local logistical centre, from where numerous porters set off round loggias all the way to Annapurna base camp. A line of porters was passing Vito, with the invariable "Namaste"; they were of various ages and had a great variety of loads, from packets of chips to gas cylinders. All the porters walked at about the same slow speed and attached their loads in exactly the same way, with the top attached to their heads with a belt or strap around their foreheads.

Vito was watching the porters with curiosity as they went past when he saw his first organised tourist group. Hitherto he had only encountered lone trekkers or pairs like himself and Angelo. To be more accurate, Vito first noticed a change in the nature of the loads carried by the porters. They carried not household items or goods but objects. At that moment, spotting the last elderly porter, Vito recognised the group of Chinese tourists from the day before, and their porters. As in Pokhara, the most outsize load, consisting of two suitcases, was carried by the oldest Nepalese porter.

"What kind of an idiot takes a suitcase on a trek!" exclaimed Angelo, emerging from their modest accommodation.

"You know, I think out of all that group, it's only the owners of the suitcases who are not here for the first time!" laughed Vito.

"Yes, with helpers like that they could carry a chest of drawers..."

At that moment the actual group, whose things the porters were carrying, started to go past the old men. The outward appearance and equipment of the Chinese tourists was so different from that of their porters that one got the impression they had different destinations. If the porters, in their rubber shoes, were fit for a gentle stroll on the plain, their clients clearly intended to conquer Annapurna. The last member of the group added to their general comic appearance by carrying on his back a coil of Alpine rope, which was absolutely useless here.

"Namaste," Angelo greeted the Chinaman loudly and pointed upwards, thus showing what he thought of the man's level of preparation.

The Chinaman merely gave a restrained nod of the head in reply. The Nepalese porter bringing up the rear, by contrast, almost died laughing. He was not a porter – he was carrying only a small personal rucksack, and his equipment was somewhere in between that of his fellow Nepalese porters and that of the tourists: good professional boots, shorts, an anorak, but no trekking poles. It was clear that he was just the sort of notorious guide eagerly offered by the agencies, whose role was incomprehensible, given there was no way one could turn off the path.

Vito finished watching the Chinese group, and was about to return to his room to get his things together when he saw that the early morning cloud had dispersed, and that snow-white Annapurna had appeared between two ridges, on one of which sat Landruk. The sight was completely unexpected, as if the mountain should not have been there at all, as if it were not the object of their childhood dreams and the place towards which they were now heading. Vito was confused. Everything was somehow too quotidian. Too simple against the backdrop of a wait of sixty years.

"You know, Vito," – it turned out Angelo had been standing behind him all this time and was also looking at the newly appeared mountain – "are you sure it's really worth it?"

"Worth what exactly?"

"I don't know – worth thinking about it, drawing up plans, dreaming…"

"We're not dreaming about it. We're dreaming about being beside it."

"Just like with a Woman."

"Exactly, my friend, exactly…"

According to their calculations, the old men were facing climbs of five hundred metres relative to Landruk, to reach Chomrong. In comparison with the previous day's climb of almost a kilometre, the day did not look so difficult, especially as the view of the valley opening up in the direction of Annapurna was very pleasant, with everything steeped in green and the hues of spring. In general, the route was so arranged that, to avoid altitude sickness, travellers didn't ascend more than six hundred metres per day. Loggias prepared to welcome guests were placed at strategic intervals. Of course, this rule was of greater significance on the second half of the journey, when the altitude of the path exceeded two kilometres. Heartened by such plans for the day, Vito and Angelo got ready quickly, had breakfast in a café by their loggia, and, overcoming the pain in their legs, set off. They jauntily covered a kilometre, passing allotments on their way. Approaching a long flight of steps, they froze in astonishment: the broad and fairly well-built steps went off into the distance – downwards.

Angelo looked at Vito.

"Is this the right way?" he asked naively.

"Do you have an alternative?" said Vito unkindly, and looked down, trying to ascertain how much height they would lose by descending. As far as the eye could see, the steps went down all the time. Further on, they disappeared among green trees; the whole scene indicated the direction of a valley between two ridges.

At that moment, they saw several figures climbing the steps towards them. The two men, acting out an unspoken agreement, sat down on a bench. Some ten minutes later, they could see that the people approaching them were tourists. There were two of them: a tall, young woman, and behind her a bearded, strong-looking man. The girl stopped by the old men, trying to get her breath back and, apparently embarrassed, merely nodded to the Italians in greeting. A moment later her companion caught up with her; despite his solid build, he was breathing fairly evenly, unlike his friend.

"Namaste." The man gave the usual greeting and smiled broadly. In this sincere smile, Vito sensed the sympathy of someone with the climb behind them towards people who as yet had no concept of what they would have to deal with in the coming days.

"Did you leave Chomrong today?" asked Angelo, thus disguising his real, and foolish, question: "Are we on the right path?"

"Almost," said the girl with a smile, by now recovered from the climb. "We spent the night by the Jinhu springs. That's half an hour's walk from Chomrong."

"That's going downhill," her companion qualified. "There's a very steep slope there. On the way there we spent two hours on the ascent."

A shadow of not the pleasantest of memories flitted across the face of the girl.

"Is it long since you left?"

"We got up early," the girl went on, trying to remove her anorak which, in the morning heat, was no longer essential. "We've been going about three hours."

"Can you see Chomrong from here?" asked Vito, still hoping they wouldn't have to go down right into the valley.

"Yes, there it is!" The man indicated a few roofs which could be seen on the opposite ridge, somewhat higher up than they were now.

"Thanks." Angelo thanked him gloomily, having lost the illusion of an easy day. "Will you spend the night in Landruk?"

"No, we don't intend to. We hope to find a car and go off to Pokhara today."

"Well, good luck with that!"

"And good climbing to you! Incidentally there's a very beautiful suspension bridge across the river at the bottom." The girl tried to cheer the old men up a bit, and again put on her rucksack.

"I can't wait to see that bridge," muttered Vito mischievously when the two had moved a decent distance away.

The old men wandered down the steps with ease, but this ease brought them no joy – the loss of height gained so hard the previous day was like the drunken loss in a casino of a sum earned by hard graft over the course of a year. Both had imagined that their route would be upwards to a definite height, and it was precisely for this that they were mentally prepared – in general, and especially this morning when their plan was to ascend five hundred metres. But to descend almost a kilometre, only to go up one and a half kilometres, was quite a different proposition, the scale of which very quickly undermined all their motivation. Meanwhile, the descent seemed endless, and with each new turn of the steps Vito grew more and more gloomy. At last they saw the bridge, which really was attractive and spanned a foaming mountain river. Interestingly, after they had crossed it and again begun a not very steep climb, their mood improved, as they became aware that they were gaining height rather than losing it. To his surprise, Vito discovered that although tough physically, the climb was more pleasant than a precipitate loss of height.

It soon became apparent that Angelo's daily game of tennis impacted favourably on his physical condition. Despite his recent illness and the shortage of breath he'd experienced during the first days of the ascent, his body was gradually adapting to the strain. Things were much more difficult for Vito – his labours in the kitchen had, apparently, not given him the same staying power. Or maybe it was simply that Vito was a bit older than his friend, and those few years told on him.

Angelo let Vito go first, so the older of the two friends dictated the speed of their climb. They often encountered indicator boards on the path, showing not the number of kilometres to the next loggia but the time it would take to walk there. It very quickly dawned on the old men that these measurements clearly did not suit them and that they were behind schedule.

Vito once again sat down on a bench built into the cliff face.

"Will you forgive them?" asked Angelo unexpectedly.

"We must forgive them," replied Vito, as if they had renewed a conversation broken off five minutes earlier.

"Now you're talking like our Sunday school teacher. Do you remember?"

"Yes, he was funny." The old man smiled at the memory. "You know, maybe I agree with him at last. But I'm not religious, just observant."

"And what have you observed?"

"I've never in my life met happy people who have been offended."

Angelo looked up at his friend:

"Why do you think that is?"

Vito groaned, and quietly set off uphill again.

"You know, it's not obligatory to make a person happy by forgiving them," Vito went on without turning round, "but you'll always feel better for it. So the ability to forgive is an egotistical skill."

"Do you think everything can be forgiven?" Angelo was trying to walk right behind his friend in order to be able to talk to him.

"I don't know. You've certainly got to try. You must yourself."

"But betrayal… Is it worth forgiving that, Vito?"

"You know, Angelo," – Vito halted and, drawing breath, turned to his friend – "you put too much into the word 'betrayal'. In fact, betrayal in its pure form doesn't exist – it's always fear, or greed, or uncontrollable ambition, or something else. Everything can be forgiven individually."

Vito turned round and resumed his climb. Angelo walked in silence for some time, thinking over what his friend had said.

"But it's more difficult with those close to you… It's one thing if an outsider deceives you – from fear, stupidity or something. You can't blame them – there's nothing that connects you. If, however one of your family betrays you, they betray not only you but everything there is between you."

Vito gave a deep sigh – either from weariness or from weighty thoughts, and went on his way in silence. Just as Angelo thought the conversation was over, Vito broke the silence.

"Maybe. Even so there are only two ways to go. One is easy – bottle up the hurt, binge on suffering, in short, be unhappy. The difficult way…"

"Is to forgive…"

"Yes." Vito halted again. "And you know what I say: forgiveness is more important than understanding. You may still not understand why they acted like that. I'll say this too: the people themselves can't always understand."

"And what then?"

"Look, to hell with all this, Angelo! Sometime simply ask yourself: do you want the truth, or happiness?"

21

APRIL 2015. ABC ROUTE:

ENVIRONS OF CHAMRONG, NEPAL

Vito had no strength left. He even felt in the last hour of the climb that he'd become indebted to the following day, the way a drunkard asks for a drink, promising to settle up tomorrow. The analogy was so real for the old man that he naively thought the Lord had given him additional strength because in his bar he never refused to give drinks on tick. Although Angelo appeared rather more cheerful, he too, in his turn, became convinced that if he'd been told in the morning what they would have to contend with, he would have said to hell with it all and gone back.

The worse thing about the route was the fact that you didn't know what awaited you round the bend: you went along, hoping that the climbing would end and there would be a flat section or, if you were lucky, a place to rest. Throughout the day the old men deluded themselves in this way, and when they did finally make it to the loggia beside the hot springs, they could not believe it.

Vito could scarcely restrain himself from lying down immediately on the tapchan, but after a moment's hesitation, he remained seated. He decided to take his boots off a bit later. The treacherous thought kept flashing through his head: "Don't take them off at all, Vito! Go to bed as you are!" If he'd been on his own, he probably would have done so, but the presence of his comrade imposed some discipline on him. He reached for his laces and threw off his walking boots with some relief. At that moment, in came Angelo.

"Are you alive?" he intoned with false cheerfulness.

"Not so sure," replied Vito with a bitter smile

"I found out something about the springs." Angelo sat down and gave a sigh of relief, which betrayed his real weariness. "They're ten minutes away. You can lie in them and give your legs steam treatment. They say it helps a lot."

"Angelo," said Vito beseechingly, "I was thinking of holding off going to the toilet round the corner until morning and you're talking about a ten-minute walk…"

"Go on with you. You'll feel better shortly and we'll have a walk, and tomorrow you'll be as good as new!" In reply, Vito merely shook his head, but Angelo persisted. "Let me get you some tea!"

"A bottle of wine would be better," groaned Vito.

"Sorry, but these are holy places! Even if they are accursed! No meat, no wine!"

"Well, I can understand no meat, but what's their objection to wine?"

"I don't know, old chap!" said Angelo, getting up with difficulty and heading for the doors. "I'll get some tea."

Angelo was away for ten minutes, and the longer Vito waited, the more firm did his opinion become that today he would not go any further.

At last Angelo did appear, holding a metal mug he'd got from heaven knows where. Vito felt the sides of the vessel with his hands and, having ascertained that the tea was not hot, took a big sip. Heat suffused his throat and then his whole inside! The heat of strong alcohol and spices.

"What's this?" said Vito, scarcely able to draw breath.

"I knew you'd like it!"

"What's this?" Vito could only repeat the question.

"My whisky plus the local tea. Oh, and some sort of rubbish I was recommended, but I haven't gone so far as to try it."

"Angelo, you bastard!"

The warmth of the alcohol or the spices, or both of them together spread through Vito's body – from his throat to the tips of his toes. His empty stomach eagerly imbibed the alcohol and quickly distilled it into blood.

"What were you saying there about the springs?" laughed Vito.

There was no possibility of Vito's forcing his swollen feet back into his boots. To be more accurate, of course if he'd had to, he could have put them on, but it would have cost extra effort. However, the promised ten-minute downhill walk to the springs did not require special footwear, and it was with no little pleasure that the old man went outside wearing rubber slip-ons. Angelo did not change his footwear and went as he was, carelessly ignoring the fact that on the way back he would be putting clean feet into dirty footwear.

The path to the springs seemed to the two friends longer than promised, and although they saw below them the pools carved out of the cliff almost at once, the path meandered towards them for about ten minutes. From bitter experience, Vito was already calculating how much time the uphill return journey would take them, and was beginning to regret agreeing to this evening activity.

The second disappointment awaited them at the bottom, in the form of the Chinese group they had already encountered twice. For the first time, the group was not accompanied by porters or a guide who, it seemed, couldn't be bothered to go downhill and, taking advantage of the fact that their charges would not wander off anywhere – the path was a dead end – had left them to it. Like children left without supervision, the Chinese were openly going crazy, filling the space around them with shouting and splashing. Angelo was on the point of leaving when he saw a second, smaller pool, more a large bath some distance away. The Chinese, whose collective spirit did not allow them to split up, all remained in the large pool.

In the bath that Angelo had spotted, just two young women were bathing. It could not really be called bathing – they simply stayed at the side, hanging on to it with their elbows.

Angelo asked if they could join them, and received a quick and positive answer. Vito's immediate reaction was that permission had been given with some relief, the cause of which were Chinese, who might well expand their presence in the resort in the direction of this pool. The old men were now an obstacle to this, given that four people filled the greater part of the pool.

The friends quickly plunged into the warm water. Angelo's first wish was to jump out immediately – he felt his body could not withstand the heat for a minute. Vito, on the other hand, stretched himself blissfully along the edge, and felt he was warming up every cell in his body. Angelo gradually calmed down and, although he could not yet properly relax, he at least stopped looking at the edge. The pool was not deep, and both men stood on the bottom. Seen close up, the walls and the bottom turned out not to be made of stone, but of ordinary polished concrete – both cheap and reliable. However, its authenticity was of no importance, and the friends found no fault with it.

Moreover, their attention had been taken by their neighbours, whose excited conversation betrayed them as Spanish. The young women were roughly the same age, and were really very curious: they were between twenty and thirty years old, with tattoos on religious subjects liberally covering much of their arms, which they were holding above the water. Apart from the tattoos, there was nothing obviously religious about them, and their behaviour was quite laid-back. Vito's surmises on this score were confirmed when one of them, with long black hair, stretched over the edge to reach for something outside the pool, revealing a bare and attractive back to the friends, without any sign of the top part of a swimming costume.

Vito glanced at Angelo, over whose face a roguish smile was creeping, and splashed some water in his direction as if to say: "Behave yourself." The behaviour of their neighbours did not seem to bother the young women, but Angelo's glance, which one of them – a young woman with a boyish hairdo – had noticed elicited a smile and a short commentary in Italian addressed to her friend. Whether by chance, or in answer to these words, the girl stretched even further and revealed sporty buttocks, clad in bikini bottoms which were certainly never intended for swimming.

The girl with short hair laughed and gave her friend a light tap on the behind, telling her friend to behave properly, as Vito had Angelo. Then something even more surprising happened: what she had been fetching from outside the pool was revealed. Of all possible variations, the old men least expected to see a bottle of champagne in the girl's hands.

"Really? This can't be happening!" exclaimed Angelo in Spanish, to the surprise of the young woman and her friend, then added in English. "But if you really want to talk to me, I'd prefer English!"

"Why?" asked the short-haired girl interestedly, still speaking in Spanish.

"My Puerto Rican nanny, without knowing she was doing it, taught me just two Spanish phrases: 'Well I never. No way!' and 'You've done that, you asshole!'"

The girls burst out laughing loudly and the long-haired one, briefly flashing the nipples of her small breasts as she turned round, went back into the water with the bottle of champagne. Vito laughed with everyone else, although he only vaguely grasped the point of the joke. However, it's not too important to get the gist of a conversation if you have the opportunity to feel oneself, for a moment, to be, not a man, but a boy, getting an eyeful of naked girls.

"Where on earth did you get champagne from here?" Despite the small difference in age with Vito, Angelo slipped more naturally into the role of gigolo. "Have the Nepalese really added this noble drink to their list of saints?"

Seeing his friend's baffled look, Angelo tactfully quickly translated his words into Italian for him.

"Champagne is as far from sainthood as we are!" the short-haired girl replied in Italian, and seeing the reaction of the old men, added: "No, no, I haven't been exploiting an Italian nanny. Much simpler than that. My father's Italian."

"That hasn't got us any nearer an answer to the most puzzling question of the last few minutes. Where did you buy the champagne?" persisted Angelo, edging round the pool towards the girls.

"Oh, there's no point looking here," trilled the long-haired girl happily, holding out the bottle to Angelo. "We brought several bottles from Kathmandu."

"I can open it but I won't drink the drink which two slim young ladies have carried on their backs." Angelo nodded involuntarily in the direction of the girl whose beautiful back he had already had the opportunity of admiring.

"Give over! We didn't carry them. You have porters for that!"

"Hiring porters in Nepal to transport champagne. That's terrific!" said Angelo delightedly and, with a nod to Vito, continued: "In all the time we've spent in the mountains, we've never come across such an exotic idea."

"Yes, we know," said the short-haired girl, somewhat embarrassed, "but from the start we wanted to do this: drink champagne here!"

"I hope you left a bottle at base camp."

"We're not going any further." The girl looked Angelo full in the face. Her friend looked away.

"Are you tired?"

"Well, you could say that. As it is, we've gone further than we were planning," the short-haired girl continued. "Time for us to go down."

At that moment Angelo finally opened the bottle, then stopped, undecided what to do. He had only just realised that they had nothing to pour the champagne into. The long-haired girl came to the rescue by taking the bottle and drinking straight from it. Then she handed it to her friend. She took a swig in her turn, then passed the bottle round the circle on to Angelo. After two such circuits of the bottle Vito felt that his head, whether from the warm water or the champagne or, most likely, from everything at once, and tiredness to boot, was beginning to spin.

The champagne was drunk, the conversation gradually switched to English and, having lost his translator, who'd forgotten him, and understanding nothing, Vito simply enjoyed the easy-going atmosphere, smiling inadvertently at his own thoughts and attempting to join in the bursts of laughter. After a while, the warm water made them all tired, and they climbed onto the edge of the pool. It was already dark, the Chinese had long since gone, and a feeling that the finale of a pleasant evening was approaching hung in the air.

Contrary to Vito's expectations, the return journey turned out not to be difficult. The group somehow split into two pairs, and Vito had the opportunity of chatting to one of the girls in Italian. Angelo wandered along in front with the long-haired girl, lighting the way with his mobile phone. While they all walked uphill, they didn't feel the cold. But as soon as they paused in front of the loggias and attempted to terminate the conversation, an icy wind, blowing from the direction of the mountains, began to penetrate their warm bodies. It became clear that the evening was over and, with many an embrace, the new friends parted.

Angelo, who seemed to Vito to be rather upset, went to bed at once, but Vito, in spite of the cold, was keen to sit on the doorstep a little longer. The starry sky was special in this place. Convex, as if in a distorting mirror, it enveloped him on all sides: it seemed there was no earth beneath him, which made him want to move his feet around to verify the illusion. Never before had he felt as lonely as he did now – and, as never before, loneliness did not scare him. He was even afraid that someone would wake up, crawl out of a warm sleeping bag, and force him to speak, if only to say what he was just thinking: thoughts taking the form of phrases would be split between speaker and listener, becoming distorted within the frameworks of verbal constructions and interpretations, avoiding taboos and seeking compromises with prejudices. Unspoken thoughts, which are always more sincere than words, led him simultaneously in two, opposing directions. Most of the neurons were rushing about in his head with thoughts that, if paradise is like the sky he could see now, one could stop being frightened about the end of the world. Sitting there, he understood for the first time the meaning of the word "earthly", which gave hope for the prolongation of his existence among the stars. These thoughts induced in him a state of calmness, close to Nirvana, into which a minority of neurons did not allow him to fully immerse himself, a minority which distracted him with primitive thoughts about a tin of meat an arm's length away in the right-hand pocket of his rucksack, which he'd left by the entrance. "Is there tinned meat in paradise?" The idiotic thought struck Vito in his slightly drunken state.

Unlike previous days, the next morning Angelo got up before his friend. Despite the drink he'd taken, when he woke up, he felt fine.

"You know, the springs really do help. I've stopped feeling pain in my legs. Probably for the first time since we started." Without waiting for a reaction from his friend, who was sitting on the step, he added: "Is everything OK with you?"

"Yes."

"Have our friends from yesterday woken up?"

"They have, and they've already gone down," said Angelo sadly.

"Admit it, you old philanderer. You're sad because of two women who could be your granddaughters."

"I admit it, old boy. That's how it is."

"Don't be sad! I don't remember everything clearly from yesterday, but what I can say is that I've invited the short-haired girl to be my guest in Montepulciano. She even put my number in her phone," said the old man, proud of himself.

"A polite girl. She even asked for your phone number."

"And why not?"

"Why not – because circumstances are such that she won't come and see you, old boy."

"How do you know?"

"She's dying, Vito."

"What do you mean?" Vito refused to understand the plain meaning of his friend's words.

"The girl's dying, Vito. Her friend brought her here. She's always dreamed of drinking champagne in the mountains of Nepal. A mad wish, isn't it?" Angelo gave a deep sigh. "So they came here, where they could."

"And she simply didn't have the strength to go any further," said Vito, dumbfounded by the news.

"No, old boy. She no longer has time to go any further."

22

1955. MONTEPULCIANO, ITALY

"Well then, shall we finish the job?!" Vito suggested cheerfully to his partner.

"Yes," said Angelo encouragingly and moved to his post behind.

Vito, of course, was expecting a triumphal victory, but somehow had not counted on its being so close: the first blow after their break decisively shifted the huge lump, demarcated by the crack in the wall, like a country on a map of the world. It fell out with a dull crash in the direction of Angelo, who just managed to get his legs out of the way of the falling stones. Vito saw his friend through the hole in the wall just at the moment when he noticed that the wall to the left of the vertical crack, which went upwards from the gap that had been formed, was tottering on the brink, as if it doubted whether it should fall or not. Still not believing that this tottering was dangerous, Vito moved his hand forward and said in a calm voice:

"Hang on, Angelo..."

The wall, as if discovering that its plans had been revealed, stopped doubting and began moving in the direction of the younger lad.

"Angelo!" yelled Vito. He needn't have bothered, though, as the boy himself, seeing a mass of stone hurtling towards him, quickly changed direction completely and began to retreat. The wall was not that big, and Angelo could have easily avoided any encounter with it by taking literally a few paces, but he was hindered by the stones which Vito had originally knocked out of the wall. Angelo stumbled over them, not actually falling, merely sitting down. The next moment the collapsing wall covered him. At least that's what it seemed like from his side to the appalled Vito. The cloud of dust accompanying the collapse contributed to this impression. Vito rushed forward, stumbling over the pile of bricks which the wall had instantly become and trying to feel for his fallen comrade in the gloom caused either by the evening or by the dust.

"Angelo! Angelo!" the terrified youth was gasping, when he heard the calm voice of his friend, sounding calm enough and coming from somewhat higher up than the place where he was looking for him.

"I'm here..."

"Good heavens! Thank God! You managed to jump clear!" Vito spotted Angelo's silhouette lying just beyond the heap of stones, and leaped quickly up to him.

"Careful," said Angelo in the same calm voice, warning his friend with a gesture to keep clear.

Vito thought this calmness was the result of his young partner's fear and, ignoring the warning, he rushed up to the place from where he had heard his voice.

"Aaah!" Angelo gave a piercing yell, which petrified Vito. In the gloom he grabbed his friend and began to examine him from the head downwards. It was only when he got to his legs that he saw that one leg was hidden from view below the knee.

"Did it get you?" asked Vito, hoping that the outcome of their adventure would not be too bad.

"Yes, I think so," replied Angelo, with tears already in his voice.

"Easy, easy." Vito stroked his friend's cheek and began to dig the leg out carefully with his hands. He very quickly came upon some wooden beam or other which had crushed his friend's leg with its weight. Still hoping for the best, Vito tried to lift the beam. However, neither his first attempt, nor his subsequent attempts, succeeded in shifting it or even budging it. To all appearances it was a load-bearing beam from the roof, to which the boys had not even paid any attention. In the intervals between his efforts, Vito feverishly scraped away at the surrounding area, trying to gauge how the beam was lying in relation to Angelo's leg.

"What is it?" groaned Angelo, beginning to cry quietly.

"Just don't cry. Don't cry!" said Vito, injecting a note of severity into his voice.

"But it hurts, Vito!" said the younger boy in quiet self-justification.

"I know, I know. I'm getting there," whispered Vito, crawling along the beam and clearing earth and rubble away from it.

"Please pull my leg out," Angelo partly demanded, partly entreated, "I can't stand it any more."

Finally, Vito unearthed Angelo's boot on the other side of the beam, and realised with horror that its position was completely out of kilter with the symmetry of the human body: the boy was lying on his side while his boot was sticking out of the earth, heels upward. The mere thought of what the hidden part of the leg must look like produced a lump in Vito's throat. Vito began to panic, maybe not outwardly but at least inwardly; for several moments, chaos reigned in his heart: his thoughts were hurtling past like the carriages of an express train, and he couldn't seize hold of any of them. But Vito fairly quickly took himself in hand. His very first, and natural, desire to pull his friend out from under the spoil heap by dragging him by the arms as hard as he could, he dismissed, His reading of the German mountaineering magazine came in handy; one of the articles had described in detail the technique for rescuing climbers if they fell from a height and were injured. The majority of such injuries entailed broken bones. The foremost recommendation was to ensure that medics came as quickly as possible to the scene of the incident; they would be able to minimize the risk that when the injured party was moved, their condition would be worsened. Also recommended was keeping the patient warm until medical help arrived. The second problem was not critical, even at the end of the Tuscan winter, and would only really become a problem if they had to spend the night in the open air. However, night was a long way off, and help could be obtained fairly quickly, and it was on this that Vito decided to concentrate.

"Angelo, hang on! You're doing well. I'll go and get Genarro now!"

"Don't leave me!" the boy implored him. "Let's do something together!"

The thought of being left on his own so horrified Angelo that he dug his arms into the earth in an attempt to push his body upwards, and immediately howled with pain.

"You mustn't move, Angelo! Don't you dare move! I need help. We've got to shift this blasted beam and see how your leg is."

"Do you think it's broken?" the lad asked naively.

Vito could not help glancing again at the heel of Angelo's boot poking out from beneath the beam, and with forced levity began to talk away:

"Not necessarily. Most likely not. It's hurting because the beam is so heavy. Well, there'll be a cut, a bruise, that's all. Keep your chin up. Give me a couple of minutes. I'll be quick, Angelo, then things'll be better."

"You... you won't be long?"

"I'll be back in a jiffy! I swear!" Vito was already on his way as he spoke.

"Vito!" He heard his friend's weak voice behind him.

"What?" Vito turned round as he ran.

"Don't dare die till you've lived your dream..."

"Be quiet, you idiot. I'll be right back."

The boys were lucky. Genarro had only just returned and was on the scene in literally a few minutes, holding a torch in one hand and a large metal crowbar in the other. En route from the house, Vito could scarcely keep up with his fast pace, endlessly repeating something about a boot, a heel, a leg, and hearing only the old man's curses in reply. Genarro's movements were clear and rational, and even seemed somewhat dilatory, although in actual fact they concealed an absolute understanding of what needed to be done. Not a single superfluous movement, not a single irrelevant word, no doubt at all about the correctness of his actions. This calm confidence conveyed itself to Vito and even to Angelo, who was in pain. Only for a moment did Genarro pause, as if undecided: the moment when the torch revealed his grandson's crushed leg. The boot heel turned upwards promised nothing good – Genarro had seen such things and realised they were dealing with a complex fracture. The main aim now was to save the leg. The problem was complicated by the fact that it was an open break, which could often lead to serious loss of blood. Genarro was surprised that Angelo had not lost consciousness from shock, and put this down to an adrenaline rush. There was no time to be lost, and Genarro, having assessed the size and position of the beam, quickly selected the best spot for lifting it with the aid of the crowbar. The very first attempt was successful – Genarro succeeded in lifting the beam several centimetres. On his own initiative Vito filled the space with some of the bricks which were lying around everywhere. Seizing the crowbar again, Genarro quickly raised the beam a second time, to such an extent that it could be moved to one side without fear of dragging the boy's damaged leg with it. Having shifted the beam, Genarro placed the torch nearer, and lit up the space he'd cleared. Genarro gave a deep sigh, Vito shrugged his shoulders, and Angelo stared with horror at his upturned boot.

"Don't look!" ordered Genarro. "Vito! Hold his head!"

Genarro carefully swept a sludge of sand and shards of stone away from the freed leg, trying not to touch the leg itself. When he got to the upturned boot, he paused.

"Angelo! You'll have to be brave, lad. I've got to pull your leg out. Vito! Hold him, so that he moves about as little as possible."

"Grandpa! Don't!" Angelo implored.

"I'll be quick."

Vito embraced his friend firmly, preventing Angelo from seeing his own leg, but could not take his eyes of the horrific picture. Genarro cautiously touched the heel, and slowly raised the boot. Angelo did not even move. Genarro continued to raise the boot, and at the moment when Vito saw that the foot in the boot was separated from the rest of the extremity, he blacked out.

A sharp slap in the face brought Vito round. Above him was Genarro's face, wearing a contented expression for some reason. Beside him, groaning slightly but also with a foolish smile on his face, lay Angelo. Vito looked fearfully towards the place where, as he understood it, the detached foot of his friend should have been. To his surprise, Vito saw not a bloody stump, but the slightly swollen, but clearly living, bare foot of his friend. Vito transferred his perplexed gaze to the old man who, instead of answering, mockingly waved Angelo's boot over him.

"You see, when Angelo fell, his boot flew off at the last moment."

"What about his leg?" asked Vito, not immediately grasping the link between these two facts.

"It's nothing. He's broken it, of course, but nothing terrible."

Vito felt that he was about to faint again, this time with relief. At least, his head started spinning, and he rushed to embrace Angelo.

"Easy, easy. Don't move me!" yelled his unexpectedly intact friend, but Vito continued to stroke him, like a favourite kitten rescued from a drainpipe.

23

APRIL 2015. ABC ROUTE: BAMBOO BASE CAMP, MACHAPUCHARE, NEPAL

The nights turned out to be the most difficult thing for Vito in the mountains. To his surprise, the nightmare was not the cold, which he had expected, but another thing entirely. The fact is that the old man had lived to a ripe old age without ever knowing what insomnia was, and the impossibility of having a good night's sleep was a personal catastrophe for Vito. It bothered him more than the shortness of breath he felt on the path. If he was gasping for breath on the climb, Vito could regulate the frequency and depth of his breathing, and thus fill his lungs with sufficient oxygen in the depleted air. But his sleeping brain could not control this process. As a result, as soon as he began to fall asleep, Vito would start gasping for breath, and jump out of bed in a panic. And every brief interval of sleep was filled with terrible dreams, in which Vito sometimes drowned, was sometimes buried in soil, and sometimes, possibly for a bit of variety, was being throttled. But, if the first two scenarios invariably took place at the bottom of a pool or the foundation pit (which is what it was until construction was complete), in the third variant his killer was invariably the hapless Maurice, whose absence of fingers did not allow him to complete his dirty business – and allowed Vito to wake up each time.

Vito had never come across this manifestation of insomnia, when you fall asleep easily and quickly but are constantly forced to wake up in order to get your breath back, and the last two nights had exhausted him. Unlike his friend, Angelo experienced no changes in his sleep pattern, sleeping for a long time and getting up with difficulty in the morning. In other respects, by the fourth day of their mountain journey the old men had begun to adapt to the challenges. Most importantly, they had finally worked out their optimum tempo, and could match their speed with the distance they had to cover in the day. The fact that practically everyone on the path overtook them did not bother them in the slightest. During their last overnight stay, Vito got hold of a detailed map of the route from one of the guides of a group going down. Importantly, it indicated not only the distances between loggias, but also the differentials in height along the way – information they had sorely lacked at the beginning, and which had a key influence on the speed at which they moved in the mountains.

Now the friends faced a dilemma: the remainder of the journey did not divide equally into days. It was obvious that the last stop before they emerged onto the lower slopes of Annapurna had to be made in the last loggia – in base camp Machapuchare, which was literally two hours' walk from the end of their route. All travellers did this as it ensured emerging onto Annapurna in the hours of dawn and afforded the opportunity of descending about one kilometre that same day – to Deurali or even Bamboo, where it was easier to breathe and significantly warmer. However, the old men could not decide whether to split the journey to the last stop into two days or to try to do it in one go.

Every attempt to get advice from people going down was ineffective, since some of them, seeing the advanced age of the two friends, automatically exaggerated the difficulty of the remaining section, while others, basking in the euphoria of the descent, minimized it. Utterly confused as to what the possibilities were, the old men decided to make their choice as they went along, depending on how they felt and the time they had left.

And, in truth, the first part of the climb was surprisingly simple – a pleasant, practically flat path in a forest. The friends made it without any particular difficulty to the loggia in Deurali, where they could spend the night if they chose the "two-day option". Having dined on the usual garlic soup, which gave Vito constant heartburn, the old men sat on the open terrace of the restaurant and warmed themselves in the sun.

The scenery had noticeably changed; the forest had ended, and the path, visible ahead, was all grass and small bushes. And although it was warm, as before, on the slopes, in the shade, there was more and more snow. The decision could no longer be delayed – the day was at its height, and in the event of the partners' deciding to go as far as Machapuchare, they would have five or six hours before darkness fell.

"You know, there's no particular reason for us to hurry. We can spend the night here of course," said Vito, still wincing from the soup. "The one thing I can't stand any more is that stinking slop."

"Look, Vito. See how you feel. Personally, I'm not tired and feel I have the strength for another go." Angelo scrutinized his friend as if trying to deduce from his outer appearance his ability to go on.

"Angelo, don't look at me like that!"

"Like what?"

"Like the vet looking at Mutu."

"What's Mutu?"

"I had a mare of that name."

"What happened to it?"

"He looked at her like that and a day later she died."

"That means we must go on!"

"Why?"

"If you're right, it's not worth dragging our climb out for another twenty-four hours!" laughed Angelo, beginning to fasten up his rucksack.

"Then let's get this finished," replied Vito decisively, rising to his feet.

Half an hour after they had left the restaurant where they had eaten, a prolonged and fairly steep climb began. Here there were no steps, as there had been lower down, but piles of huge boulders. The path was now marked by splodges of red paint on stones. However, as before, it was impossible to go wrong, since there were simply no alternatives. In addition, the number of people on the path had increased: it turned out that several routes came together here, all of them leading finally to Annapurna. In view of the fact that it was after dinnertime, most of the tourists were heading downhill towards the old men.

With barely concealed envy, Vito contemplated the people – for the most part young – skipping lightly over the stones on their way downhill. Their excited faces and multilingual chatter clearly indicated that just this morning they had stood at the end of the route in base camp Annapurna and had been photographed many times against the background of the sinisterly splendid mountain. As he stepped high over the next rock, Vito tried to imagine himself in that place, but each time he had to dismiss this picture and again concentrate on his own breathing, which was threatening to burst his lungs.

Angelo, who was walking behind him, felt cross: At the start of the trek, the majority of the looks he had received expressed delight and respect for them, as persons of such advanced years who had decided on such an expedition. Now, though, practically no one they met on the path concealed their pity for them. It was obvious, but Angelo could not understand what was prompting the sympathy – the pitiful spectacle of the two old men or the knowledge of those coming down of what they would shortly be in for. Furthermore, he felt more and more waves of nausea to add to the headache that had plagued him for two days. The aspirin he had taken during their stop only helped for a short time, and the pain again settled in in his temples.

After some two hours of almost continuous climbing, the friends unexpectedly found themselves in a valley. Ahead, as far as they could see, the path was absolutely flat – it wound slightly, following the outline of a small river, and only somewhere in the distance ahead did it hit the mountain massif. The map gave the friends optimism. Judging by the map, two thirds of their remaining journey would be in this valley. The sun had already begun to sink behind the mountains, but the friends were not particularly worried, given the flat path ahead of them.

Vito emerged onto the level section of the path with relief, and began to walk briskly and without pausing along the river. His head was buzzing – something he had only noticed now that he'd stopped focussing on the climb. His legs, grateful that they were no longer compelled to go upwards, carried the old man easily forward. Vito felt a surge of new strength, despite the accumulated weariness of recent days. Furthermore, for the first time since setting off along the path, he found himself thinking that undertaking this trek had been the correct decision, despite everything. Vito turned round to say so to Angelo, but could not see him.

It turned out that Vito, in his happy contemplative mood, had gone a couple of hundred metres beyond the end of the climb, and managed to lose sight of his partner. Suddenly concerned, Vito took off his rucksack and walked quickly back.

Reaching the beginning of the level section and still unable to find his friend, Vito began to panic:

"Angelo! Angelo!"

"I'm here," Vito heard, coming from behind a large boulder just off the path.

"Good Lord! Thank God! You're here!" The old man sighed with relief.

"Careful." Angelo's voice was calm, but all the same there was something strange about it. "Don't come round here. I've been sick."

"Do you feel bad?"

"Seems so."

Despite his friend's warning, Vito went round the boulder. Angelo was on his knees, not sure whether he could stand up or whether he would have another bout of sickness. Vito took a bottle of water from Angelo's rucksack, which was standing nearby, and handed it to his friend. Angelo rinsed his mouth out and poured some water onto the back of his neck, which at once made his back wet.

"How are you now?"

"A bit better, I think. I'll try and carry on."

Leaning with one hand on a stone and with the other on his friend's arm, Angelo stood up. He stood for a while, as if listening to his own body, then moved uncertainly towards the path. When he got there, he sat down on another stone and raised his eyes to Vito.

"What happened?" asked Vito anxiously.

"I don't know myself."

"How did you come to be off the path?"

"Well, I went for a leak and all this began." Angelo gestured vaguely.

"Have you got a headache?"

"Well, I've had a splitting headache for two days."

"Do you still feel sick?"

"I can't be sure." Angelo was clearly confused.

"Well, let's not hurry," said Vito soothingly. "It's still light, and the way ahead isn't difficult. We'll make it somehow."

Angelo sighed, and tried to get up. He succeeded, but when he started off, his walk was very uncertain. Vito grabbed his friend's rucksack and followed him.

"But where's yours?"

"My what?"

"Rucksack."

"I left it up ahead."

Angelo gradually increased his pace, but as soon as they drew level with Vito's rucksack, he dashed off the path and again fell to his knees. He got to his feet a second time, with much more difficulty, but, despite this, grabbed his rucksack.

"Leave it, Angelo. Let me carry it!" said Vito defiantly.

"It's OK. You'll have too much to carry. I can still manage." However, the spiritedness was all in Angelo's words and not at all in his voice.

Vito gave in, thinking that Angelo could carry the rucksack as far as he was able, but if he felt worse, Vito himself would take over – hopefully, his own strength would not desert him before then.

Their progress slowed to a crawl, and both were somewhat peeved that they had had to overcome such difficulties on this beautiful, and in all respects, easy stretch. Angelo halted periodically, but in view of his meagre diet in recent days, the contents of his stomach were exhausted and he had nothing left to bring up, although he still felt sick. As luck would have it there was no one else in the valley apart from them. There was nothing surprising about this, since the majority of tourists, restricted by how far they could climb in twenty-four hours, managed the daily kilometre norm before dinner, while those who were coming down had long since gone past in the first hours of daylight and were now a long way below.

It had already begun to get dark when the old men got through the valley and approached the cliffs on the other side. The friends sat down briefly on a stone which marked the next climb. Vito was unable to judge its severity and complexity as the path quickly spiralled away beyond the cliffs.

Vito began to panic. In addition, it seemed to him that Angelo's calmness was only a result of his feeling so bad that he had no strength left to get agitated. Despite all his growing anxiety, Vito did not chase his friend along and waited patiently for him to decide to continue.

"Time to go," Angelo ordered tersely, and moved forward.

On the climb the friends' halts became even more frequent. Angelo no longer ran off to the side but merely lowered his head between his legs in a fruitless attempt to squeeze something more out of himself. To make matters worse the old men began to run out of water. Vito stopped drinking himself and gave Angelo a swig each time he had an attack of sickness.

At the next stop, Vito decided to take Angelo's rucksack. While he was thinking how to suggest the idea tactfully, Angelo stood up and tottered off. The rucksack remained where it was, on the ground. Five minutes later Angelo shouted in horror:

"My rucksack! Vito! I've forgotten my rucksack!"

"Don't worry. I've got it," puffed Vito behind him.

"I'm sorry," was all his friend could say.

About an hour later it became completely dark. The path was not very steep, but for the first time it became twisting and fairly narrow. To their right there was a cliff the whole time, to the left a precipice. Well, not exactly a precipice, but a steep gradient, which nevertheless guaranteed any tourist who stumbled a hundred metre fall and more, over pebbles. It was difficult to make any assumption how such a fall might end in view of the fact that in the darkness one could not make out precisely where the slope ended.

Vito got out his head torch, and walked behind, trying to illuminate the path for both of them. Only now, as he lit up the

IGOR ZAVILINSKY

path in front of Angelo, did he become aware how bad his friend was; he was describing dangerous zigzags and his feet kept hitting stones or each other. To go on was dangerous, both for health reasons and for the risk of misstepping in the darkness. Angelo halted, and Vito caught him up, intending to discuss their next move with him.

"Going on…"

"Look!" Angelo did not raise his head but merely pointed somewhere ahead.

Vito's eyes followed the direction which his friend was indicating, and he saw lights in the windows of several buildings. In the darkness it was difficult to estimate the distance to them, since it was not clear whether the path to the loggias was straight or whether it contoured. Angelo sat down heavily, and it became clear that the lights of the stopping place, which had just appeared, had robbed him of his last strength to move on. Vito realised this at once. He did not even try to ask his friend whether he could go on for a little.

"Angelo! I'm going to get help! I'll be quick."

"Yes. Only leave the rucksacks."

"You're not cold."

"A bit. But that's good. I don't feel so sick."

"I'll be quick!"

"So you said."

"Yes. I'll leave the torch with you."

"You don't need to. My mobile's still working. I'll switch its light on."

"Right. Only don't switch it off."

"Off you go."

"I'll be quick…"

"Vito!"

"Yes. Enough. I'm on my way."

Vito set off, all the time looking round at the light from the mobile, which Angelo had simply put on the ground in front of him.

Fortunately, there turned out to be a loggia nearby. Some five minutes later, Vito was faced with the steep wooden steps leading to the houses. His anxiety for the abandoned Angelo added adrenaline and, despite the fact that Vito had been in the mountains all day, he simply flew up them. In the common room the evening was in full swing, and it was full of tourists and porters. Vito was lucky in that when he, and a dozen people who had volunteered to help him, emerged onto the path, he saw the light from Angelo's mobile below, and did not have to go down himself. Within half an hour, Angelo was lying in his own room being fussed over by doctors who had appeared from heaven knows where.

Later Vito explained that they were Swiss doctors who had come to Nepal to conduct a seminar on altitude sickness. However, since neighbouring India had imposed an embargo on fuel deliveries, the seminar had been cancelled, and in order to put their time to good use, four of the doctors decided to go on a trek. Thus, instead of a theoretical course, the young people and their director – a woman who looked to be over fifty – had the chance to demonstrate their skills in practice.

At the time, though, Vito was unaware of all of this. Persuaded that Angelo was in safe hands, he put the remaining pair of self-heating insoles in his socks and simply crashed out.

IGOR ZAVILINSKY

24

APRIL 2015. ABC ROUTE:

MACHAPUCHARE BASE CAMP, NEPAL

"Vito!"

Vito did not immediately understand whether the voice calling him was a dream or real.

"Vito!"

Vito opened his eyes; now he did not realise where he was as he surveyed the dilapidated ceiling of his room. A second later and he remembered all the events of the day, although it was actually yesterday.

"How are you, Angelo?"

"I need the toilet badly." Angelo's voice was quite weak.

"Yes, the doctor did say that might happen." Vito remembered the Swiss giving him instructions in his sleep.

"Vito…"

"What?"

"I'm afraid I won't manage it. I mean, I won't make it to the toilet."

"I'll help you."

This was easier said than done. The very thought of crawling out from under the blanket, and then out of his sleeping bag, and then out of the room, was agonising. Despite promises in the instructions about five hours of warmth, Vito couldn't feel the heated insoles at all. He felt carefully for the boundary between the insole and his foot, but everything in his boot felt like a single lump of ice. Inside Vito, charity struggled with his fear of cold. Fully aware of this, Angelo graciously waited. With an abrupt movement, Vito sat down on the bed, keeping on for the time being the weight of the blanket and sleeping bag. It was pitch dark, and the only light was coming from the gap under the entrance door. Vito listened – there was no wind. At least something good. He threw off the blanket, and remained sitting in his sleeping bag. The treacherous cold hurled itself at his back, like hungry dogs at a hunk of meat. Vito realised it would hurt less if he did everything quickly.

"Let's go, quickly," he ordered, offering Angelo his hand.

Angelo sat up, summoning up his strength for the dash. Judging by Angelo's hesitant movements, his friend's hand was a substantial addition to his own motor skills.

"Are you ready?" urged Vito.

"Yes."

"Then stand up slowly."

Angelo stood up. The walls of the room began to come and go before his eyes, and he needed some little time to stop them revolving. Leaning on each other, the old men moved towards the strip of light coming under the doors. Vito hesitated a little as he felt for the bolt, the presence of which was dictated not so much by considerations of security as by the necessity of closing the door. Without this primitive lock, the door opened each time with a loud creak and let in the cold from outside.

The friends went out onto the open veranda, shared by all ten rooms of the loggia. In the left-hand corner of the veranda, in a room which was both a bar and sleeping quarters for the porters, could be seen the sole source of light, a very dull source at that. To all appearances, it was some kind of night light. The exhausted Angelo hurried towards the light – the toilet was opposite the entrance to the common room. Just for form's sake, Vito supported his elbow, thinking with some annoyance that Angelo could have managed the expedition to the toilet on his own. The cold, on being encountered, turned out to be less fierce than it had seemed under the blanket, and his body was gradually getting used to the temperature of the Himalayan night. Of course, the total absence of wind was a help. A minute later the toilet door creaked and Angelo began to emerge. Only now did Vito see his face, illuminated by the light in the toilet –

it was uncompromisingly green. The return trip was worse for him – in the absence of motivation from his bladder, Angelo's legs would not obey him, and Vito's support now played a key role. Without hurrying, the friends reached their room. Vito was about to open the door when Angelo asked:

"Can I sit here for a bit?"

"You won't get cold?"

"Strange though it may seem, the cold distracts me from wanting to puke."

"It's simply the fresh air. Wait, don't sit down."

Vito opened the door and pulled out two thick blankets. He folded the first several times and laid it on the step, then prepared to cover himself with the second. Angelo sat down uncertainly. Vito sat down beside him and covered them both with the one blanket. The old men were so focused on their actions that they did not once raise their heads. Only when they had sat down did they do so, involuntarily. They were both astounded.

It was as if they were inside a glass Christmas decoration, filled, not with snow, but with stars, which were not so much above as to the sides. They seemed to be everywhere bar on the step on which the old men were sitting. From time to time, meteor trails crossed the sky, now here, now there. Through force of inertia, Vito continued to support Angelo by the arm, although the latter, squeezed between his friend's shoulder and the edge of the veranda, was unable to move anywhere. Vito was the first to speak:

"This is probably what our childhood dream is supposed to look like."

Angelo grinned.

"I can't remember any more what I dreamed about."

"About a motorbike."

"Yes, that's right."

"So, did you buy yourself a motorbike?"

"Yes."

"What did you do with it?"

"I did a lot of travelling. Very fast. Then I gave it all up."

"Why?"

"I had an accident."

"A bad one?"

"Yes. Well, I got away with fractures." Angelo was choosing his words carefully. "Someone died. A girl."

"She was with you?"

"Uh-huh."

"I'm sorry."

"It was a very long time ago."

Angelo made it clear that he wanted to drop the subject.

"And what about your dream, Vito?"

"What dream?"

"You dreamed of going away to Rome."

"Or Milan... Yes, somehow the dreams vanished. The bar was my responsibility. I thought once of installing someone at the helm but, as you know, where we are everyone's got their own business to attend to. Then things kind of got going. We began to build. Nothing kills a dream like building!" laughed Vito.

"So you stayed there?"

"And to my shame never made any attempt to change anything. And how could I have done? Alessandro soon came along. He was very ill as a child, and that took up a lot of time and money. Then he outgrew the illness and everything calmed down. For a couple of years we lived quietly, until Massimo was born. While I built the house and raised children, life passed. So, unlike you, I never had a career."

"True enough, I did have a career, remarkably quickly and easily. By the time I was thirty, I'd already founded my brokerage company."

"Everything went OK for you?"

"It depends what you mean by that. You know, at times I thought I wasn't living, but fulfilling a business plan. I'd go to a party – because the birthday boy was a big shareholder. I'd play tennis to show clients I was in good health. The women I met came through a filter."

"How so?"

"The shareholders were afraid that the decrepit old man might exchange his share for sex." Angelo laughed bitterly.

"What about your wife? And Cristina?"

"To all intents and purposes they weren't included in my business plan. We lived together for a long time, but it wasn't a marriage. More a picture of domestic bliss, advantageous to both sides. My daughter became so used to doing without concerned parents that when I tried to play father, it turned out she'd already grown up."

Both men fell silent. They were so close to the sky that everything on earth sounded strange. They even talked about their lives in a kind of abstract fashion, as if they weren't talking about themselves. It seemed the old men were four thousand metres above not only the earth, but above life too. Gazing from a height, they felt no bitterness, disappointment or other emotions. They simply looked and drew conclusions.

"It's easy to dream when you're a child," said Vito thoughtfully. "What's more, there's always a choice: in the first place, what to dream about, and you can always put it off. Then dreams gradually fade in an unbelievably big mass of problems."

"You know," Angelo replied, "my partners once – I think it was on my fiftieth birthday – gave me a present: a game of tennis with a girl who at the time was ranked in the world top 50. While we were getting acquainted, chatting, getting ready for the game, like any normal male, what didn't I dream about her. I watched her knock up, I watched her first serves, I admired her strong shapely legs in their short little skirt and, of course, I thought what chance there was of sex with her. And then... then such a hail of balls landed on me that I was rushing from corner to corner, scarcely returning any of them and dreaming of only one thing – for this whole thing to end as quickly as possible. Throughout the whole game I scarcely recalled her startlingly attractive body or what pleasure possession of it might afford me; I simply didn't see it; all I could see was tennis balls. It's like that in life – the most beautiful dream gets lost in a hail of problems which descend on you."

Vito said nothing. It felt strange for him to be disabused of Angelo's image as a successful man, an image he had lived with all his life since the latter departed across the ocean. It wasn't that Vito often recalled his friend, but all the same, he existed in his consciousness and came to mind whenever Vito mused about life, as they say, on a grand scale. On such occasions, for Vito Angelo was the background against which his own life was grey and singularly uneventful. Moreover, it sometimes seemed to Vito that Angelo had, as it were, stolen his own dream; he had gone away from Montepulciano and had success, imaginable and unimaginable. This was so like what Vito had planned for himself in his youth that the point about theft had lodged itself firmly in his brain and was the cause of general and undeserved resentment towards his friend.

"How do you feel in yourself?"

Angelo was slow to respond, at first not realising that this was not a question about life as a whole but about his current condition.

"While I'm sitting in the fresh air it's tolerable. But standing up is scary."

"So don't stand up. You're not cold?"

"I'm OK. Maybe you should get some sleep. I'll sit here a bit longer."

"I won't be able to sleep. I still can't get used at all to the time difference. Everything's gone haywire in my old noddle. Another couple of hours and we'll get ourselves ready. The doctor said the earlier we go down, the better you'll be. There's a couple of porters here – they'll help with the rucksacks."

"Vito."

"What?"

"I was thinking." Angelo did not know how to begin. "Listen, we've still got two hours' walking."

"Not quite, Angelo. Of course, it's easier going downhill, but I suppose in your condition we can't move too quickly and we've got to lose a minimum of one kilometre altitude. I realise you have doubts about the porters, but I'm sure we need them. Not so much on account of our things as that I want two young lads to be alongside us. I got scared yesterday."

"I'm not talking about that."

"Not about the porters?"

"No. We need porters. I agree."

"That's good. What were you talking about then?"

"Let's leave earlier. While everyone's asleep. We'll leave the things here. And we'll go up."

"What?! Are you thinking what you're saying?"

"I know, I know, Vito, it won't be very good for me."

"No, Angelo. Not only will it not be very good – it'll be positively dangerous! It would even be dangerous for a young person, but at our age we can't fool about with it."

"I know all that, old boy…"

"So act according to what you know. We're not kids. That bloody Annapurna has surrendered to us. These are the terms – there she is! We'll see her shortly, as soon as the sun rises. Who's bothered whether we see her from here or from a few kilometres nearer."

"Vito, listen…"

"No, I won't listen, Angelo! Don't make yourself out to be a mountaineer. We're not mountaineers! And we're not climbing to the summit but to base camp. We're tourists! And, unfortunately, we're not the optimum age for that. And I certainly don't want to explain to Cristina afterwards what cerebral oedema is and why I didn't protect her dad from it. You know what? Let's tell everyone we were there. The sun will soon be up. Let's take a couple of photos of sodding Annapurna and go down. Not a living soul will find out where we turned round!"

"Vito, let me speak."

"What do you want to say, Angelo?"

"I've not cared for a long time what people think of me. And I didn't come here for anyone. I came for myself and, you'll not believe this, for you too. Vito! If we do this now, I'll fulfil at least one of my dreams. Do you understand? Maybe I'll fulfil my sole dream. I'm over seventy, Vito. I won't have any more chances to complete something significant in my life. This is the only thing left…"

"Don't, Angelo…"

"I must, Vito! To hell with fear! It's better to die up there than at a meeting in my office!"

"Why in your office?"

"Recently I collapsed unconscious in the middle of a meeting. I don't want to die like that. It's revolting when people mill about you and, out of respect, can't touch you. Even to save your life."

"How do you know?"

"Know what?"

"That they were afraid. You were unconscious."

"I got the record off security afterwards – so that no one saw it. Well, I didn't hold back. I had a look. Revolting."

"Angelo, when you die for real, you won't care how you did. No one will show you the record in the next world."

"Yes, Vito, I know, but I need this. And you know, you need it just as much."

"Why?" asked Vito, more from inertia than any desire to hear the truth, which was obvious to him.

"You and I have wasted our lives, brother. Have you not yet realised that? I earned everything I could, except love for myself. And, forgive me, but you stayed put where I left you sixty years ago – in a bar! Of everything we dreamed about, there's just this mountain left! Nothing more! And, Vito, if we go back now, we'll be left with nothing. We must do it. To hell with fear. It's too late to be afraid."

Vito sat, his head sunk in his chest. There was a scarcely perceptible light in the sky, but the stars were not hurrying to go away. Angelo waited for his friend's answer.

"We'll take water and your pills, a pair of socks each and money. We'll have lunch at base camp. I'm off. I'll put all that in my rucksack."

Vito stood up abruptly and went off to his room while Angelo remained, contemplating the stars as they gradually dissolved in the sky. The outline of Annapurna began to show through to his right.

Some five minutes later, when the friends were ready to leave, the path could already be seen without the need to illuminate it with the torch. Vito took the unusually light rucksack on his back and turned to Angelo, who was leaning his shoulder against the building.

"Are you ready?"

"Yes. We must get going before that lady doctor wakes up – she'd be bound to kick up a fuss about me."

"So you go in front. I'll be right behind you."

"God be with us."

Angelo pulled himself away from the wall of the building, like a big ship casting off from its mooring. For a while he tried to stop the world spinning before his eyes, but then set off uncertainly along the path. Vito followed his friend at the minimum possible distance, in order to catch his arms if the need arose. The stretch to base camp was fairly short and without big changes of altitude. The last section took trekkers on average no more than an hour and a half of easy and fairly pleasant walking through a valley with absolutely no dangers. Angelo had to stop every fifteen or twenty metres and make prolonged efforts to normalise his breathing.

"Are you sure you're not getting worse?" asked Vito.

"No."

"Do you feel sick?"

"I'm all right now."

"We can't spend long at the top: we'll climb up there, have lunch and hurry down. Today we need to lose at least a thousand metres. Or more. Although I'm afraid we won't manage more."

"Vito…" said Angelo, breathing heavily.

"What is it, Angelo?"

"I was sure you'd support me!" Angelo stood up with difficulty from a rock.

"Your confidence was misplaced. I don't understand myself how I agreed to this."

"I had confidence in you… Thanks."

"All right – you've said it all before."

"I'm so confident that I've ordered a helicopter to come to base camp for us." So saying, Angelo trudged off along the path without turning round. Vito stood rooted to the spot, and set off only when Angelo was a long way ahead.

"When did you manage to do that?" asked Vito, pursuing his friend.

"Yesterday, while you were going for help," replied Angelo, neither stopping nor turning round.

"And I thought you were dying there!" said Vito in surprise, as he caught up with his friend.

"Well, as you can see, not quite." Angelo turned round with a sly smile. "And, unlike you I get on with phones."

"You know what I'm going to say to you?" Vito's voice sounded threatening.

"Well, I can imagine," Angelo muttered without stopping.

"No, you can't begin to imagine… That's the best thing you've done for me this whole time," laughed the old man. "For the last two days I've been dreaming of nothing but your helicopter and thinking with horror about the return journey."

Angelo halted. Turning round, he saw his friend's contented face.

"Angelo, tell me truthfully: have you ordered lunch in Pokhara."

"No," replied Angelo, leaning heavily on his stick and waggling his head, "in Kathmandu without delay!"

"You crafty bastard!"

The old men took just under five hours to climb to base camp. Other tourists overtook them, including the Swiss lady doctor, who walked with Angelo for twenty-five minutes, upbraiding him for his negligence. At some point the flood of people overtaking them dried up – seemingly all those who had spent the night with them in the same loggia had gone on to the top. An hour later all these people began their descent, greeting the old men again. On the return journey, the Swiss lady doctor merely looked at Angelo, launching into Vito instead, telling him everything she thought about him. After this she bade them farewell, saying they'd meet again at the bottom, to which Vito muttered: "Like hell you will – I've got a helicopter."

When the old men reached base camp, there was almost no one there except two Russians finishing off a bottle of whisky. The Russians were saying something irritably to their porters and indicating the summit. The two young porters were, as usual, pretending they did not understand their clients' obvious desire to go to the summit. The Russians were raising their voices, supposing that at that volume the Russian language would become more comprehensible to the Nepalese.

The sun was already high in the sky, and it had become quite warm. Vito was smiling blissfully, and it was obvious that this was not so much because they had reached the finish as because for the first time in recent days he felt warm. The old men were sitting at the last table before the mountain and drinking tea. As far as they could judge, their table stood at about the same spot where Maurice had been when he had been photographed before his ascent. They needed to have something to eat, although they did not feel like it. As a result, the friends decided to take one plate of plain rice for the two of them. As they looked at Annapurna, off which the wind was tearing snowy protuberances, each sought, but failed to find in his innermost depths, a moment of triumph. Everything around was beautiful, but somehow ordinary. A Nepalese brought the rice and asked whether they'd be spending the night there. To which Angelo replied, pointing towards the Russians:

"No, we and our friends are beginning our assault straightaway."

The astute waiter countered with:

"In that case you've ordered the wrong drinks."

Everyone laughed, thus attracting the attention of the Russians, who rather lacked Tibetan serenity. Vito waved to them companionably, with a loud cry of "Namaste". They merely shrugged.

"They'd probably forgotten to explain to those lads that conquering the summit is not included in the price," joked Vito, almost abstractedly, continuing to contemplate Annapurna as if he really were preparing for an ascent and was surveying the optimum route. Somewhere in the distance could be heard the sound of a helicopter.

25

1955. MONTEPULCIANO, ITALY

In the event, the leg did indeed turn out to be broken, although without complications. Despite such a favourable result to the evening's adventure, Angelo was faced with spending the coming months in plaster. However, both friends were euphoric for several days, and regarded all complications light-heartedly, considering, justifiably, that plaster was a small price to pay compared with what had threatened the younger partner.

They gradually sobered up. Angelo began to resent his limited ability to move, and Vito began to think seriously about how to finish the business they had begun with the stones. They had just a few days left in which to complete the delivery of the materials – not an easy task for two people, but when one of them was incapacitated, it turned into a problem. The whole enterprise with the stones had from the outset been simple, not requiring any inventive decisions. This was still the case. Vito had a choice: carry twice as much each time, or make two trips a day.

Vito inclined to the first alternative, and a couple of days after the accident he had had a plan and made an attempt carry it out. He could not find a more capacious container, and so tried ways of carrying Angelo's sack himself. For the first few hundred metres, he carried the second sack in front of him and, as a result, was in danger of falling, since he could not see where he was going. Next, he thought about putting the second sack on top of the first, but on its side. In theory this did not look like a bad idea, but in practice the boy could not fathom how to arrange them, and, even more important, how to stand up once he had them sorted. After several attempts, Vito succeeded, by leaning against a small stone wall, in getting himself under the piled-up sacks and lifting them. His legs shook treacherously, and, just as at the beginning of their demolition of the barn wall, he was gripped by panic: "I won't be able to do this." And although darkness was still a long way off, Vito's proximity to the starting point of his journey killed his hopes. What was more, after fifty metres the top sack began to slip to the left over the bottom one. Vito increased his pace as if he were considering running to Montepulciano and getting there before the top sack fell. However, the sack had a mind of its own, and other plans. And despite the boy's attempts to keep his balance, the stones fell with a crash, raising dust from the path. Cursing, Vito sank to the ground. Breathing heavily, he turned round, looking for a springboard for a fresh start. However, the wall he'd used before was already nowhere to be seen, and there was nothing else suitable between the lines of olive trees.

Vito made three more attempts to adapt himself to the tall arrangement on his back, but each time the top sack fell off even more quickly. The boy had not yet covered even half his journey, and his strength was running out. His lack of strength was more than compensated for by an excess of anger. It was just a pity that anger could not carry sacks. It seemed to Vito that his anger was enough to take him to Florence. As happens, his anger was not selective, and gradually spread to everything: to parsimonious Genarro and dozy Angelo, both of whom were at this very moment enjoying a life of ease at home; to the old barn, three walls of which had been not enough for them to achieve their goal, and the fourth wall of which had nearly killed his friend; to the climb which began a bit nearer the town; to the sacks, which were unsuitable for transporting heavy loads; and especially to the string, which cut into Vito's fingers as he balanced his load, and to the pebble which had found its way into his boot. The dimensions of the pebble were big enough to cause discomfort, but at the same time too small for him to stop because of it. He was angry, too, at the rapidly falling cool night, at his unknown father, who had done nothing to avoid going to the front, thus condemning Vito to orphanhood, at the whole of Tuscany, which had not released him to enjoy a full and beautiful life, and even at the museum expert from Florence, who appeared on his hate list at the last moment and who was to receive the goods in five days' time. The appearance of the latter on this list was so unexpected for Vito that he grinned, as if debating with his own anger and saying "I'm overdoing it. What has he to do with it?"

His back hurt. Not in one particular place, but all over. Vito sat helplessly on one of the sacks by the side of the dusty path and indulged in self-pity; he felt sorry for his strained back, for his fingers ground down by the string, and especially for his legs, which continued to shake even after he had stopped and thrown off the sacks. At such moments of pain he realised he could have been sitting quietly in the bar, surreptitiously finishing off the remainder of the wine at the bottom of a bottle left behind by a visitor and talking to Angelo about any old rubbish. Left on his own, without the need to save face in front of Angelo or Genarro, for the first time Vito doubted the wisdom of the goal they had chosen: the mysterious snow-capped peak was a particularly long way away from him. It now seemed to him that common sense had mercilessly swept away his naïve notions about the beauty of life on the slopes, about the grace of heroism, and the pleasure of mastering oneself. Sweaty and grimy, Vito sat on the dusty ground in the gathering darkness of Tuscany, and simply wanted to go home. Genarro and the Frenchman Maurice seemed madmen to him; he and his friend Angelo seemed foolish milksops, and the whole enterprise of the journey to Nepal seemed completely irrational and a sheer waste of money. And there was the money they hadn't earned. And there was Genarro himself... Now Vito forgot about his weariness and leapt to his feet.

"He's a crafty old so-and-so!" yelled the young man. "A crafty old so-and-so."

Vito angrily kicked a small pebble from under his feet. It only now occurred to him that through his uncompromising attitude, Genarro had not been trying to teach them anything but had simply wanted to wean the lads off the idea of travelling to the Himalayas. How he'd learned of their plans was not known, but something else was absolutely clear – he'd known from the outset about the friends' decision to prepare for the expedition and was now very subtly preventing the realisation of those plans, hoping that in the end the lads would give up on the enterprise and return to their usual domestic pleasures and plans. It had to be admitted that he had almost succeeded: Angelo was lying in plaster with a heap of unhappy thoughts, while Vito was cursing himself and the whole of Nepal on the approaches to Montepulciano. Of course, the wall which had fallen on Angelo had unexpectedly helped Genarro, although it had scared him a good deal. Only now did Vito understand the reason why Genarro himself had been cursing that evening on the way to the barn.

Why had he opposed the boys? Out of fear for his grandson, or out of envy that they would do something he had not managed to achieve? More likely, something in between. He did not actually consider that the two boys would be able to get nearer to his dream than he had. He didn't believe it, and was trying to shield Angelo from disappointment, as a minimum, and from death in the mountains, as a maximum.

Vito was angry. Not so much at Genarro, whose behaviour, whatever his motivation, was explicable, as at himself. He was angry at his own weakness, at his readiness to give up at the first complication, and at the naivety with which they had, step by step, followed Genarro's scenario. The surge of adrenaline was so powerful that in a flash Vito had leapt to his feet with his sack on his back, holding the second in front of him, as he had done originally. Scattering curses all round, the boy began the climb along the winding path to the walls of Montepulciano. He reached them having stopped only once for a rest.

When Vito returned, it was fully dark. The anger caused by his unexpected surmises was gradually subsiding, but was replaced by perplexity: he did not know what to do. Should he talk to Genarro, or should he tell Angelo of his suspicions? The first alternative was completely pointless, and the second might completely sap the strength of his friend, who was already suffering. The evening chill cooled not only Vito's body, which the climb had made hot, but also his burning thoughts. Towards the end of his journey, he was already rejoicing in the fact that he'd rumbled Genarro's strategy and taken the decision to say nothing to Angelo, at least until he'd recovered. Vito felt like a card player who had managed to glimpse his opponent's cards and was convinced that his opponent was bluffing.

In the days that followed, Vito decided to go back to two trips a day. Taking into account the speed with which he covered the distance to the town with a double load, he didn't actually lose that much time, and he quickly hit on a timetable which guaranteed he would finish the job on time.

Angelo took his enforced inactivity badly, and felt he had let his friend down. He dragged himself along on his crutches behind Vito each time the latter went to the ruined barn. Sitting on the dreaded beam, he pushed bricks towards the sacks with his crutch. This was awkward, was of no great help, and, it seemed, only served to salve the conscience of the injured partner by indicating he was present in the action. When he'd filled a sack, Vito would set off towards Montepulciano. Angelo would remain where he was, following him with his eyes until he disappeared behind the olive trees.

Overall, the broken leg turned out to be the ideal injury for the boy: it didn't hurt, but made going to school and fulfilling his bar duties impossible. Angelo slept in as he'd never allowed himself to do so throughout his whole life, while his appetite grew in proportion to the excess of free time. His lack of mobility led to a situation in which, after a couple of weeks he, always as thin as a rake, began to fill out. This was particularly noticeable in his youthful cheeks. The idleness, which first had irritated him mightily, fairly soon became to the boy's taste, and the only unpleasantness in his new mode of existence was that he was tormented by itching under the plaster. Having a great deal of time at his disposal, Angelo concentrated on solving this problem, and equipped himself with a whole arsenal of means for doing so. Like a golfer with a range of clubs, Angelo had a selection of devices which allowed him to scratch his leg under the plaster. The most painful sites of the itching were most distant parts of his leg, for which Angelo had special sticks for the awkward shape round the heels, sticks with broad ends, like shovels, to offer maximum coverage of the area near the edge of the plaster, and a special soft twig covered in leaves for light, calming, stroking.

For those areas which remained inaccessible even in theory owing to the shape of the plaster, he had a special stick which he simply banged on the affected spot. If this didn't stop the itching, it did at least reduce it. Undoubtedly, if Angelo had had something to do, he would have spent less time on such trifles, but the absence of any external distracting factors automatically created the problem, which was a primary one at this stage of life. It was, however, possible, that such "sufferings" somewhat allayed his pangs of conscience regarding his inactivity.

The day of the last trip with the bricks arrived. All through the months of daily treks with the sacks, Vito had pictured this day as being, for some reason, definitely sunny, and not just sunny, but especially sunny. The boy didn't understand how the special nature of this sunniness would be manifested, but he was certain that when the time came, he would be able to pin it down accurately. When he arrived at the place where the barn had stood previously and where now there was just a small heap of rubble, Vito looked towards heavy rain clouds coming in from the direction of the fortress walls of Montepulciano and was rather disappointed. These clouds were the only thing distinguishing this morning from the previous one. It was clearly not the "special nature" on which he had counted. Vito tried, without success, to capture the triumph of the moment. Somewhat foolishly, he even felt some regret that he would not have to lug sacks to the mountain next day. The feeling was entirely irrational, and irritated Vito. His soul stubbornly refused to celebrate and, as a result, the boy had a new feeling. He did not yet know that it was called "desolation", and was felt by everyone who achieved a long-awaited goal.

Angelo was, as usual, sitting on the beam. Beside him stood a solitary sack, already filled up – according to the latest calculations that one would be sufficient. Vito looked at it, and gave his friend a surprised nod.

"Did you do that?" he asked.

"Early this morning Genarro was clearing up here. He's probably done the sums," said Angelo, looking past his friend.

"Why did he do that?"

"Ask him. I don't always understand grandfather."

"Who?"

Angelo merely looked up at Vito, who was hearing the word "grandfather" for the first time from his friend. Genarro had always been Genarro, or at least, in American fashion, "boss"; his blood link with one of the boys had never been stressed – either by Angelo or by the old man himself.

"All right, we'll put it down as a riddle," drawled Vito coolly, sitting down beside Angelo and, as usual, hitting the plaster cast with his knuckles as if ascertaining whether or not there was something in there. "When does it come off?"

"In two weeks exactly, I think. I'll ask the doctor tomorrow."

"I'll see him in town today. I can ask him myself."

"No you can't. Tomorrow I'll be seeing a doctor in Milan."

"How so?" said Vito in surprise.

"To please Mum. Mum wants to take me back while I'm not going to school anyway."

"Are you going today?"

"Straight away."

"For long?"

"Who knows? Genarro only told me this morning that he's sending me off today."

"Why the urgency?"

"I don't think it is urgent. He's known for a long time that mother wanted me back. He simply didn't tell me. But there's a car going that way today."

"Well, well. You'll miss the share-out of the money." Vito attempted to joke, but the joke was only in his words and not in his tone.

"You'll owe me," replied Angelo.

"What will you do in Milan?"

"You know, I haven't thought yet. Given this plaster, the choice won't be much bigger than here."

The friends' conversation somehow did not gel – and there were reasons for that: the end of their work, Angelo's unexpected departure. The air was heavy, and every word seemed to have difficulty in going through it. Both boys found this hard. It was time for Vito to go. He knocked on the plaster cast again, and, entirely inappropriately, asked: "Does it still itch?" Angelo got as far as opening his mouth in reply, but his friend, heaving a sack onto his back, was already going down the hill. To answer his retreating back would have been out of place.

"Bye!" yelled Angelo instead of answering.

Without turning round, Vito merely raised the hand not occupied holding the string.

In the years that followed, the thoughts of both boys frequently returned to that moment: what would they have said if they had known it was their last conversation? Certainly Vito would not have asked his friend whether his leg itched under the plaster, and Angelo would have said something more meaningful than that idiotic "Bye". What words do you say when you know that you won't see someone ever again? And why did they not sense that their friendship was to end on that day? Both of them sifted through many more "ifs" and "buts" – the curse of subjunctive mood – until, layer by layer, time covered their memories with new impressions, new friends, new experiences, new misfortunes, turning an open wound first into a painful scar, and then merely into a pink stripe, the origin of which has largely been forgotten.

26

APRIL 2015. NEW YORK, USA – KATHMANDU, NEPAL

The old men had gone incommunicado, but it was not difficult for Cristina to ascertain where they had got to. No one in her father's hotel could help her, but a pleasant young man called Nava from Vito's hotel told her in some detail how two very elderly gentlemen had set off for the mountains on their own.

Hearing this, Cristina voiced her alarm, which old Aaron, cynical as ever, quickly quashed, declaring:

"Child! If he'd died on the path, you would have already been informed. You haven't been, so he's already on his way to Annapurna. I don't think there's any point in equipping an expedition just now. Wait a couple of days."

The old man's words quickly cooled Angelo's daughter anxiety; she calmed down, and merely rang Massimo in Italy and told him everything she knew. Five days of waiting lay ahead for her; according to Nava, her father and Vito had reserved a room in his hotel and planned to stay there after their climb.

Cristina had five days not only to wait for her father but also to explain her actions to him. She realised how awkward the conversation awaiting her was going to be, and prepared herself for it more than she had ever done for her numerous business meetings.

To begin with she approached her preparation for the conversation from the point of view of finances and, as was her wont, made a very restrained, but informative presentation of all the benefits which would accrue to the company with the purchase of an internet store. The final slide presented all the personal advantages Angelo brought to being the main shareholder. She started by drawing up a ten-year plan for the growth of his capital, but then, as if seeing her father's ironical look, made it a five-year plan. Cristina polished the presentation for two days, bringing it to financial perfection and external elegance. If presentations were nominated for Oscars, she would have been more certain of receiving one than she was of receiving a favourable review of it from her father.

On the third day, Cristina realised that she had killed two days in vain. Her father would not even open the presentation. And he knew these figures as well as she did. Possibly, as always, somewhat better. In a panic, she even cast an eye on the medical file supplied by Aaron, but quickly composed herself and didn't spend even a couple of minutes on it.

Angelo had his own peculiar attitude towards his health. It might have appeared that he treated it very seriously and attentively but, on closer inspection, it became clear that what was important to him was not his health itself but what other people would say about it. As Angelo saw it, his body was one of the indices which influenced the share price of his company. That meant he had to keep tabs on it. Even now, having been retired, he would regard any attempt to press him on his health as blasphemy. Time was short, and Cristina still did not know how to greet her father, and relied more and more on chance or playing it by ear.

A major earthquake began on April 25 2015 at 11.56 Nepal time (6.11.26 universal time) 34 kilometres east-south-east of Lamjung (Central Nepal) at a depth of approximately 15 kilometres and lasted around twenty seconds. The US Geological Service originally calculated its magnitude as 7.5, but soon raised this to 7.8.Mw. According to the US Geological Service the cause of the earthquake was a sudden release of accumulated tension along the line of a geological fault in a region where the Hindustan tectonic plate is slowly sinking beneath the Eurasian plate. The city of Kathmandu, which stands on a block of the earth's crust measuring approximately 120 by 60 kilometres, shifted three metres south in the space of 30 seconds. Casualties of the earthquake in Nepal, according to data released on 12 May, stand at 8151 dead, 17868 injured. Earlier, the Prime Minister of Nepal, Sushil Koirala, announced that the casualty figure could reach ten thousand.

The UN estimates that the earthquake affected 8 million inhabitants, of whom two million lived in the eleven most severely affected regions.

For Cristina the morning news was in the nature of a muted visualisation, while she performed a round of female rituals. As she hurried past a live screen, she could see reportage of the latest disaster, but did not pay much attention to what exactly it was, and, more importantly, in what part of the world it was. Big city cynicism came into play, which does not allow one to empathise with everything that appears on TV screens. Probably every one of us perceives such events as the contents of the television, bearing no relationship to the real world in which people live. Moreover, the more dreadful the TV pictures, the better people feel their own lives to be, free as they are from the sufferings of mourners in TV reports.

That morning everything was like that; Cristina paid no special attention to pictures with red "Breaking News" strap lines, openly despising footage spattered liberally with blood. Somewhere at the back of her mind flashed the image of the latest terrorist atrocity in a third-world country. Cristina was already in the doorway when her mobile rang. In other circumstances, possibly, she would not have accepted a call before the beginning of the working day, but this was Vito's son, Alessandro. This immediately struck Cristina as odd, since all lines of communication with that family went through Massimo, and she couldn't remember any calls from the elder brother.

"Cristina, have you seen the news?" the young man asked, without any preliminaries.

"No," she replied, searching with her eyes for the TV remote, which she had been using a second before.

"There's been an earthquake there," said Alessandro, calmly enough, which prompted Cristina to imagine that the next sentence would be something along the lines of "but they're OK." However, that sentence did not follow. Instead came a question:

"When did you last speak to your father?"

The question annoyed Cristina. It seemed a mere formality, given that literally a few days previously she had told Massimo everything about her investigation.

"Massimo is up to speed. They refused a helicopter, went off into the mountains, and should have returned to Kathmandu..." Cristina paused for thought, thinking what the date was yesterday. "Where exactly was the earthquake?"

"I'm not sure where precisely. Information is patchy. But Kathmandu suffered badly. Very badly."

No, that can't be right! It's just a TV picture with no relevance to my life, Cristina tried to persuade herself.

"I'll ring you back!" Cristina cut short the conversation in order to ring Nava, in whose hotel the old men had planned to stay. There was no connection – just a voice recording from some nice girl in an incomprehensible language.

Even given all the financial and organisational opportunities at Cristina's disposal, even given the fact that that their company had become one of the biggest private sponsors of a rescue operation, even given the presence of reliable partners in neighbouring India, given all that, she only got to Kathmandu three days later, on board a military aircraft which was bringing in special equipment.

Cristina had never been in Kathmandu before, and had nothing to compare with the impression she now received: the city, with its chaotic mass of small buildings, had turned into one great rubbish tip of building materials. At first it seemed to her that nothing remained intact, that everything had been destroyed. Only when she calmed down and looked closer did she realise that some buildings had survived, and her first impression was down to the dust and debris, which was everywhere. As a methodical person, Cristina subconsciously sought some sort of logical continuity in this ruination, some sort of principle by which buildings fell. Finding no such, her brain became despondent: alongside practically intact houses were ruins; it was impossible to know what had stood there before. It was total CHAOS – perhaps the thing that Cristina was most afraid of in her life.

In such a city, the car was of little use. Realising this, Cristina, not without difficulty, found a tuk-tuk, whose owner agreed to take her for the whole day. Getting to the hotel turned out to be far from easy, even though Cristina had been given a precise location and the tuk-tuk owner had an excellent knowledge of the city. That particular part of the city had been damaged more than most, and from whichever direction they tried to approach, they were blocked off by rubble or cordons of police and rescue workers. The most they succeeded in doing was to get as close as possible to the place, in order to do the rest of the journey on foot.

The driver was struck by Cristina's anxiety, and undertook to accompany her. This turned out to be vital in view of the complex relief of the locality after the earthquake. When, according to all indications, they arrived at the right place, Cristina could not work out for a long time which heap of rubble was the hotel she was looking for. Finally, through her joint efforts with the driver, who questioned local inhabitants wandering about in circles distractedly, looking for their own, and, to all appearances, other people's things, they succeeded in identifying, in a heap of ruins resembling a house of cards, the hotel where rooms had been booked for Vito and Angelo.

There was no great rescue activity there. It seemed to Cristina that the rescue workers did not know where to begin and were scurrying unsystematically through the ruins, responding to calls from various directions. For this reason, more attention was being paid to the apartment blocks, whose surviving inhabitants asked the rescue workers to dig through their houses first even if they knew for certain that there could be no one alive beneath the ruins. Less attention was paid to the hotels, with whose guests no one had had any dealings. The appearance of Cristina, vested with considerable authority by dint of her financial clout, changed the situation, and after a couple of hours, work was going on frantically around the collapsed hotel. Parallel with this, Cristina constantly tried to call Nava, on whom were based her hopes of getting at least some information about her father.

An hour later the worst part began. The rescue workers were pulling the first victims out of the shattered hotel. Cristina was forced to remain on the spot, hoping not to recognise the next body as either of the old men. By evening, she remembered she had not slept for two days, and her diminishing supply of adrenaline was unable to keep her on her feet any longer.

Fortunately, by this time the rescue workers had set up a small camp in a school yard and assigned one of their tents to Cristina. Cristina did not even fall asleep; her consciousness was merely switched off.

In the morning, when she went to what remained of the hotel, she noticed some especially heightened activity. A dozen or so rescuers had gathered in one part of the ruins, two of them with dogs. They were all excited, and paid no particular attention to Cristina. Even so, from their conversation she gathered that the dogs had indicated there was someone still alive underneath.

Cristina eyed the dimensions of the spoil heap, and the thought that someone could be alive beneath this mass sent a shiver down her spine. Just for a second, she imagined what a person trapped beneath this heap of stones and wood was feeling, and it made her feel ill.

It was only towards the end of the day that the rescuers succeeded in reaching the person whom the dogs had found. It was a man who, to all appearances, worked in the hotel or had simply been going past when everything happened. The victim was unconscious, although without external signs of severe injuries. He was carefully pulled to the surface and set down on a stretcher. One of the rescuers poured a bottle of water over him, which wiped the dust from his face and the upper part of his clothing, and Cristina, who had come nearer, saw a small badge on the lapel of his shirt bearing the name "Nava". He was the last to be brought out alive from the ruined hotel. The next morning the rescue workers gave the go ahead for excavators to begin work on the site.

It was twenty-four hours before Nava came round. As it turned out, he had got away with fractures to both his legs, a crushed rib cage, and severe dehydration. He was out of danger but still very weak.

Cristina did not leave him, and as soon as he showed the first signs of life, she approached him with a photo of Angelo:

"Nava! Was my father in the hotel?"

The young man looked uncomprehendingly at the photograph.

"Were there two old men in the hotel?"

Nava tried to understand what was wanted of him.

"Nod your head! Were there old men in the hotel?"

Nava nodded. For the first time in recent days Cristina burst into tears and, leaving the still weak Nava in peace, turned to leave. He was clearly trying to say something, choosing English words.

"Yes," whispered Nava and, taking in air, added, "but they left the day before."

"How do you mean – the day before? They had a reservation for the 24th to the 25th of April."

"They did, but they returned early from the trek. One of them got ill in the mountains so they came down two days early. They spent the night here and our car took them to the airport."

"On the 24th, that is?" said Cristina in bewilderment.

"Definitely," whispered Nava wearily.

"Nava, you're not getting things mixed up?" asked Cristina apprehensively.

"I printed out their boarding passes for them. For the 24th."

"Where did they fly to?"

27

1955. MONTEPULCIANO, ITALY

Vito, twice deceived that day, first by the false expectation of pleasure at completing the saga with the bricks and then by the unexpected separation, stomped off to the fortress, trying to distract himself with commercial calculations.

Angelo poked the earth with his crutch and desperately did not want to go to Milan, which he disliked, to people with whom his relationship was purely formal.

Watching all this from his house, Genarro figured that he was the only one who understood the seriousness of what was happening.

However, even Genarro, for all his wisdom, was not aware of the scale of events which, in essence, had already occurred and towards which they were all being carried, like a rudderless ship is carried towards the rocks. Changes unconnected with one another but arranged in random order for no particular reason, as if for fun – in order to do the heads in of those who enjoy looking for logic in the trajectory of a falling leaf.

Genarro knew what the boys had not guessed at: Angelo was going away for a long time. But Genarro himself did not realise that for him "a long time" meant two weeks, and that, by an irony of fate, without symbolism or melodramatic links, he would not wake up the night Angelo, trembling with fear, would fly across the Atlantic.

No one could believe that these two events were a chance coincidence: neither Angelo, who, only learned of his grandfather's death a month later for the simple reason that no one, apart from Genarro himself, knew how to contact his daughter and grandson, nor the neighbours, to whom it was obvious that grief for the loss of his grandson had killed the old man, nor Vito, sitting distractedly in the empty bar while his aunts washed up from the wake.

But now, two weeks before this, full of life and ideas, Genarro was thinking least of all about himself or his fate, and was certainly not thinking about his own death. All the old man's thoughts revolved round the boys, who were uniquely dear to him.

That evening a weary Vito returned to the bar, somewhat annoyed with Angelo who, by his sudden departure, had unwittingly sullied celebrations for the end of their project. The lad sat in the bar, which the old man had tidied up, looking out of the corner of his eye at the window of Angelo's room, as if hoping to see movement there. Maybe the boy thought first about the inappropriateness of the expensive fork with which he was poking at his modest rustic supper. Seeing his torment, Genarro put several pieces of cheese on a plate and sat down opposite him.

"Will he come back?" asked Vito unexpectedly.

"Who?" said Genarro, as if not understanding who Vito was talking about, but in fact simply putting off the need to give an answer.

"Angelo."

"Who knows? Possibly. Sometime."

"And you're saying that just like that? 'Possibly. Sometime.'"

"There are some circumstances, Vito, which don't depend on us. It's best to take them as they come."

"Reconcile oneself to them?"

"I'd say: 'Accept them.'"

Vito's eyes treacherously filled with tears, and he was afraid to move lest one of them drop onto the table.

"Why is everything so complicated, Genarro?"

"What is complicated?"

"Everything. Life, happiness." Vito stared at the plate with its uneaten food.

"No, son, on the contrary. One day you'll understand that happiness is not complicated. It's sometimes difficult to achieve

IGOR ZAVILINSKY

it, but in itself, in its essence, it's always simple. And happiness never consists of a lot of parts, but when life's puzzle finally takes shape, you are frequently left, as it turns out, with a multitude of superfluous pieces, in searching for which you spent so much time previously."

Vito raised his eyes to Genarro.

"How can one understand what is superfluous."

"You can't, dear boy. You can't outwit life. In that lies its essence: first you become happy, and only then do you understand why."

2016-2019

ABOUT THE AUTHOR

Igor Zavilinsky was born in 1969 in Kiev (now Kyiv). After military service, he graduated from the Kyiv Polytechnic Institute and then went into business. He began writing for electronic media in 2000 but his first printed publication was a collection of novellas *Boatman, I love you* (2018). A second collection, *Lighthouse* followed in 2019, the year in which his first novel, *A Dream of Annapurna*, was published by Samit (Summit, Kyiv). A second novel, *Five Days with Lauren* was published in 2021.

Zavilinsky, who lives in Kyiv, numbers travel and the fortunes of Kyiv Dynamo Football Club among his other interests.

ABOUT THE TRANSLATORS

Michael Pursglove is a UK-based translator specialising in the works of Ivan Turgenev, and in modern Ukrainian literature. He also writes and reviews for a number of journals, notably *East-West Review*.

His son Jonathan graduated in History from the Open University and is a translator from Russian.

Glagoslav Publications Catalogue

- *The Time of Women* by Elena Chizhova
- *Andrei Tarkovsky: A Life on the Cross* by Lyudmila Boyadzhieva
- *Sin* by Zakhar Prilepin
- *Hardly Ever Otherwise* by Maria Matios
- *Khatyn* by Ales Adamovich
- *The Lost Button* by Irene Rozdobudko
- *Christened with Crosses* by Eduard Kochergin
- *The Vital Needs of the Dead* by Igor Sakhnovsky
- *The Sarabande of Sara's Band* by Larysa Denysenko
- *A Poet and Bin Laden* by Hamid Ismailov
- *Zo Gaat Dat in Rusland* (Dutch Edition) by Maria Konjoekova
- *Kobzar* by Taras Shevchenko
- *The Stone Bridge* by Alexander Terekhov
- *Moryak* by Lee Mandel
- *King Stakh's Wild Hunt* by Uladzimir Karatkevich
- *The Hawks of Peace* by Dmitry Rogozin
- *Harlequin's Costume* by Leonid Yuzefovich
- *Depeche Mode* by Serhii Zhadan
- *Groot Slem en Andere Verhalen* (Dutch Edition) by Leonid Andrejev
- *METRO 2033* (Dutch Edition) by Dmitry Glukhovsky
- *METRO 2034* (Dutch Edition) by Dmitry Glukhovsky
- *A Russian Story* by Eugenia Kononenko
- *Herstories, An Anthology of New Ukrainian Women Prose Writers*
- *The Battle of the Sexes Russian Style* by Nadezhda Ptushkina
- *A Book Without Photographs* by Sergey Shargunov
- *Down Among The Fishes* by Natalka Babina
- *disUNITY* by Anatoly Kudryavitsky
- *Sankya* by Zakhar Prilepin
- *Wolf Messing* by Tatiana Lungin
- *Good Stalin* by Victor Erofeyev
- *Solar Plexus* by Rustam Ibragimbekov
- *Don't Call me a Victim!* by Dina Yafasova
- *Poetin* (Dutch Edition) by Chris Hutchins and Alexander Korobko

- *Forefathers' Eve* by Adam Mickiewicz
- *One-Two* by Igor Eliseev
- *Girls, be Good* by Bojan Babić
- *Time of the Octopus* by Anatoly Kucherena
- *The Grand Harmony* by Bohdan Ihor Antonych
- *The Selected Lyric Poetry Of Maksym Rylsky*
- *The Shining Light* by Galymkair Mutanov
- *The Frontier: 28 Contemporary Ukrainian Poets - An Anthology*
- *Acropolis: The Wawel Plays* by Stanisław Wyspiański
- *Contours of the City* by Attyla Mohylny
- *Conversations Before Silence: The Selected Poetry of Oles Ilchenko*
- *The Secret History of my Sojourn in Russia* by Jaroslav Hašek
- *Mirror Sand: An Anthology of Russian Short Poems*
- *Maybe We're Leaving* by Jan Balaban
- *Death of the Snake Catcher* by Ak Welsapar
- *A Brown Man in Russia* by Vijay Menon
- *Hard Times* by Ostap Vyshnia
- *The Flying Dutchman* by Anatoly Kudryavitsky
- *Nikolai Gumilev's Africa* by Nikolai Gumilev
- *Combustions* by Srđan Srdić
- *The Sonnets* by Adam Mickiewicz
- *Dramatic Works* by Zygmunt Krasiński
- *Four Plays* by Juliusz Słowacki
- *Little Zinnobers* by Elena Chizhova
- *We Are Building Capitalism! Moscow in Transition 1992-1997* by Robert Stephenson
- *The Nuremberg Trials* by Alexander Zvyagintsev
- *The Hemingway Game* by Evgeni Grishkovets
- *A Flame Out at Sea* by Dmitry Novikov
- *Jesus' Cat* by Grig
- *Want a Baby and Other Plays* by Sergei Tretyakov
- *Mikhail Bulgakov: The Life and Times* by Marietta Chudakova
- *Leonardo's Handwriting* by Dina Rubina
- *A Burglar of the Better Sort* by Tytus Czyżewski
- *The Mouseiad and other Mock Epics* by Ignacy Krasicki

- *Ravens before Noah* by Susanna Harutyunyan
- *An English Queen and Stalingrad* by Natalia Kulishenko
- *Point Zero* by Narek Malian
- *Absolute Zero* by Artem Chekh
- *Olanda* by Rafał Wojasiński
- *Robinsons* by Aram Pachyan
- *The Monastery* by Zakhar Prilepin
- *The Selected Poetry of Bohdan Rubchak: Songs of Love, Songs of Death, Songs of the Moon*
- *Mebet* by Alexander Grigorenko
- *The Orchestra* by Vladimir Gonik
- *Everyday Stories* by Mima Mihajlović
- *Slavdom* by Ľudovít Štúr
- *The Code of Civilization* by Vyacheslav Nikonov
- *Where Was the Angel Going?* by Jan Balaban
- *De Zwarte Kip* (Dutch Edition) by Antoni Pogorelski
- *Głosy / Voices* by Jan Polkowski
- *Sergei Tretyakov: A Revolutionary Writer in Stalin's Russia* by Robert Leach
- *Opstand* (Dutch Edition) by Władysław Reymont
- *Dramatic Works* by Cyprian Kamil Norwid
- *Children's First Book of Chess* by Natalie Shevando and Matthew McMillion
- *Precursor* by Vasyl Shevchuk
- *The Vow: A Requiem for the Fifties* by Jiří Kratochvil
- *De Bibliothecaris* (Dutch edition) by Mikhail Jelizarov
- *Subterranean Fire* by Natalka Bilotserkivets
- *Vladimir Vysotsky: Selected Works*
- *Behind the Silk Curtain* by Gulistan Khamzayeva
- *The Village Teacher and Other Stories* by Theodore Odrach
- *Duel* by Borys Antonenko-Davydovych
- *War Poems* by Alexander Korotko
- *Ballads and Romances* by Adam Mickiewicz
- *The Revolt of the Animals* by Wladyslaw Reymont
- *Poems about my Psychiatrist* by Andrzej Kotański
- *Someone Else's Life* by Elena Dolgopyat
- *Selected Works: Poetry, Drama, Prose* by Jan Kochanowski

And more forthcoming . . .